The car came out of nowhere

It shot past Bolan on the shoulder, racing down the ramp, and he had only a fleeting impression of gray primer. It hurtled down the line of idling vehicles and made a kamikaze rush straight toward the roadblock.

"Down!" Bolan snarled.

Both James and Encizo reacted without hesitation. The Cuban sprawled flat in the back of the minivan as James threw himself between the front seats, landing next to Encizo.

The vehicle-based improvised explosive device detonated. Shrapnel cut through the air like steel rain and shattered the vehicle's windows, spraying glass shards on the Stony Man team.

Shaken by the concussive impact and sudden violence, Bolan pushed himself into place behind the steering wheel and grabbed the AK-104 carbine.

Welcome to Baghdad, he thought grimly.

Don Pendleton's Mack Bolan®

Appointment In Baghdad

A GOLD EAGLE BOOK FROM

WORLDWIDE®

TORONTO • NEW YORK • LONDON
AMSTERDAM • PARIS • SYDNEY • HAMBURG
STOCKHOLM • ATHENS • TOKYO • MILAN
MADRID • WARSAW • BUDAPEST • AUCKLAND

First edition May 2008

ISBN-13: 978-0-373-61523-0
ISBN-10: 0-373-61523-X

Special thanks and acknowledgment to
Nathan Meyer for his contribution to this work.

APPOINTMENT IN BAGHDAD

Printed in U.S.A.

Once we have a war there is only one thing to do.
It must be won. For defeat brings worse things than
any that can ever happen in war.

> —Ernest Hemingway,
> 1899–1961

War is a special kind of hell. There are no winners.

> —Mack Bolan

For the men and women of the U.S. armed forces

CHAPTER ONE

Toronto, Ontario, Canada: 0146

The mosque had been defiled.

Mack Bolan studied the building. A place of worship had been transformed into a forum for hate. A place where the devout and faithful had once found expression had now been subverted into a recruiting ground for blasphemers killing in the name of religion.

The rest of the street lay quiet.

Earlier that evening, Bolan had pored over an architect's blueprints of the structure procured for him by computer expert Carmen Delahunt at Stony Man Farm. Like most of the buildings in that area of downtown Toronto, the old building was aesthetically unappealing. The mosque was not beautifully gilded, nor did it possess a dome and minaret. Only the placard sign announced what the squat bricked building housed.

A red flag had risen immediately when ownership of the building was traced to Syrian business magnate Monzer al-Kassar. The Syrian's dealing had been on

Stony Man's radar for almost a decade. However, the Syrian facilitator had such a diverse, worldwide portfolio that his mere ownership of certain real estate was not considered a primary cause for action in and of itself. But that had all changed.

The mosque occupied two floors of a four-story brownstone in the run-down neighborhood. On the street level there was a Korean grocery store, and the top floor housed five apartments rented to people, as far as Delahunt could find, who had no connection to the radical activities going on beneath their feet.

Bolan looked at the dive watch on his wrist. It read 0148. Gary Manning, the Canadian-born Phoenix Force commando, would be in his overwatch position by now. Bolan had requested the operator as a readily available asset already long familiar with the Toronto area. For this brief operation Manning monitored Toronto police communications and stood guard against the possibility of outside forces arriving after Bolan had penetrated the building.

Bolan slid the earpiece into place so that the microphone was resting against his cheekbone. He placed a single finger against the device and powered it on.

"You ready?" he asked.

Manning answered immediately. "Copy that, Striker. I'm up. I've got eyes on your approach and the area. Radio chatter is good."

"Let's do it."

Bolan eased open the door to his nondescript Toyota 4-Runner and stepped out into the street. It was very late winter in Toronto and still cold. There was dirty slush on the ground, and everything was cast in a gray pallor.

Streetlights formed staggered ponds of nicotine-yellow illumination. In the building facing the street a single light burned in the window of the third floor.

Bolan closed the door to the 4-Runner and fixed the stocking cap on his head before walking to the rear hatch of the vehicle. Despite the chill bite in the air, he left the zipper to his heavy leather jacket undone. The deadly Beretta 93-R hung in a shoulder holster customized to accommodate the sound suppressor threaded onto its muzzle.

He opened the rear hatch, reached down and pulled up the lid over the compartment that held his spare tire and jack. He moved it to the side and pulled out a hard, plastic-alloy box of dark gray. His fingers quickly worked the combination locks and the case popped open.

Inside, snugly held in place by cut foam, was a Heckler & Koch MP-5 SD-3, the silenced version of the special operations standby weapon. Bolan pulled out the submachine-gun, inserted a magazine, chambered a 9 mm Parabellum round and then secured a nylon sling to the front sight and buttstock attachment points. He thumbed the selector switch to 3-round-burst mode. When he finished he shrugged his jacket off his right arm, slung the weapon over his shoulder so that it hung down by his side and slipped the sleeve back into place.

Bolan slammed the rear hatch shut and looked around the quiet street. No one moved in the early morning hours. He clicked on the alarm to the Toyota and shut the automatic locks as he crossed the street.

He turned left, away from the mosque set above the Korean grocery store. A used-furniture store stood next to the store and beside that was a run-down apartment building six stories high. On the other side of the tenement, next to the intersection, was a tire store.

Bolan turned down the sidewalk next to the apartment building and circled the tire store, entering a narrow alley that ran behind the businesses fronting the street. He slowed his pace as he entered the alley, senses alert as he neared the target.

Bolan kept his gaze roving as he moved closer to the back door of the mosque's building. A couple of empty beer bottles stood among wads of crumpled newspapers. It was too cold for there to be any significant smell. Slush clung to the lee of brick walls in greater mounds than out on the open street. Several patches of slush were stained sickly yellow. Halfway down the alley Bolan drew even with the building housing the mosque.

The devout entered the building through the rear entrance, avoiding the grocery store all together. An accordion-style metal gate was locked into place over a featureless wooden door, and a padlock gleamed gold in the dim light. Bolan approached the security gate and pulled a lock-pick gun from his jacket pocket.

He inserted the prong blades into the lock mechanism and squeezed the lever. The lock popped open. Bolan reached up with his free hand and yanked the accordion gate open. The scissor-gate slid closed with a clatter that echoed in the silent, cold alley. He quickly inserted the lock-pick gun into the doorknob and worked the tool.

He heard the lock disengage with a greasy click and put the device back into his jacket pocket. He grasped the cold, smooth metal of the doorknob and it turned easily under his hand. He made to push the door inward and it refused to budge. Dead bolts.

Bolan swore under his breath. He placed his left hand on the door and pressed inward. From the points of resistance he estimated there were at least three independent security locks attached to the inside of the door.

His mind instantly ran the calculations for an explosive entry. He factored in the metal of the bolt shafts, their attachment points on the door frame and the density of the door itself. He was able to sum up exactly how much plastique he would need and ascertain the most efficient placement on the structure.

But Bolan had no intention of blowing the door of a building in downtown Toronto. Not until he was exactly sure of what he would find inside. He was well versed in various forms of surreptitious entry and had been thoroughly schooled in the techniques of urban climbing, or buildering as it was sometimes called.

Bolan lifted his head and looked up. As per the city's fire code, a means of emergency egress had been placed on the outside of the building to aid occupants above the ground floors. The fire escape was directly above the back door and ended in an enclosed metal cage around the ladder on the second floor.

"Change of plans," Bolan said into his throat mike. "I'm going up."

"Your call, Striker," Manning answered. "Everything is good at the moment."

Bolan looked around the alley. He thought briefly of pushing over one of the large green garbage bins and climbing on top of it to reach the fire escape. He rejected the idea as potentially attracting too much attention. He looked around, evaluating the building like a rock climber sizing up a cliff face. Above the first floor five uniform windows ran the width of the building along each floor.

Bolan made his decision and zipped his jacket. It would keep him from getting to his concealed weapons quickly, but it was a necessary risk if he were to attempt this climb. He opened the scissor-gate again and grasped it at the top. He stuck the toe of one boot into a diamond-shaped opening and lifted himself off the ground. He placed his other hand against the edge of the building, using the strength of his legs to support him as he released one handhold on the gate and reached for a gutter drain set into the wall.

He grabbed hold firmly and held on before moving his other hand over. The drain was so chill it almost seemed to burn the flesh on the palm of his hand and fingers. He pulled himself up despite the great strain of the awkward position and grasped the vertical drain with both hands. He moved his right leg and stuck his toe between the drainpipe and the brick wall, jamming it in as tightly as he could.

Once he was braced Bolan pulled his boot from the scissor-gate and set it on top of the door frame. It was slick along the top and he was forced to knock aside a minor buildup of slush along the narrow lip. Confident with the placement of that foot, the soldier pushed down hard against the lip at the top of the door frame and shimmed himself farther up the drainpipe.

Bolan's muscles burned, and he forced himself to breathe in through his nose. Squeezing the frigid, slick pipe tightly, he inched his way up until his knee touched the second-story window ledge.

His body stretched into a lopsided X, Bolan carefully pressed his hands against the windowpane and pushed upward, testing to see if the window was open. He met resistance and realized it was locked. Bolan eased his head back and looked up. Light shone from the window on the floor directly above his position. Above that the fourth floor was as dark as the second. Directly above that was the roof.

From his careful study of the architect's blueprints Bolan knew the internal staircase rose up to a roof access doorway. He debated breaking the glass on the window and working the lock mechanism from inside. He decided the risk was simply too great and made a decision to keep climbing.

"This is a no go," he whispered. "I'm going all the way up."

"Roger," Manning answered.

He chose this route for the same reason he had decided not to use the fire escape. The metal structure was as dated as the building and ran directly next to the softly lit third-floor window; he feared the occupants in the lighted room would be aware of the rattle as he climbed and be alerted to his presence.

Decision made, he shimmed his way up to the third floor despite the toll the physical exertion was taking on him. Bolan was in exceptional physical shape, but the task of urban climbing was extremely arduous. Hand over hand and toehold to toehold, the soldier ascended the outside of the building, working himself into position by the third-floor window.

Bolan paused. He could hear the murmur of voices and sensed shadowed movements beyond the blind, but not enough for him to gather any intelligence. Moving carefully to diminish any sound of his passing, Bolan climbed the rest of the way up the building.

He rolled over the edge and dropped over the low rampart onto the tar-patched roof. He rose swiftly, unzipping his jacket and freeing the MP-5 submachine-gun. Exhaust conductors for the building's central air formed a low fence of dull aluminum around the free-standing hutch housing the door to the fire stairs.

Bolan crossed the roof to the side opposite his ascent and reached the door. He tried the knob, found it locked and quickly worked his lock-pick gun on the simple mechanism.

"All right," Bolan said. "I'm going inside."

"Be careful," Manning's voice said across the distance.

Bolan glanced quickly around to see if the occupants of any of the other nearby buildings had witnessed his climb. He saw no evidence of either them or Manning in his overwatch position and ducked into the building, leaving the door open behind him.

The Executioner descended into darkness.

CHAPTER TWO

Bolan moved down the stairs and deeper into the building. He moved past the fire door leading to the fourth-floor apartments and down toward the two levels housing the mosque.

NSA programs had intercepted calls originating in the An Bar province of western Iraq with their terminus in this area of Toronto. Official procedures had been followed and contact with Ottawa made in the offices of both the Royal Canadian Mounted Police and the Canadian Security and Intelligence Service, known as CSIS.

Because the intercepted cell-phone call had been made to the twenty-seven-year-old son of a Syrian diplomat stationed in Canada's capital, the response from the government security services had been to decline the request for mutual cooperation. Subsequent investigations made by CSIS had concluded that the foreign jihadists were not threats domestically and served only in administrative and supportive roles to insurgents operating in the Middle East, much as American representatives of the Sinn Fein had served nonviolently to facilitate IRA activities during the 1970s.

The Canadian position became an official posture of low-key overwatch. The mosque in question would remain unmolested.

To an embattled and besieged America, the Damascus-Toronto-Ramadi connection represented a treasure trove of information and a clear and present danger. The Hiba Bakr, who ran the center for Islamic studies was a known Whabbist, and the Syrian diplomat in question was a man frequently associated with the top levels in the Idarat al-Mukhabarat al-Jawiyya, or the Syrian Air Force Intelligence known as the IMJ.

The IMJ had evolved into Syria's most covert and ruthless intelligence agency and was, despite its moniker, not primarily concerned with gathering intelligence for the nation's air force. Hafez al-Assad, the former president of Syria, had once commanded the air force and upon his assumption of power in 1970 had frequently turned away from the nation's other three intelligence services in favor of one filled with men he personally knew and had in most cases appointed himself.

As Syria, like Saddam's Iraq, was a Baathist state, IMJ's internal operations had often involved operations against elements of Islamist opposition domestically. Externally, international operations had focused on the exportation and sponsorship of terrorist acts and causes the regime was sympathetic to, such as interference in the internal politics of Lebanon. Its agents operated from Syrian embassies and in the branch offices of Syria's national airline. Dozens of terrorist actions had been attributed to them, including the attempted bombing of an Israeli airliner at London's Heathrow Airport in April of 1986.

The IMJ's position as favored attack dog had not changed with the death of Hafez al-Assad and the ascendancy of his son, Bashar.

Most importantly for Stony Man, the IMJ had been at the spearhead of the pipeline operation moving foreign fighters and equipment into western Iraq. Even if the Toronto cell was a passive operation, its communications, records and computer files could prove to be vital. Two days earlier a known courier, monitored by the CIA as an informational node between disparate jihadist cells, had disappeared after disembarking a plane in Toronto's Pearson International Airport.

The runner's face had shown up in a routine situation report filed by an Army counterintelligence unit working out of the Pentagon and in close liaison with the Defense Intelligence Agency. The report had put him outside an extremist mosque mostly unpopular with the larger Toronto Muslim community. Stony Man had been put on alert.

Mack Bolan had once again been placed at the sharp end.

The MP-5 SD-3 was up and at the ready in his grip as he ghosted down the staircase toward the third-floor landing. Intelligence targets were worth more alive than dead. However, as had been the case with al-Qaeda-in-Iraq's leader, Abu Musab al-Zarqawi, it was often more expedient to simply take them out when other means could not be readily facilitated. In this case a snatch operation under the eyes of CSIS had been deemed imprudent and traditional American assets too much of a potential political liability.

Bolan stepped softly off the staircase and stopped by

the interior door on the narrow landing. From his check of the blueprints Bolan knew the third floor housed offices, a small kitchen and bedroom apartments while the second floor, directly above the grocery store, was a wide-open place of worship housing prayer mats, a lectern and screens to separate male and female faithful.

Bolan tried the knob to the fire door. It turned easily under his hand and he pulled it open, keeping the MP-5 submachine-gun up and at the ready. The door swung open smoothly, revealing a dark stretch of empty hall. Bolan stepped into the hallway and let the fire door swing shut behind him. He caught it with the heel of his boot just before it made contact with the jamb and gently eased it back into place.

Down the hallway, in the last room, a bar of light shone from underneath a closed door. Bolan heard indistinct voices coming from behind it, too muffled to make out clearly. Occasionally a bark of laughter punctuated the murmurs. The soldier stalked down the hall. Prudence dictated clearing each room he passed before he put those doorways at his back, but it was an unrealistic expectation for a lone operator in Bolan's circumstance.

He eased into position beside the closed door and went down on one knee. Keeping his finger on the trigger of the MP-5, Bolan pulled a preassembled fiber-optic camera tactical display from his inside jacket pocket. He placed the coiled borescope cable on the ground and unwound it from the CDV display.

It was awkward working with only his left hand, but the voices on the other side of the door were clearly audible and speaking in what he thought was Arabic, though Bolan's own skill in that language was low enough that it might have been Farsi. He turned on the display with an impatient tap of his thumb and then slid the cable slowly through the slight gap under the door.

The display reflected the shifting view as Bolan pushed the fiber-optic camera into position. A brilliant light filled the screen, and the display self-adjusted to compensate for the brightness. A motionless ceiling fan came into focus and Bolan twisted the cable so that the camera no longer pointed directly up at the ceiling.

A modest kitchen set twisted around on the slightly oval-shaped picture, and Bolan could clearly distinguish four men sitting around the table. All wore neutral colored clothes and sported beards, except for a younger man seated to the left, whose facial hair was dark but sparse and whispery.

Bolan was able to identify all of the men by the photographs that had been included in his mission workups. One man was Hiba Bakr, the imam of the Toronto mosque, a radical Whabbist cleric with ties to the Egyptian-based Muslim Brotherhood. Sixty-three years old, veteran of the Soviet occupation of Afghanistan where he had served as spiritual adviser to the mujahideen, Bakr was a man intimately plugged into the international jihadist network, and had been for decades. His fiery rhetoric and extreme interpretation of the Koran had earned him followers among the disaffected Muslim youth of the area and the interest, albeit passively, of the RCMP.

The next man at the table was the youth with the wispy beard. Bolan identified him as Aram Mohammed Hadayet. It was his cell-phone calls that had been intercepted. An automatic pistol sat on the kitchen table in front of the youth. He listened as the cleric spoke, but his eyes kept shifting to the pistol on the table.

Next to Hadayet sat the man who had so excited the DIA—Walid Sourouri. A known graduate of al Qaeda training camps in Afghanistan under the Taliban, Sourouri had impressed his trainers with his nondescript demeanor and language capabilities. No glorious death by suicide for this warrior. Instead he was employed to help the networks circumvent the technical superiority of Western intelligence agencies by keeping things primitively simple. Sitting at the imam's kitchen table was the foot messenger of al Qaeda.

The third man was Raneen Ogedi, a blunt-featured man with a large reputation within the intelligence community. It was a gruesome reputation that had somehow failed to capture the attention of the news media for one reason or another. Despite this, Bolan realized he had stumbled upon a killer from the Iraqi A-list of wanted men.

Ogedi was a former cell commander of Saddam's fedayeen, and an operator who had exploited his Syrian intelligence contacts to funnel in foreign fighters during the earlier stages of the American occupation and to later on target Iraqi consensus government Shiite officials in hopes of exacerbating a civil war. He had been a virulent Baathist until the fall of Saddam, after which he had suddenly found his Muslim faith again, most specifically its very radical and extreme fringe elements.

The man was almost never accompanied by less than a squad of Syrian-trained bodyguards, but Bolan saw no evidence of them in the kitchen. Like the youth Hadayet, Ogedi had a weapon positioned in front on him on the kitchen table. The wire-stock of the Skorpion machine pistol had been collapsed, and the automatic weapon was barely larger than a regular handgun.

The resolution on the borescope was state-of-the-art, and Bolan was able to make out several books on the table as well as the weapons. One was a copy of the Koran, another a modern arms book and the third a U.S. Army munitions manual.

Bakr was speaking directly to Hadayet, his words impassioned. The youth nodded in agreement and muttered something in a low voice. The cleric's blunt finger tapped the worn copy of the Koran for emphasis, and Sourouri nodded in enthusiastic agreement. His bulky parka fell open when he did, and Bolan got a flash of the nylon strap supporting the man's shoulder holster.

Out of the jumble of conversation Bolan suddenly heard several words he recognized from his intel briefings at Stony Man Farm. Someone said Monzer al-Kassar's name, which he'd already known. Then Hadayet said a different name: Scimitar.

The code name was cliché but iconic and was used as the calling card of a man believed to be at the center of the web of an international network of violent jihadist and criminal enterprises that stretched across the Middle East and southwest Asia.

Bolan slowly pulled his borescope out from under the lip of the door. He coiled the fiber-optic camera cable back up into a tight loop and attached it behind the heads-up display with a little Velcro strap designed for the purpose. He slid the device into the inside pocket of his jacket and shifted the H&K MP-5 SD-3 around.

Gary Manning's deep voice came across the com-link. His voice remained calm but his urgency was obvious.

"We've got trouble," Manning said. "There was nothing across the scanner, but I got an unmarked sedan with a dashboard light that just pulled into the alley."

"Roger," Bolan whispered.

"Get out!" Manning's voice suddenly gritted. "Get out, they just rushed the door and a request for backup call just went out over the scanner. My boys had a surveillance operation. Get out."

At that moment Bolan heard the downstairs door break open and the shouts of men as they entered the stairway on the first floor.

"Get Jack into the air and over the rally point," Bolan ordered.

"Roger," Manning acknowledged.

Then everything began to fall apart.

The voices in the kitchen went silent then burst into frantic curses, and in the distance Bolan heard the wail of police sirens. He knew with sudden intuition that a storm had just arrived in Toronto.

CHAPTER THREE

Bolan heard chairs scrape across the floor from inside the mosque's kitchen and backpedaled from the door as it was thrown open. Light spilled into the gloomy hallway like dawn rising, and Bolan dropped to one knee and swung up the MP-5.

The first of the kitchen cabal rushed into the hallway. Raneen Ogedi held his Skorpion machine pistol at hip height as he emerged from the cramped room, his head already turning toward the far end of the hall where the footsteps of numerous men could be clearly heard thundering up the fire stairs. He looked stunned to see the black-clad Bolan crouched in the hallway. Ogedi leveled his weapon. The chugging sound of the silenced MP-5 was eerie as Bolan pulled down on the terrorist. His spent shells were caught in the cloth-and-wire brass catcher attached to the weapon's ejection port. A 3-round burst of 9 mm Parabellum slugs ripped into the Iraqi's face with brutal effect.

Blood splashed like paint onto the wood of the door and stood out vividly against the pale linoleum of the kitchen floor behind the man. Ogedi turned in a sloppy half circle and bounced off the kitchen door before dropping onto the ancient carpet of the hallway.

The next figure in the frantic line stumbled into the door frame. Bolan cut loose again and put a tight burst into the chest of the pistol wielding Sourouri, who had raced into the hallway directly behind the Iraqi killer. The man's eyes were locked on the fallen form of his jihadist brother, and they lifted in shock as Bolan's rounds punched up under his sternum, mangling his lungs and heart.

Blood gushed in a waterfall over the lips of the man's gaping mouth and he tripped up in Ogedi's legs and went down face-first. Bolan saw Bakr frozen at the edge of the kitchen door, hands held out and empty, his eyes locked on the grim specter of the Executioner.

Down the hallway the fire door burst open and Bolan glimpsed three men in suits, pistols drawn, as they raced into the hall. The lead man had a leather wallet open in his left hand and Bolan caught the dim flash of an RCMP badge.

Bolan rushed forward, hurtling the tangled mass of the two fallen terrorists. He slammed his shoulder into Bakr and knocked him out of the way. The old man grunted under the impact and spun off Bolan, stumbling backward over a chair and falling heavily to the kitchen floor. Something in Bolan, some sense of mercy or propriety, kept him from killing the man.

The soldier used the momentum of his impact with the man to spin to one side, putting himself at an angle to the fumbling Aram Hadayet, who was attempting to bring his pistol to bear. Bolan gripped his MP-5 in both hands and chopped it down like an ax, using the long sound suppressor like a bayonet.

The smoking, cylindrical tube struck the youth in his narrow almost-feminine wrist with a crack, and he dropped his weapon in surprised shock. Bolan swept the submachine-gun back and then thrust it forward, burying it in the Syrian's soft abdomen. Hadayet folded as he gagged, and Bolan cracked him across the back of the neck with the MP-5's collapsible buttstock. The youth went down hard to the floor. A cell phone skidded out of his hand and slid across the floor to bounce off the stove before sliding back to Bolan's feet.

The Executioner heard footsteps pounding in the hall and sirens wailing outside as more police cars raced into the alley below the kitchen window. In the hall men were shouting, identifying themselves as police officers. Bolan caught a flash of motion out of the corner of his eye and turned to see Hiba Bakr scrambling to escape the kitchen.

Bolan let the man go, hoping he would slow the plainclothes police officers outside as he made good his own escape. Two hardcore killers had been put down and two intelligence coups left for the authorities to question. Bolan's code of ethics wouldn't let him fire on the police, even in self-defense, and he had an aversion to killing holy men.

He heard Hadayet moan at his feet, and he twisted to fire a burst across the room, shattering the glass. Beyond the window he saw the spiral reflections of flashing red emergency lights. In the hallway officers ordered Bakr to "Get down! Get down now!"

Bolan used the distraction to bend and secure the

loose cell phone dropped by Hadayet. He rose and sprang toward the window across the kitchen. An RCMP officer, rushed the door with his pistol up, a mini flashlight attached below the barrel of the handgun. As Bolan passed the kitchen table, he turned and flipped it up so that it flew back and landed in the doorway.

The officer ducked back around the corner of the kitchen door to avoid the flying furniture. Bolan dropped the MP-5 and let it dangle from its sling as he scrambled up onto the counter. The leather sleeve of his jacket protected his arm as he knocked splinters of glass away from the window frame.

He stuck a leg through the window and prepared to duck out onto the fire escape. He looked back toward the kitchen door as he slid out and saw the officer he had distracted swing back around the corner, his service pistol held in both hands.

Bolan threw himself to the side as the man fired his weapon. A 10 mm slug cracked into the wall just to the soldier's right, creating a pockmark, and the roar of the pistol was deafening in the acoustic chamber of a tiny room.

There was a frenzy of activity beneath him. Two separate police cruisers had entered the alley behind the mosque from either direction, and more sirens heralded the arrival of backup. Men shouted up at the fire escape from below, excited by the pistol shot.

"I have sights on. I have sights on," Manning said over the com-link. "You want me to put their heads down?"

Bolan kept rolling as he fell, turning over his shoulder. He reached out with his hands and pulled himself upright by grasping the cold iron bars of the fire escape ladder. He hauled himself up and gathered his feet under him. Set, he scrambled upward, running hard up the rungs.

"Negative, negative," Bolan snarled. "I'm still good."

Below him the Canadian cop thrust his body out of the window and shouted for Bolan to stop, raising his weapon. Bolan ignored him, his lungs burning as he scrambled upward. Sparks flew off the metal rung in his grasp, and the fire escape rang as a bullet ricocheted away. An almost indiscernible second later he heard the pistol bark.

"Your call, Striker. Copy," Manning said.

At the fourth floor Bolan spun and raced up the last length of fire escape. Bullets peppered the walls around and below him as police officers on the ground began to fire. The sharp barks of the pistols echoed up between the narrow walls of the alley.

Diving over the edge of the roof, he hit the tar-papered platform and rolled across his back, coming up quickly. He crossed the roof and looked down onto the main thoroughfare. Three more police cars had pulled up in front of the mosque, their occupants running forward to the storefront.

Bolan turned away from the edge. He knew the police would be hard on his heels, and he felt a certain admiration for their tenacity and courage. He crossed the rooftop at a dead sprint, heading for the next building, a long, two-story, used-furniture store.

The soldier hit the waist-high wall circumventing the roof like a rampart. He lowered himself and slid his chest across the cinder-block divider, swinging his feet over until he dangled off the wall, holding on by only his grip. Bolan looked down to make sure his landing area was clear and then let go.

He fell straight down, struck the lower roof and rolled over hard onto his back. The maneuver, left over from his paratrooper training, absorbed much of the force of his fall but he still struck hard enough to nearly drive the air from his lungs.

Bolan gasped in the frigid air and forced himself to his feet. He rose, setting his sights on the tenement building rising up on the other side of the used-furniture store's roof. Windows faced out from the apartments onto the roof, and lights were snapping on in response to the gunfire and police sirens.

"I'm heading for the tenement," Bolan barked into the phone.

"Roger. Jack says he's over the rally point. You want me to come get you?"

Bolan began to run toward the tenement building, starting to skirt a large skylight set in the middle of the rooftop. From behind him he heard the voice of the policeman who had dogged his every footstep since the hallway. A white pool of light from the officer's mini-flashlight cut through the night. The officer shouted his warning.

Bolan refused the cop's third warning and the officer began to fire.

"Negative. I'm going to try for my vehicle for now, stay in overwatch," Bolan answered.

"Okay, but you got a street full of good guys."

Bolan didn't have time to answer.

Bullets struck the roof as the Executioner ran, and he knew he'd never make it. Already the bullets were falling closer, and if the RMCP officer settled down, he had a very good chance of striking the fleeing Bolan.

The soldier pushed back the edge of his jacket and swept up the MP-5. His heart was pounding as he leveled the submachine-gun. He heard the crack of the officer's pistol behind him as Bolan squeezed his trigger. The H&K submachine-gun cycled through a burst, and the skylight just ahead of him shattered.

Bolan felt a tug at the hair on his head as he ran, followed by the pistol report and he knew how close he'd come. He hunched down and dug his legs into the sprint. The lip of the broken skylight rushed toward him and Bolan leaped into the air.

Bolan hurtled across the open space. The black hole of the broken skylight appeared under him as he jumped, and he brought his legs together. At the zenith of his leap he plunged through the broken window.

Glass shattered under his feet, and he could feel sharp glass spikes tear at his leather jacket as he smashed through the smaller opening he'd initiated with his gunfire.

The bottom of his jacket fluttered up behind him as he dropped into the darkness, and he felt a jolt of apprehension as he fell, completely unaware of where he would land or on what. Splinters of glass scattered and fell around him like shards of ice, and the buildup of icy slush on the window cascaded down in an avalanche.

Bolan tried to prepare himself for the impact, knew it could be considerable enough to snap his legs or even kill him if he landed wrong, but it was impossible because of the tomblike darkness of the store interior to know for sure.

The soldier grunted with the impact as he struck a countertop and it was unfeasible to roll. His legs simply folded under him and his buttocks hit the hard wood with enough force to snap his teeth closed.

He spilled out on his back, and if not for the sling around his shoulder he would have lost the MP-5. His head whipped down and bounced off the countertop so sharply he saw stars before his momentum swept him off the counter. He fell another five feet onto the ground, striking his knee painfully on the concrete floor under the thin, rough weave of the cheap carpet.

His outflung arm made sharp contact with something large and the object was knocked to the floor. The item landed with a crash beside him and an internal bell rang, telling Bolan he had just tipped over the store cash register. The empty door on the register shot open with a pop like a gunshot as he landed, and the flesh of his palms split as they made rough contact with the floor. He winced at the sudden sting.

Forcing himself to his feet, Bolan clung to the counter for support. Adrenaline filled him and he gritted his teeth as he forced himself up. Once he was standing he ripped off his balaclava and stuffed it inside his coat. Through the store's big front windows he saw police lights flashing. They cycled through the dark store, illuminating the interior briefly.

Bolan hobbled into a pile of furniture and out from underneath the broken skylight. If he knew the character of the cop on his tail, the man would be there soon. He saw other cops moving out in the street, their attention focused on the building housing the mosque.

The Executioner forced himself forward, heading

directly toward the front of the building, dodging around furniture displays set up to look like living rooms or bedrooms or dinning areas. He spoke into his throat mike with blood-smeared lips.

"Striker, here," he said. "My ride is a no-go. You ready for extraction?"

"Affirmative," Manning answered.

"Copy," Bolan said. "As soon as it's clear, I'll blow the distraction."

"I'm coming now."

Bolan moved forward until he was clear of the furniture displays and could see out onto the street unimpeded. Five police cars were visible, most of their occupants out of their vehicles and storming toward the grocery underneath the mosque.

The soldier looked at his own Toyota 4-Runner. No one appeared to be standing near the vehicle. He looked down the street and saw a black Ford Expedition abruptly round a corner three blocks up, lights blazing.

Bolan made his decision.

From the skylight behind him a beam of bright illumination shot out from the flashlight attached beneath the barrel of the RCMP officer's 10 mm pistol. It cut through the shadows inside the furniture store and swept around, hunting for Bolan.

The soldier dived out of the way as the light tracked toward him and the officer fired. A 10 mm round burrowed into the floor with relentless force. Bolan desperately needed something to rattle the Canadian officer's aim. He fell into a shoulder-roll, away from the illumination of the big front windows.

He came up out of his somersault and shoved a store

mannequin toward the searching light. The figure toppled and the cop triggered his gun twice. The man's second round struck the mannequin in the head, and the soft lead slug hammered a crater into the plastic statue.

Bolan shoved a hand into the pocket of his leather jacket, grasped his key ring and pulled it clear. He looked down and located the electronic fob on the end. His thumb pressed the vehicle's remote start option.

Out in the street the Toyota exploded in a sudden ball of flames with a deafening boom. The chassis leaped straight up, engulfed by fire and pouring black smoke. It came down hard and sent metal car parts scattering in all directions.

The ruined 4-Runner came to a rest in the middle of the street and burned like a bonfire. Up the street Gary Manning's Ford Expedition locked its brakes with an angry squeal. Bolan swept up his MP-5 and fired at the plate-glass window. Spent shells clanged together as they rattled into his brass catcher.

The window shattered and heavy shards of glass cascaded like icicles to burst against the concrete outside the window. Bolan slung the weapon as he raced forward.

He heard pistol shots from behind him, but had no idea if they came close or not as he stepped off his lead foot and sprang into the air.

He hurtled the bottom of the window like a track star and landed outside. He heard shouts coming from his left and risked a look as he landed in a crouch. He saw a squad of Toronto uniformed policemen, most of them on the ground and disorientated by the car bomb he had just detonated.

One patrolman was sufficiently together to lift an arm and point, shouting out a warning as Bolan pivoted and began to sprint up the slushy sidewalk toward the Ford Expedition gunning straight for him. His breath billowed out in front of him in silver plumes as he charged forward. His breathing was loud in his ears, and he could feel his heart hammering in his chest.

He saw Manning clearly through the windshield of the Expedition. The Phoenix Force commando locked up the emergency brake, and the tires screeched in protest as he swung the back end of the SUV in a smooth bootlegger maneuver. Bolan dived toward the passenger door.

Pistol shots rang out from behind him.

He saw Manning lean across the front seat and open the passenger door. A bullet struck the rear windshield and pebbled the safety glass. Another round sparked off the bumper. Bolan reached the front of the SUV and threw himself inside.

Manning didn't wait for his passenger to close the open door but instead stood on the gas. Tires screamed, turning fast, digging for traction. Then they caught and the Expedition lurched forward like a bullet train leaving the station, throwing Bolan back into the seat.

"Grimaldi ready?" the soldier panted.

"Always," Manning stated as he sent the SUV into a power slide that took the fugitive vehicle off the street and out of sight of the policemen firing on them. "He's put the Little Bird down on the top floor of a parking garage six blocks over. We'll be in the air in two minutes." He looked down at a digital clock display. "One minute," he corrected.

Bolan nodded. He reached inside his jacket pocket and checked for Hadayet's cell phone. If they moved fast, he thought, they just might have a crack at Scimitar.

CHAPTER FOUR

The Stony Man team switched out the Little Bird for a clean JetRanger at the Buffalo Niagara International Airport and proceeded south. In a reasonable amount of time the helicopter was following Skyline Drive along the backbone of the rugged Blue Ridge Mountains in Virginia. The base for the Special Operations Group was only fifty-odd miles southwest of Washington, D.C., and dawn was breaking as the aircraft approached the installation.

A Chevy Blazer was waiting beside the landing strip where Jack Grimaldi put down the JetRanger.

"You guys go on ahead," he told Bolan and Manning. "I'm going to do some postflight checks."

"Thanks, Jack," Bolan said.

He and Manning ducked under the slowing props and crossed over to where Buck Green, chief of security, waited behind the wheel of the SUV. He smiled as the Stony Man commandos approached.

"How was Canada?"

"Chilly," Bolan replied.

"He warmed it up a bit," Manning noted, his voice dry.

"So they tell me," Greene laughed. "Get in. Gary, you've got some time off coming. Later tonight David wants your help running an op-for exercise against the blacksuits," Greene said, using the slang term for Stony Man's security detail.

Manning grunted. "What have you cooked up?"

Greene grinned. "It'll be good. I want to focus on the orchard approach to the compound."

Manning shrugged his acceptance and climbed into the back of the Blazer. If he'd wanted a life of leisure, he could have chosen a thousand other occupations. He was dedicated to the Stony Man cause without question. Even the covert action inside his homeland hadn't bothered him. He'd operated surreptitiously under the nose of his host country, the U.S., on many occasions. Slaying dragons was a pannational vocation.

"What about me?" Bolan asked.

He climbed into the front seat and slammed the door shut. He gave a lazy salute to Grimaldi as Greene pulled the Chevy onto the narrow road leading from the airfields toward the central complex and the Stony Man farmhouse.

The security chief snorted. "Oh, no rest for the wicked, I'm afraid."

"Hal?" Bolan asked, knowing the answer.

"Yep, Hal's here. He's very interested to hear what you got in Toronto."

"I got time for breakfast? Maybe some coffee? Most of what we'll decide will depended on what Aaron can get out of this cell phone I recovered."

Greene nodded and reached down to pick up the

Blazer's radio. "I'll call ahead to Barbara," he said. "She'll make sure the kitchen gets you what you want."

Greene meant Barbara Price, the honey-blond mission controller and sometime Bolan paramour. She ran Stony Man with cool competence and considerable ability. If she gave the word, the Farm's kitchen would prepare a feast. She was also the only one likely to keep Hal Brognola quiet about waiting.

After the fall he'd taken from the skylight in Toronto, Bolan wanted nothing more than a long, hot shower and to eat a good meal before his debriefing. However, the link he had discovered to Scimitar was tenuous. Most high-ranking insurgents in the Iraq theater never stayed in one location for more than twelve hours.

If Stony Man was going to have a shot at Scimitar, the clock was already ticking.

BOLAN SAT in the War Room.

The multimedia compatible meeting room was as secure as anything one could find at the NSA or CIA headquarters and as comfortable as a New York City law firm's boardroom. It took up approximately one-half of the basement space of the main house, and Bolan knew the room intimately after all his years at the Farm.

Hal Brognola sat at the head of the conference table, chewing on an unlit cigar. Price and Bolan occupied two other chairs, while Aaron "The Bear" Kurtzman sat in a wheelchair off to one side. Nearby was a high-tech console that controlled the War Room's media displays and lights.

Bolan had brought his breakfast with him. He pushed

his empty plate away and pulled a large mug of coffee closer.

While eating he'd gone over the details of the Toronto takedown. Brognola acknowledged that an inquiry had been made to the Department of Homeland Security regarding an operation against Hiba Bakr. Official channels had been able to respond honestly that they had neither authorized such an illegal incursion nor were they aware of such an ongoing operation.

Since Bolan had chosen to leave Bakr to Canadian intelligence, the CIA had requested that an agent join CSIS for the interrogations. Brognola had learned that the diplomat father of the Syrian youth had already filed a protest with the government in Ottawa and the UN regarding the arrest of his son. The company of known international terrorists notwithstanding, it was likely his request for release would be granted.

"This means Scimitar could already be alerted. In fact we have to assume so," Brognola said. "Carmen is running those cell numbers into Iraq right now, cross-referencing NSA databases. We're hoping for a triangulation. When we're done here I intend to fly back into D.C. and follow up on some things Barb has put into motion." He looked over at Barbara Price whose face was carefully neutral, a sure sign of her displeasure. "Certain operational contingencies we've already had in place, in the event that Stony Man was ever called upon to act in Iraq."

Bolan nodded and sipped his coffee. He'd taken 800 mg of ibuprofen on arriving at the farmhouse and was beginning to feel less banged up.

"What kind of contingencies?" he asked.

"Barb, this was your brainchild," the big Fed said.

Price nodded and set her mug of coffee on the conference table.

"If the need should arise, we've worked out several scenarios to get Mack into Iraq under operational cover. Our most promising cover is dual. We can coordinate your activities through the DNI and CIA. CENTCOM will think you're Pentagon spooks. Your 'cover' for that cover will be employment as private military contractors working for a prestigious international company breaking into the lucrative southwest Asian market."

"What company would that be?" Bolan asked.

"A Montreal-based firm called North American International, headed by one certain Gary U. Manning," Kurtzman stated.

"I take it the background check for such contracts was expedited?" Bolan asked.

"I hand-carried the forms through channels myself," Brognola admitted.

"This means," Price continued, "that we'll be able to funnel out special access program funds into legitimate government contracts paid to North American International."

"Clever," Bolan stated.

"It is a court of last resort," Price said. "As far as I was concerned, this was a contingency plan that was never meant to be used. The U.S. government has plenty of assets in place already to deal with conventional problems."

"But Scimitar isn't conventional anymore, is he?" Bolan observed.

"No, he's not," Brognola said.

The big Fed leaned forward. He nodded once to

Kurtzman. The head of Stony Man's cybernetics team pressed a series of buttons on the table's console. The lights dimmed and a slab of paneling in the wall behind Brognola slid back to reveal a six-foot HD wall screen. Immediately an olive-skinned, bearded face with blunt features and a patrician nose appeared on the screen. Bolan recognized the man as the individual known as Scimitar.

Brognola took his chewed up cigar out of his mouth and held it between his blunt fingers.

"He realized more quickly than most of his compatriots that no matter what happened in Iraq, post-Saddam, a return to Baathist rule in any form was extremely unlikely. He rapidly morphed his activity away from American resistance into establishing a power base for himself, using the insurgency as a cover with his jihadist allies. His method was, as most effective plans are, simple. Barb?"

Stony Man's mission controller smoothly took over the briefing. She rose and crossed the room, placing a folder on the conference table in front of Bolan before continuing.

"Initially he set up a small regional base manned by Fedayeen subordinates in the Baghdad slum of Amariyah, along Route Irish," Price began, using the U.S. military designation of the road running between the Baghdad International Airport and the Green Zone, often referred to in the media as the "Highway of Death."

Price took a drink of her coffee and continued speaking. Bolan began to leaf through the file as he listened. His fatigue and physical discomfort began to bleed away as his interest in the mission grew with his realization of how important it was.

"Scimitar then withdrew to the west, into An Bar province in proximity to the Syrian border," Price said. "He used his Fedayeen troops to control the area, then exploited his contacts with Syrian intelligence as well as secret caches of equipment, weapons and cash to outfit foreign fighters.

"All pretty run-of-the-mill. He maintained credibility as anti-American with both former Saddam supporters and the international jihadists movement. However, Scimitar is no ideologue. He used his connections with jihadists in southwest Asia to begin moving heroin into Iraq. From there he used Albanian mafia connections given him by the Syrian IMJ and the freelancer al-Kassar, to move the heroin out of Iraq, through Istanbul and on to points west in both Europe and America. Ostensibly the funds were used to fund insurgent activity. Mostly it went to purchasing Sunni members of Iraq's government to give him immunity from scrutiny. He now operates out of a section of the city of Ramadi completely under Iraq national control. He used his connections in the Iraqi government to give up rivals in the area when the National Army moved in. The area, under his orders, remained 'pacified' and the National Army was mostly supplanted by local Iraqi police units."

"Its ranks filled with members of his personal militia," Kurtzman added.

Price nodded in agreement. "Scimitar owns that city, or that neighborhood anyway. The imams answer to him there, foreign agents take his direction and the police forces are essentially his private militia. It is a quiet sector, a success story for the Iraqi national army in an otherwise blatant embarrassment. He moves funds for operations in Baghdad out of the city and heroin in through it."

Bolan was silent. If ever a target or network had needed taking out, Scimitar's rated right up there. The problem was not clear-cut, however. The soldier had adhered to an iron-fast rule during his War Everlasting. Cops were off limits.

"I'll take down the network," he said slowly, "but crooked or not, I don't want to draw down on police officers."

"Mack, this isn't the bad old days. This situation isn't even one of corruption per se. Scimitar's militia hasn't infiltrated or corrupted the Iraqi police in western Ramadi. His militia simply put on those blue uniforms," Brognola said. "In the initial months there *were* honest Iraqis in that police unit. They were found, one by one, hung by their heels from lampposts with their heads cut off. Look for yourself." Brognola indicated the file in front of Bolan. "Those uniforms don't represent good street cops gone bad. It's more like the Gestapo or some kind of disguise. This isn't New York City, or even Chechnya. It's like calling those butchers, the Fedayeen, police officers when they operated under Saddam."

Bolan sat silently. He considered Brognola's words as he mulled over this worst-case scenario. When he spoke he chose his words with careful deliberation.

"Scimitar has a network. I'm on board with taking that network down. I'm on board with bringing Scimitar down. But I reserve the right to call this off at any time. If I don't like what I see going on when we get into Iraq, I walk. That's the deal, Hal."

"Wouldn't want it any other way, Striker," Brognola answered.

CHAPTER FIVE

Carmen Delahunt entered the room at that moment, bearing a slim file containing a computer printout. She also carried the cell phone he'd taken from Aram Hadayet.

Delahunt was an attractive middle-aged redhead who had been recruited from the FBI to become a vital member of Aaron Kurtzman's cybernetics team.

She smiled and nodded her greeting to everyone in the room, then handed her findings to Barbara Price, who nodded her thanks.

"What did you find, Carmen?" Price asked.

"The Ramadi connection is now dead. I couldn't discover whether that was because the people at that end knew about the raid or because the numbers are changed daily. However, overall the phone was a treasure trove. We were able to triangulate several geographic locations and assign specific personnel to those coordinates. I did a quick run up on them from our files. We've got several known players, and it gave us a pretty good idea about Scimitar's network, if not his specific location."

"If he has the Iraqi government bought off," Bolan asked, "is he still underground?"

"Technically he's still wanted by U.S. interests. He keeps a low profile, but it's mainly the fact that the Iraqis run interference for him that keeps him operating outside of the notice of the U.S. CENTCOM there," Price answered. "Either way, his network is in place. Simply cutting off the head of the dragon would do us only so much good."

Bolan nodded his agreement with Price's assessment, then turned his attention back to Delahunt.

"Three numbers proved to be of the most interest," she said. "The first was confirmed to be that of an arms dealer named Mirjana operating out of Croatia. I have a file worked up on him. He's known to Interpol but is well connected to the government there. He moves in the same circles as our friend Monzer al-Kassar, but we haven't connected them specifically, yet.

"The second number is to a former commander in Saddam's Special Republican Guard. He's living with relatives in Amman, Jordan. He left Iraq immediately after Baghdad fell and has given no indication of having been involved in anti-American activities. The Defense Intelligence Agency had a workup on him they shared with Homeland Security, and he was given a pass.

"Perhaps the potentially most significant one is to the number of a Syrian National Airlines branch office in the former Soviet Republic of Azerbaijan. It is, of course, well-known that certain elements of Syrian intelligence services operate frequently from these branch offices. I've pulled everything we have on the region and that airport for the report." Delahunt paused, she seemed almost apologetic.

"It's pretty sparse," she admitted. "It's obvious the Syrian diplomat to Ottawa was using his son as a plausible deniability cutout. However, what is unrelated Syrian interest and what is specific to Scimitar remains uncertain at this point. If the youth was using the Toronto mosque to expand Scimitar's network then such a disparate web as the numbers seem to indicate is a very bad sign. The network is most definitely global and apparently reaches beyond either the jihadist movement or Syrian intelligence."

"Thank you, Carmen," Price said, and Delahunt exited the War Room.

"There you have it," Brognola said. "Not much to go on. Despite that, they're the best leads we've ever come across concerning Scimitar-specific information. Because of his links to the Iraqi government and what the press would do if they found out, the Man wants this kept Stony Man quiet."

"I guess the sooner I start, the sooner Scimitar gets taken down," Bolan said.

"This couldn't have come at a more inopportune time, Mack," Price said.

"Able Team is tied up in South America and Phoenix Force has been tapped to provide security on a high-profile VIP working on nuclear proliferation in—" Kurtzman added.

"It's important," Brognola interjected.

"That op was set up a while ago through—" The computer wizard started.

"I know." Brognola cut him off again. "If this trail

takes Striker into Iraq, I don't want him operating in that cesspool alone."

"I'm somewhat used to working alone," Bolan said, his voice as dry as an old grave.

"I know, Striker. But this could get damn ugly, and I know you're used to that, as well," Brognola said.

He turned to Price. "How many of Phoenix can you peel off that detail?"

Price pursed her lips, obviously conflicted. She was a mission-first person, and she ran Stony Man that way. Still, both operations were obviously of importance.

"I can't drop the ball on that security detail, Hal," she said. "I can give him two and that's stretching it. Not Manning, though," she added, thoughtful. "He's my ballistics and explosives number one. He can handle the matter with North American International over secure communications if he needs to."

Brognola turned back to Bolan. "I can give you two from Phoenix Force. Take them, Striker."

Bolan nodded. He was pensive for a moment, weighing out the various specialties of each man. McCarter was out, obviously, as he was the team leader. The soldier trusted each man in Phoenix Force with his life; it wasn't a question of trust. All of them were equally capable in their own ways. It was a question of pure pragmatism that guided his decision now.

"Give me Calvin and Rafe," he said, referring to Calvin James and Rafael Encizo. "I'd like a dedicated Stony Man pilot if the need comes down to that," Bolan said. "That could expedite things a lot. Jack, of course, if you can spare him."

Brognola shifted his eyes to Price. Such matters were her domain.

"I'm sorry, Mack," she said. "I know how much you trust Jack, but I need him down with Able Team. I can give you Charlie Mott."

"He's a good man," Bolan agreed.

"All right," Brognola stood. "Now that that's settled we'll get Rafe and Cal in here and get them up to speed. I have a meeting at Pennsylvania Avenue I'm late for." He came around the table and shook Bolan's hand. "That was good work in Toronto, Striker. You keep yourself safe on this one."

Bolan smiled back. If he had a dollar for every time he'd heard Brognola tell him to stay safe…well he'd be ahead by a lot.

"Thanks, Hal," he said. "I'll see you when I get back."

SEVERAL HOURS LATER Bolan sat in the Stony Man Computer Room.

Price manned a telephone, deeply immersed in a conference call. Across the room Aaron Kurtzman worked at his station. He typed on a keyboard with a blunt, staccato rhythm. Maps, weather reports, intelligence bulletins and classified military reports scrolled across his multiple screens.

Bolan shuffled through his travel papers. He had identification as a North American International employee and another set as an Associated Press freelance reporter. His kit held passports, open tickets and visa receipts to bonded warehouses around the region. At his feet there was a black leather satchel that reminded him of a bowling ball bag which was tagged with a Diplomatic Pouch ID.

The suitcase was filled with stacks of money in several currencies. There was no functioning bank system in Iraq, no money wire transfers. Most people, from the government to the U.S. military to street vendors and terror agents, dealt in cold, hard cash.

In the War Room Rafael Encizo and Calvin James were being given their briefings. Bolan looked up as the door opened and Carmen Delahunt rushed in.

She held up a fax sheet and waved it at Price, who nodded and hurriedly cut her connection on the telephone. Bolan slid his paperwork together and put it in the black satchel with the cash before zipping the suitcase closed.

"We just got a break," Delahunt said.

Price walked over to where Bolan was sitting and sat on a corner of the desk. Bolan leaned forward, resting his elbows on the desktop. Delahunt slapped the fax printout in front of them.

"I had a hunch," she said. "So I did a keyword search of the integrated system. I came across an oblique reference to 'Scimitar' in an Interpol Asian Liaison report. It was pretty vague, but it was in reference to the Shimmering Raindrop Triad, known to operate out of Hong Kong. The interesting part is that the Agency," she said, referencing one of the slang terms for the CIA, "has them pegged as a sometime mercenary cutout for China's Central Control of Information."

Bolan grunted in recognition at the name. The CCI was a branch of Communist China's foreign intelligence services. It was mostly known for economic and industrial espionage. It operated out of Silicon Valley and Hong Kong the way the KGB had operated out of Berlin during the cold war.

"Good work, Carmen," Price said. "What else?"

"Apparently the agency had a middle management mole in the triad. It was a report about that asset, Jigsaw Liu, that mentioned Scimitar. Jigsaw Liu was given control of triad gambling operations in Hong Kong. He was briefly the focus of an Immigration and Customs investigation into human smuggling with the FBI. The Agency stepped in and asked the DNI to squash it, despite the various crimes, because he represents a backdoor into the CCI.

"I have a contact number for Jigsaw Liu's handler if you want to make contact before you go overseas," Delahunt finished.

"Might give us a little more to go on before we commit," Price said, thoughtful.

Bolan nodded. "Every little bit helps," he agreed. "Check with the Agency man, set up a meet." He turned to Price. "Go ahead and send Rafe and Cal to Zagreb," he said. "Have them set up and start initial recon. I'll handle the meet alone. It'll expedite the whole operation."

Price pursed her lips. "Rafe and Cal are probably our best choice for moving through Baghdad unnoticed, but they won't exactly blend into the Croatian crowds."

"I'm going to approach Mirjana as a representative of North American International. Don't have them pretending to be local. We'll set them up as company reps since they'll obviously be pegged as foreigners."

"Good point. I'll send Rafe and Cal over on a commercial flight. You three can fly into Jordan from Zagreb later and then take a commercial flight into Baghdad International."

"I'll call the Agency handler and set up a meet with Jigsaw Liu," Delahunt stated.

"Let's make it happen," Bolan said.

Things were starting to click. He just couldn't tell if the pieces were falling into place or if this was the beginning of an avalanche.

CHAPTER SIX

Special Administrative Region, Hong Kong

Bolan stood in the alleyway behind the Mandarin restaurant.

Several streets over the sound of a busy Hong Kong night met his ears. Along the waterfront it was quiet. There were no streetlamps, the only illumination coming from bare bulbs set over the back doors of various businesses.

It was quiet enough that he could just make out the gentle lapping of harbor water against the wooden pilings of the piers. The alley he was in stank of urine, rotting vegetables and fish guts. Under a naked bulb casting a weak light, Bolan faced an old wooden door. The paint was peeling and the wood had grown soft with age and the erosion by salty air. A Chinese ideogram had been spray painted in the center of the door.

Bolan recognized the symbol from Carmen Delahunt's report as standing for the Shimmering Raindrop Triad. Down the alley three Chinese men in their early twenties crouched and smoked, talking rapidly. One of them watched Bolan, dragging on his cigarette. The Executioner thought the youths likely to be security forces. Soldiers in the triads were differentiated by the slang numeric code 426.

Hong Kong had changed a lot since 1997 when the British had returned it to the control of the People's Republic of China. Hong Kong formed one of only two Special Administrative Regions, the other being Macau. Despite the PRC's take over, Hong Kong had maintained a high degree of autonomy and was China's richest city, operating in accordance with terms laid out in the Sino-British Joint Declaration, existing under not Beijing rule, but the Basic Law of Hong Kong.

Under this "One Country, Two Systems" policy Hong Kong kept its own legal system, customs policy and currency until 2047. As a result, the city had one of the most liberal economies in the world and had maintained its status as an epicenter for finance and trade. It had long been a seat for the People's Republic of China's espionage efforts. In many ways it had come to replace old Berlin as the spy center of the world, though Islamabad and Amman gave the Asian metropolis a run for its money.

In spite of all this, or more accurately, *because* of all this, Chinese crime syndicates flourished in the environment. Bolan was about to enter living proof of that as he prepared to attend the meet set up by a junior Hong Kong case officer in the CIA.

Bolan turned the knob on the door in the alley and let it swing open. A concrete staircase, littered with multicolored stubs of paper and crushed cigarette butts, ran down to a small square landing. From this landing a second set of stairs led even deeper into the earth under the Mandarin restaurant.

The soldier walked through the door and descended the stairs. The door swung shut behind him and the gloom on the steps thickened. Another naked bulb hung from a cord above the landing below him, and Bolan carefully moved toward it.

The smell of the raw earth around him was dank. He could faintly hear the squeal of rats moving behind the packed dirt walls and rotted timbers. The earth had absorbed decades' worth of body odor, spilled alcohol and cigarette smoke. He was entering the pit, an underground warren of small rooms and low tunnels devoted to the greatest vice of the Chinese: gambling.

The only legal gambling permitted in the Special Administrative Region of Hong Kong was the horse races sanctioned at the Happy Valley tracks since 1846 or at the relatively newer Shatin facility. This fell far short of satiating the traditional penchant for wagers and games of chance, and in the spirit of ruthless entrepreneurialism the Hong Kong triads had stepped in to meet the need.

Bolan turned the corner in the narrow staircase at the landing. Below him the second staircase halted at a sturdy metal door. A Chinese male sat on a tall, three-legged stool, guarding the door.

As he moved closer in the uncertain light, Bolan saw the butt of a Beretta 92-F sticking out of the guard's waistband. On the back of the man's right hand was a tattoo of the same ideogram painted on the door in the alley above them. More ideogram tattoos crawled up the man's fat neck in precise, if sprawling, patterns. From through the cast-iron door Bolan could hear muted but obviously raucous activity.

The man scrutinized Bolan with narrowed eyes. He barked something in what Bolan took to be Cantonese. The soldier shrugged helplessly, then held up a thick wad of Hong Kong dollars. He said Jigsaw Liu's name.

The doorman took the bank notes and thumbed through them suspiciously. He looked back up at Bolan and repeated Jigsaw Liu's name.

"Jigsaw Liu," Bolan agreed.

The wad of money disappeared into a pocket and the guard rapped sharply against the metal door. It swung open immediately and a skinny, sallow-skinned man with a hand-rolled cigarette clenched between crooked, yellow teeth eyed Bolan up and down. From behind him the noise of the room spilled out.

He said something to the doorman, who grunted and repeated Jigsaw Liu's name. The skinny 426 nodded once and stepped out of Bolan's way. The soldier ducked his head and stepped into the chamber beyond.

His senses were fully assaulted as he stepped through the door. The ceiling was low on the long room. The haze of cigarette smoke was thick in the air and looked like a gray-blue fog above the heads of the shouting gamblers. The cacophony of chattering, arguing, belligerent voices was punctuated by the sharp clacking of mahjong tiles. He saw numerous tables filled with frantic men, many clutching their own wads of HK dollars.

Bolan's gaze wandered across the room, noting additional exits and the hard-eyed men standing sentry on the edge of the gambling pits. Other than the pistol tucked into the waistband of the outside doorman, Bolan saw no other weapons on flagrant display, though he was positive they were present. He'd been somewhat surprised not to have been searched at the door, but he assumed most customers here were local and, from the look of it, older.

The sallow-skinned Chinese man repeated Jigsaw Liu's name and indicated a gloomy tunnel leading off the main, cavernous parlor. Bolan began to make his way across the crowded room, sticking close to the back wall as he did so. More than one pair of suspicious eyes followed him.

He crossed the chamber and ducked into the narrow tunnel running off at a sharp angle from the parlor. He felt at once exposed and claustrophobic in the hallway. The pit was a perfect place for a trap, and he had a hunch that its proximity to the harbor made the disposal of bodies an uncomplicated matter.

Bolan stepped over the sprawled and unconscious body of an opium smoker. The ancient Oriental habit had become modernized and had morphed into the use of more current narcotics in Hong Kong, as it had in the rest of the world, but there were still more "traditionalists" of opium in Hong Kong slums than elsewhere on the globe. The man's eyes stared dully, pupils glassy and out of sync with the gloomy light in the tunnel. The man's filthy, short-sleeved, button-down shirt was stained with vomit. His breathing was so shallow that Bolan at first thought him a recent corpse.

Bolan turned a corner in the hallway and exposed metal pipes suddenly erupted from the packed earth, ran for a length of several yards then just as abruptly turned back into the wall. Up ahead he saw two heavyset Chinese men standing in front of a door set back in the hallway wall. Both 426 grunts openly sported Beretta 92-F pistols. Despite the damp, they wore stylish black T-shirts and tan slacks with shiny dress shoes. Their arms crawled with tattoos.

Though the hallway ran down a ways past them and split off into an intersection, Bolan felt sure he had found Jigsaw Liu's office. He walked up to the men, who watched him from beneath hooded lids, their hair slicked back in pompadours.

"Cooper," he said, giving his cover name. "Jigsaw Liu."

They seemed to recognize the name, and Bolan sent a silent thanks to the Agency case officer who had cleared the way. One of the guards knocked softly on the door. At a muttered response from within the man opened the door and stuck his head inside.

Bolan heard a rush of whispered Cantonese, the name "Cooper" and then a gruff response from deeper within the room. The bodyguard pulled his head out from behind the door and indicated with a curt gesture that Bolan should enter.

The soldier stepped forward and crossed the threshold. The interior of the office couldn't have been more at odds with the general atmosphere of the pit. Bolan stepped onto thick carpet accented by tasteful lighting. A massive desk of Oriental teak dominated the room. The narrow, vertical paintings popular in Asian cultures hung from walls made of the same teak as the desk.

The desk itself could have belonged to any successful businessman. It was neatly organized and two separate laptops flanked the main PC screen, all done in a lacquered ebony sheen. One of the screens was turned in such a way that Bolan could see it. He recognized software designed to track up-to-the-second stock market variations.

The man behind the desk regarded Bolan with the eyes of a reptile. He did not rise as the big American entered. His dark, Western suit was immaculate and in sharp contrast to the jigsaw patterns of scars that traversed his almost moon-shaped face. Bolan knew from Jigsaw Liu's file that the Hong Kong mobster had gotten the scars when he'd been propelled through the windshield of his car during an assassination attempt. In the parlance of his kind, Jigsaw Liu was the Red Pole of the Shimmering Raindrop Triad.

Behind him a long, low cabinet ran the length of his office wall. Books in stylish and expensive leather bindings took up one side. The other held two closed-circuit television monitors. The screens were divided into four squares, each revealing a different image as captured by Liu's security system.

Bolan noted that one screen showed the alley where he had first entered the pit. The three youths he had witnessed loitering there were now gone. Another screen showed the mahjong parlor Bolan had cut through. On a third, potbellied and middle-aged Chinese men lounged as young girls in skimpy costumes and heavy makeup pampered them. On the other screen one of the picture sets showed the two men standing guard outside of Liu's office door.

Set on the wall above the cabinet was a plasma-screen

television. The HDTV was on with the volume turned down. Bolan was surprised to see that it was turned not to a Hong Kong or even Chinese station but to Al Jazerra. To the left of the plasma screen a single door made of dark wood was set into the wall. Bolan could tell at a glance that the door was very heavy and solid in construction.

"You come with impressive introductions," Liu said.

When the Red Pole spoke there was a slur to his voice that Bolan immediately attributed to the facial scars and not to alcohol or drugs. The man's black eyes glittered like a snake's.

"As do you." Bolan inclined his head.

The soldier had no use for the excessive manners common in the Orient, or the preoccupation with "face" that was almost stereotypical but still entirely prevalent. However he had a larger agenda than a Hong Kong kingpin. He had no intention of stepping on the CIA's toes unless it became very necessary.

Because of that he remained standing until Jigsaw Liu indicated he should sit. When the Hong Kong gangster gestured, Bolan took a seat in a comfortable, wingback chair set on Liu's right side. Bolan inquired after Liu's health. The Hong Kong killer snorted his laughter.

"I appreciate the effort," he continued in heavily accented English. "But I assure you it is unnecessary. I know how important it is for you *gwailo* to get down to business. So—" Liu templed his fingers in front of his double chin "—let us get down to business."

"Good enough," Bolan said.

He reached into his jacket and pulled out an envelope and a photograph. He leaned forward in his chair and casually tossed both onto the top of Liu's desk. The gangster reached out with one hand and pulled the items toward him, his eyes never leaving his visitor.

Bolan leaned back in his chair and absentmindedly scratched at his new beard. It was filling in nicely, and more quickly that he'd hoped.

Liu opened the envelope and ran a thumb across the tightly packed bank notes. He opened a drawer in his desk and slid the money into it.

Only after he had securely closed the drawer did Liu look at the picture. His eyebrows furrowed slightly as he inspected the image on the photograph Bolan had given him. He looked up and his eyes were quizzical.

He grunted. "I recognize al-Kassar, but who's this with him?"

"Scimitar."

"Scimitar?" Liu snorted.

"Isn't it?"

"I wouldn't know."

"You know Scimitar, don't you? My people think you do."

Liu regarded Bolan, his face expressionless, but a certain low, animal cunning made his black eyes glisten. He reached out and pushed the photograph back across his desk in Bolan's direction.

"My establishment is a good place to hear rumors, you understand?" Liu said carefully. "I have heard that certain men of…influence, sometimes move certain contraband products out of Laos and into the Middle East. As I do not engage in such illicit activities, I do not have firsthand knowledge of these things myself, you understand?"

Bolan nodded. If Liu was uninterested in admitting

his part in moving heroin out of the Golden Triangle and into Europe, then Bolan wasn't going to challenge him. At the moment, anyway. Everything he learned would go into Stony Man files, and Bolan new that sooner or later such a heavy hitter as Liu would screw up and the Executioner would have him.

"Go on," Bolan said.

"I can tell you that none of the people involved in that enterprise have ever dealt with the men in that picture."

"But they have dealt with Scimitar?"

Liu held his hands up as if to say "who can tell" and smiled. "So they say. I am told, and I'm quoting now," he continued. "I am told 'Scimitar is a lie.'"

Bolan pondered Liu's words and their implications. He felt deeply dissatisfied. He looked away from Liu's sneering mask of a face and tried to decide on a fresh avenue. His gaze drifted to the CCTV monitors and a flurry of motion caught his attention.

The guards outside Liu's office door staggered backward, their bodies jerking in crazy, disjointed dances. Blood spurted from their blossoming wounds. One 426 sentry stumbled back against the door and simultaneously Bolan heard the thump from behind him.

Liu cursed at the interruption and turned to look at his CCTV displays. He nearly screamed at what he saw.

Three men with balaclava masks burst into the camera view. One wielded a cut-down Remington 870 pump-action shotgun. He was flanked by a man with a mini-Uzi machine pistol, the sound suppressor nearly as long as the weapon itself. This man was still firing, and he raked the downed bodies of Liu's 426s with ruthless abandon.

Behind the two men a third stepped into view. He wielded twin Beretta 92-F pistols, and he fired one several times back down the hall toward the mahjong parlor and off camera.

Bolan was going for the Beretta 93-R under his shoulder when he saw the shotgun-wielding hit man level his weapon at the door to Liu's office and begin pumping blasts into the wooden structure. Behind Bolan 12-gauge slugs slammed through the lock mechanism and he heard the booms of the Remington 870.

Hell had found the Executioner one more time.

CHAPTER SEVEN

Time seemed to unfold in slow motion. Bolan came up out of his wingback chair as the door to Liu's office banged open, Beretta in his hand. Behind the desk Liu had grabbed a custom-engraved .45ACP pistol.

Bolan swept up the Beretta in a two-fisted grip. The shotgun-perforated door had swung wide and bounced off the inner wall of the office. The hit man wielding the mini-Uzi rushed into the room, his silenced subgun cycling fast, flame spitting from the muzzle.

Bullets sprayed the room. Liu's computer exploded with a shower of sparks and his laptops were torn apart and swept to the floor. The twin CCTV screens caught a single 9 mm slug apiece and went dark as the glass cracked open like eggshells.

The fusillade continued unabated until the room was destroyed.

Jigsaw Liu went out like a warrior.

No matter how despicable his crimes, the triad Red Pole showed courage as he died. Bullets struck him in rapid-fire torrents. Blossoms of scarlet bloomed on his expensive dark suit, spilling blood in surging fountains across his wide desk. Liu shook under the impact, and the sound of lead slugs burning through his torso was clearly audible to Bolan.

Liu was rising as he caught the first burst, swinging around his .45 ACP pistol. The six rounds that struck his chest and gut knocked him back into his seat as he leveled the pistol. The Hong Kong crime lord triggered his handgun twice, the reports sounding like a cannon in the confines of the room. The shots flew wide as more of the submachine-gun rounds drilled into him.

Liu's jigsaw face disappeared in a splashing wave of crimson and flying bone chips as a 3-round burst smashed into his head. The force of the 9 mm bullets bounced him off the back of his seat and he pitched forward, a bloody ruined mess sprawled across his desk.

Blood gushed across the flat expanse of the table top and spilled over the edges to stain the thick carpet burgundy. As he tumbled forward, Liu's hand jerked on the trigger and the pistol fired one last time.

The .45 ACP round burned across the office and struck the submachine-gunner in the thigh, causing the man to crumple and almost fall. Blood spurted bright against the dark material of the hit man's pants. He looked up from behind his balaclava mask and tried to bring the mini-Uzi back under control.

Bolan's single pistol shot from off to the side and just behind the wingback chair took the assassin in the temple. The man's head snapped sharply on his neck, and blood spurted from the wound as a red halo appeared behind his ruined skull.

As the first hit man fell, Bolan's perception of time

caught up with his adrenaline and everything began to unfold in fast forward. The gunman folded at the waist, his submachine-gun bouncing off the carpet. From behind him the shotgun-wielding killer charged into the room. The man moved in with the Remington 870 held out in front of him, the weapon's stock tight against his shoulder.

The cavernous muzzle of the 12-gauge swept the room for a target. Bolan stepped forward and kicked his heavy chair across the room. The hit man tried to swivel as he caught the motion, and the barrel of the shotgun dipped as the shooter instinctively drew down on the object. The chair bounced off the floor and struck him in the shins, causing him to stagger, one hand slipping off the shotgun.

Bolan fired three times in rapid succession on semi-auto. His rounds burrowed through the flesh of the second hit man's throat to pulverize his spine.

The gunner fell, and Bolan dropped to one knee as he shifted aim with the Beretta 93-R. The third hit man was already entering the room, his arms extended straight out in front of him and his hands filled with blazing automatic pistols. Bullets passed harmlessly through the space where Bolan had been standing, whizzing over his head.

The soldier's pistol barked and the face showing in the balaclava mask became a gaping red gash. The dead man's momentum carried him farther into the room until his feet tangled up with corpses of his crew and he pitched forward, his head rapping against the floor.

Through the ringing in his ears Bolan heard angry shouts from the hallway. He knew there was no way that members of the Shimmering Raindrop Triad would believe that he'd had nothing to do with the death of their warlord. They'd shoot first and ask questions later.

Bolan quickly crossed to the desk and grabbed the picture of the individual Stony Man had thought was Scimitar. Whether Liu's reaction was an indication that his intelligence was wrong or that Scimitar was simply cagey, Bolan had no way of verifying at the moment.

He stuffed the picture into the pocket of his jacket, yanked open a desk drawer and plucked the envelope full of cash he'd given Liu for the information. He saw a little black address book and took that, as well.

As he shoved the book into his pants' pocket, he heard a rush of movement outside of the door and dropped behind the desk. The slap of footsteps became muffled on the carpet, and he stood out of his crouch. A Chinese gangster with a ponytail and an M-4 carbine held at port arms stood in the doorway, stunned by the carnage. Bolan took him down with a single Parabellum round.

Hearing more shouts from the hall, the Executioner spun and tried the door set in the back of Liu's office. It was locked. He shifted the fire selector switch to 3-round-burst mode.

Checking first to ensure that the hinges were on the other side of the door, Bolan fired two bursts into the wood around the polished silver handle. The knob burst apart, and the soldier kicked the door open before darting through the opening.

As he passed into a small antechamber at the foot of a short staircase, an automatic weapon cut loose behind him. A storm of bullets cracked into the door frame.

Bolan twisted in the cramped space of the stair landing and thrust his pistol around the corner of the door, triggering two bursts of blind harassing fire, hoping to drive back the triad gunmen. He pulled his hand back and sprinted up the stairs, taking them two at a time, soaking in his environment on the run. Liu's private access stairs were plush and well lit. Bolan's pounding footsteps were absorbed almost completely by the thick, luxurious weave of the carpet. He could see the top of the stairs just ahead and the teak door to the right of the next landing. Before going on, he dropped the clip from the Beretta and rammed home a fresh one.

The door from Liu's office had swung shut behind him, and Bolan heard it slam open. He whirled and leveled the Beretta, tracking for a target. Below him on the stairs a wild-eyed triad gunner leaped through the doorway, an MP-5 submachine-gun in his fists.

The 426 screamed and lifted the weapon. Bolan stroked the trigger on the Beretta 93-R, putting a burst just to the left of the thug's sternum. The gunner buckled at the knees and pitched forward, triggering a burst into the carpet on the stairs.

Knowing the Red Pole had to have fielded numerous 426s in defense of the pit, Bolan spun and continued racing back up the stairs. He bounded to the top and tried the door. It was locked, but this time he could see the lock on his side of the door. He worked the latch and pushed through. His plan was fluid. From the harbor he would make his way to Ladder Street. Once he had climbed that steep incline he'd make his way to Tak Ching Road and begin extraction procedures.

Questions swirled in his mind. Had that hit been a

triad business dispute? Had Bolan been the target? Or had it been designed to keep Liu from talking to him?

The Executioner moved through the door and stepped into a crowded kitchen. The room was big and white, and filled with staring Chinese cooks and bus-boys alerted by the gunfire on the stairs. They shouted in fear and began to scramble over one another in pan-icked efforts to escape.

Sensing no threat, Bolan cut through the kitchen, heading for a swing door set in a far wall. He followed close behind two teenage dishwashers who were run-ning screaming through the exit just steps ahead of him. Bolan burst into a crowded restaurant filled with stunned Chinese couples and a smattering of Occiden-tal tourists.

He raced up an aisle between semiprivate booths, head-ing for the front door of the restaurant. He caught a flash of motion and tried to turn. A lithe 426 in a heavy leather jacket leap toward him from around a decorative support beam, a long-bladed knife naked in the snarling man's fist.

Blocking the wild thrust with the hand holding his Beretta, Bolan twisted at the waist, diverting the man's energy. The triad gunner was tossed around Bolan's center of gravity and crashed into a deserted table, spill-ing bowls of steamed noodles and Kung Pao chicken. The man's blade sliced a six-inch shallow wound along Bolan's arm, splitting the sleeve of his jacket.

The pain was sharp and intense and his clothes were soaked with blood, but the wound was superficial and Bolan was able to raise the Beretta. The 426 twisted smoothly as he slid across the table, recovering with the agility of a cat.

A slim dagger flew from the thug's hand and tumbled smoothly. Bolan managed to jerk his head to one side as the knife spun past him and stuck in the support beam, pinning a narrow silk painting to the lacquered wood.

Bolan's finger was already on the trigger as he ducked, and the Beretta spoke once. Avoiding the knife throw pulled the soldier's aim and the rounds meant for the heart punched through the gangster's upper abdomen instead.

The man shrieked at the sudden agony and Bolan put a second burst under his jaw, silencing the knife fighter before turning and running toward the front door of the restaurant. He could see a knot of panicked people blocking the entrance. Desperate men and women clawed at one another to escape as a tight group of 426s attempted to punch and kick their way into the restaurant. A tall 426 gunner fighting through the doorway recognized Bolan. The man's eyes widened in the shock and he raised his Type-64 Chinese submachine-gun.

Civilians screamed and parted like the sea in front of the 426 death squad as the man unleashed a blast of 7.62 mm rounds. Bolan turned and dived backward over the corpse of the knife fighter as the submachine-gun began to chatter.

Bullets chased Bolan, 7.62 mm slugs tearing into the dangling feet of the 426 knife fighter's corpse. As the Executioner rolled over the table and landed in the next aisle, the 426 he'd killed soaked up more submachine-gun rounds.

Bolan hit the ground, rolled over a shoulder and came up with the Beretta in a two-handed grip. He put the sights on the submachine-gunner and drilled him with a neat 3-round burst. The man fell and Bolan shot the man standing directly behind him. The third 426 staggered backward as the weight of his dead brother in arms pitched back into him. He fired a sloppy shot that sang wide and tried to turn and run. Bolan's next triburst struck the gunner in the neck, knocking him into the street.

Bolan struggled to his feet, reloading on the run. He passed huddle knots of terrified people who watched his rapid progress with wide, unblinking eyes. He stepped over the sprawled corpses of the men he'd shot and left the restaurant to emerge onto a quiet street. No cars moved on the thoroughfare. He could discern no sound of approaching sirens. No other Triad soldiers rushed him. The third 426 he'd killed lay in the gutter.

Bolan lowered the smoking Beretta to his side and jogged across the street. He had rented a nondescript Isuzu Rodeo at the airport under his cover name and parked it several streets over. Once he was at his rendezvous point on Tak Ching Road he'd prep for exfiltration.

The scream saved him.

He heard the angry cry and flung himself flat in the middle of the street. Even as he hit the ground shards of gravel kicked up from the road as bullets slammed into the street all around him. He heard the high chatter of a submachine-gun and caught the muzzle flash blinking out of the darkness at the mouth of the alley.

He saw the shrieking 426 walking toward him, eyes narrowed into slits like an angry cat's, the Type-64 bucking wildly as the man fired from the hip. Behind the gangster two more triad soldiers, each armed with twin Beretta 92-Fs, spilled out onto the street.

Bolan rolled up onto his left side and swung out his right arm, triggering the Beretta. His rounds cut into the crazy 426 just under the man's bucking submachine-gun, ripping open his stomach. The man staggered to one side and fired his weapon into the ground. He stumbled then went down, dropping his weapon to the street.

The two 426 gunners behind him stood their ground, side by side, each man blazing away with the 9 mm Beretta pistols they held in either hand. Bolan sighted in on one, moving too fast for anything other than instinct, and drilled the man through his open, screaming mouth.

The gangster's head jerked and a bloody halo framed his head as he pitched over backward. The triggerman beside him stopped firing as his partner went down. His face registered horror, and he thrust out his arms as he began to run back into the cover of the alley, his pistols belching flame and lead in a sporadic, indiscriminate pattern.

Bolan drew down on the man and put a burst into his torso under his waving arms. The man shook with the impact and staggered, then went down like a tree in a high wind. His pistols fell from slack fingers and clattered on the pavement.

The Executioner pushed himself up from his prone position, weapon at the ready. He shuffled backward across the street, his eyes scanning the restaurant and alley for even the slightest hint of hostile movement. He made it across the street and onto the sidewalk, then turned and sprinted down a small side street, putting solid cover between himself and the battlefield.

The CIA would be unhappy about a back door source into the People's Republic CCI being shot to pieces, but

Bolan could legitimately argue that it hadn't been his fault. Gangsters killed off one another on a frequent basis. The higher the profits at stake, the more likely violence became.

Jigsaw Liu worked a dangerous profession but Bolan didn't believe in coincidences. It was a very real likelihood that Liu had been silenced because of him, which meant his mission was compromised from the very beginning.

The Executioner would be leaving Hong Kong with unanswered questions.

CHAPTER EIGHT

Bolan took a commercial flight into Zagreb International Airport.

He navigated the transglobal route with an almost mechanical competency. Weapons and identification were dumped with the CIA in Hong Kong after he made one report to the case officer and a second one to Stony Man. A layover in Manila was followed by a connecting flight to Bangkok, Thailand. In Thailand he destroyed his papers and obtained new ones from a dead drop in an airport locker.

Under his new papers he flew out of Bangkok and into Riyadh, Saudi Arabia. There he noticed a marked increase in Westerners in both the airport and on his own flight to Izmir, Turkey.

In Izmir, Bolan used a safehouse to shift identities once again while he waited during a four-hour layover for a flight into Zagreb on Turkish Airlines. At the safehouse he was able to utilize secure communications to catch up on the progress Encizo and James had made so far. After a nap and a shower, Bolan was in the air to Croatia.

As the plane veered into its runway approach, Bolan was able to see the gleaming ribbon of the Sava river just to the south of the city. Zagreb, Croatia's capital, was situated between the southern slopes of the Medvednica Mountains and the north bank of the Sava river. The commercial flight touched down and Bolan was able to sail through customs with his immaculate paperwork and only a small carry-on to check.

Outside the modern terminal Calvin James and Rafael Encizo waited for him in the passenger pickup area. The two Stony Man commandos greeted Bolan like old friends and the three "representatives" of North American International climbed into their waiting Ford Excursion.

"That beard's coming in nice," Calvin James said with a smile.

"Thanks. It itches like hell," Bolan replied. "You wait, once we finish dealing with Mirjana you'll get your chance."

After sliding into the shotgun seat, Bolan saw immediately that the Excursion was a diplomatic special, possibly left over from the days of violence in the former Republic of Yugoslavia. Such a vehicle would be outfitted with upgraded communications, executive armor, a more powerful engine than factory stock and concealed compartments for prohibited equipment such as weapons or surveillance devices.

Encizo pulled the big SUV into traffic and headed northwest out of the village of Pleso toward the congestion of Slavonska-Držićeva Avenue some fourteen kilometers away.

"How was you flight, Mack?" Encizo asked from behind the vehicle's steering wheel.

The stocky, square-faced Cuban commando was an experienced underwater warfare specialist and urban operator who had cut his teeth in anti-Castro actions before joining the Stony Man team.

"Good enough, though I was feeling about as incognito as a circus clown on some of my flights out of Hong Kong."

James snorted his laughter from the backseat. "Hell, try being *us* being *here* if you want difficulty blending in."

Bolan smiled and nodded. Such problems had been a consideration when he'd chosen how to staff the operation. While he'd almost picked others from Phoenix Force, Bolan had finally decided that what was a hindrance for the minor action in Croatia would become an advantage once the team reached Baghdad.

"You have trouble with Mirjana because of that?" Bolan asked.

Encizo shook his head. "No, he bought it completely that we were purchasing agents for North American International. We played up the whole running-wild-on-an-expense-account thing."

"Sounds like you had more success than I did," Bolan noted. In precise, clipped details he ran down the events that had unfolded in Hong Kong and Jigsaw Liu's final words.

Encizo let out a long, low whistle as Bolan finished describing what had happened in the Hong Kong pit.

"Scimitar's a lie?" James asked. "Does that make sense?"

"Only in context," Bolan said. "Unfortunately, we don't understand that context."

Encizo steered the Excursion down an off-ramp and exited onto the modern expressway that encircled the city. From the expressway Bolan could look out and see the most notable landmarks of Zagreb's skyline: the Euro, HOTO and Cibona towers. On the expressway Encizo began to speed toward the northwest corner of Zagreb.

"Well, Mirjana is the real deal," James said.

"He offer you weapons?" Bolan asked.

"Yep, get this. Once I made my introduction and gave him the information for North American International, he verified our employment with the company through standard channels."

"Typical."

"Sure, Gary's people vouched for us no problem. But then the Croatian government asked for information on the company from the State Department as a 'diplomatic favor.' Gary has his network security tied into Stony Man. Aaron said he was able to detect an info-snatch worm originating from the HIS that cracked our cover personnel files and North American International's authorization package to operate as a private military contract company in Iraq."

"HIS?" Bolan grunted. "No one told us Mirjana was that well connected."

The HIS, Hrvatska Izvestajna Sluzba, or Croatian Intelligence Service, was the youngest agency in the former Yugoslavia republic's espionage community. It had been first commissioned in the winter of 1993 and dealt exclusively with the collection and analysis of foreign intelligence for coordination and dissemination to other branches of the Croat government and intelligence community.

As the majority of information collected by the HIS was utilized through the office of the president and his closest advisers on the cabinet, their involvement with Mirjana was potentially ominous.

"Apparently this is news. Aaron doesn't want to share what this proves with the DNI because he's afraid that once the Agency finds out, they'll call Mirjana off-limits and try to exploit him," James said.

"Oh, we were here first," Bolan said. "That crooked Syrian bastard al-Kassar might have a pass for now, but Mirjana is all ours."

"That's what Barb says, too," James agreed. "Hal's going along with it for now. Part of the confusion is that we aren't really able to tell where Mirjana pulls his arms from. It isn't Croatian stocks except in small numbers."

"I thought he was initially an executive with RH-Alan?" Bolan questioned, referring to the infamous Croatian arms company.

"He was, until 2000. Made his millions off government contracts during the conflicts, then he retired. Most intelligence reports had him figured for getting his supplies through them."

"Looks like they figured wrong," Encizo said. "Either way, we can purchase light or heavy infantry weapons, parts for armored personal carriers, including the electronics for cutting-edge systems, night-vision equipment and engineering explosives. He hinted he could go larger, but we really didn't have a reason to be asking about laser-guided bombs. Still, most of the stocks are not Croatian armed forces mainstays."

"He didn't ask why you need black-market weapons with a U.S. government license to operate?"

"We told him there were restrictions we wanted to circumvent on numbers and types of munitions. He saw a sale and greed did the rest."

Bolan nodded. "Betting on greed usually works."

"Only to a degree in this case," James said. "He flatly refused to discuss anything beyond business transactions. If we want information from him, we're going to have to take it."

"That's not a problem," Bolan said.

KARL MIRJANA'S SPRAWLING estate sat nestled in a gentle saddle among the foothills of the Medvednica Mountains. In some ways it reminded Bolan of Stony Man Farm, with a large dacha-style main house, attached garages and numerous outbuildings. One of the structures was a luxurious hunting lodge—set at the edge of the estate on the woods leading to the southern slopes of the mountains—where Mirjana was known to conduct his business. A small paved airstrip was set on a patch of level ground on the river side of the estate.

Just beyond the airstrip Mirjana's property abutted a bend in the river. A two-story yacht was moored to a man-made jetty of boulders that sheltered the craft from the river current.

James and Encizo had done preliminary reconnaissance of the Mirjana estate. The man's defenses were considerable and appeared left over from the 1995 battles with Serbian forces: ground surveillance microphones, electronic sensors, commercial alarms and land mines along certain approaches.

Mirjana kept a small cadre of former members of the Serbian Special Police Units, the SMJ, as bodyguards.

It was at first confusing why a Croatian arms dealer would be using Serbian commandos who had been accused of war crimes against his own people.

On further reflection it made a certain, cynical sense. Serbs were a minority in Croatia. Former Serb military veterans were hated and the SMJ most of all. The social animosity kept Mirjana's private army isolated and thus loyal to him. He paid them well, they lived in luxury and were kept busy.

In addition to duties as security for shipments, action as bodyguards and sometime strike force for underworld disputes, the ex-SMJ troopers served as estate sentries. Armed with modern weapons and equipment, they patrolled the interior of the property and responded to any alarms or other disturbances.

Bolan sat in a rest area just off the northern expressway where it turned into a more rural highway. From that position the Stony Man team could overlook the entrance to Mirjana's estate. Behind it the Sava ran in an almost perfectly straight diagonal line up toward the northwest.

It was night, and lights from Mirjana's estate cut through the dark to illuminate expansive lawns and the purple tree copses on the mountain slopes behind it. At the front gate a sentry worked a brick booth, controlling entry.

Bolan lowered his night-vision binoculars.

"These are good," he said.

"I thought it would be ironic if we took him down using equipment and weapons he'd sold us as part of our preliminary package," James said.

Bolan smiled. "All this gear is from him?"

"Yeah. He took us to a warehouse in Pleso to show off his selection. We pulled exactly what we needed off the shelves. It was like Home Depot, dudes with electric forklifts and everything," James said.

"When's my meeting?" Bolan asked.

"About thirty minutes," James replied.

"And he always does his business meets in the hunting lodge?"

"He claims it's easier to ensure his electronic countermeasures are working against surveillance," Encizo stated. "Like I told you, he even has an airport metal detector in the entrance hall."

"I doubt you can get a piece in," James said.

Bolan nodded. "I don't intend to. I'll rely on you two to shut the place down. I'll keep Mirjana busy until you get in, Cal," Bolan replied.

The two Phoenix Force commandos had thought Bolan's plan for the Mirjana takedown risky. They were men used to danger, and Stony Man missions were run on extraordinarily narrow margins to begin with, but the news that Mirjana was tied into the Croatian government had changed everything for Bolan.

A straight assault could result in a distress alert making it out. The Stony Man commandos could find themselves trapped in the compound with SMJ killers while a Croatian government rapid-response force surrounded them, a diplomatically unacceptable situation. Smuggling their own weapons into the estate was also unfeasible due to Mirjana's extreme security precautions.

Bolan had instead decided on a multipronged strategy. He would meet with Mirjana as the top purchaser of overseas acquisitions for North American International. The man who could sign the checks for big orders. Once Bolan was in proximity to Mirjana and could control his movements, Encizo and James would begin their assignments.

Encizo would approach from the Sava River and provide security overwatch across the lawns between the hunting lodge and the rest of the estate. He would neutralize any reinforcements moving to assist their boss.

James would infiltrate across the estate and bring in the weapons to secure the lodge. With Mirjana under wraps and Encizo providing security, the two men would begin their interrogation of the Croat arms dealer.

Bolan had brought hell with him to Croatia. He was about to introduce the Zagreb arms dealer to a fiery term of retribution.

Karl Mirjana had information the Executioner needed. Saying no was not an option.

CHAPTER NINE

The Stony Man team readied its gear and climbed into the Ford SUV. Bolan drove the Excursion now and he navigated through the outskirts of Zagreb, dropping James and Encizo at predetermined locations before heading directly toward Mirjana's estate.

Headlights stabbed through the pitch darkness as Bolan rolled to a stop and switched them off for the first insertion. Calvin James, dressed in a sniper's ghillie suit and armed with a Croatian-made APS-95 assault rifle, rolled out of the back of the vehicle and into the woods. The forest ran unbroken up into the southern foothills that formed the northern perimeter of the arms dealer's remote estate and private hunting preserve.

Bolan pulled the SUV away from the spot and sped toward a secluded section of highway that ran next to the Sava River.

Outfitted in a neoprene drysuit, Encizo quickly disappeared into the low hedges along the riverbank, equipped with combat swimmer fins and a rebreather as well as an oilskin shoulder bag containing his long weapon and a silenced machine pistol. A double-edged dive knife was secured to the knotted muscle of Encizo's calf and ankle.

Bolan was gone long before the Cuban-born commando had entered the water. With the members of his team deployed for their assault, the soldier guided the Ford Excursion back toward Karl Mirjana's estate.

Bolan had dressed in upscale casual for his meet with the Croat. He wore sturdy but stylish khaki pants in black. Under his jacket he wore a crew-necked black pullover of expensive material and weave. He wore his Rolex Submariner watch and a pair of low-cut loafers with thick tread. The loafers were steel-toed and he hoped this would go unnoticed. Except for those steel caps he would be unarmed going into the death merchant's lair.

After several minutes Bolan pulled off the main highway and took an unmarked paved private road. The long drive wound through several gentle curves cut through a dense copse. After nearly a full mile Bolan caught sight of the gate complex set across the road like a military checkpoint.

The fence was constructed of deeply red brick, ten feet high, and ran into the forest on either side. The heavy wrought-iron gate was electronically controlled, and heavy enough to resist ramming by even a semi-truck.

Bolan slowed as he approached the cinder-block gatehouse. Through the window he saw a tall man in blue coveralls rise from behind a desk. The black nylon pistol belt secured around his waist held a Glock handgun secured in the holster.

As the soldier stopped the SUV beside the gatehouse and powered down his window, the sentry came out, a telescoping metal pole with a mirror fitted on the end in his left hand.

"Mike Cooper, North American International," Bolan said. "I have an appointment with Mr. Mirjana." He wondered if the man spoke English, though the names should get the message across if he were expected.

The man nodded. "*Ja,* moment." His English was broken and accented but passable. "I check the vehicle. If you have weapons, I request you turn them me, now."

Bolan grinned. "I'm clean."

The sentry seemed to accept his word and focused on playing the mirror across the vehicle's undercarriage. As he went about his security check, Bolan was able to get a better look at the pistol in the man's holster.

Calvin James had been correct during his earlier briefing to Bolan. The Glock was a specialized model only available to military and police units. The Glock 18 fired 9 mm Parabellum ammunition and, like Bolan's Beretta 93-R, could operate in either semiautomatic or 3-round bursts. The pistol had a 31-round extended magazine and a theoretical rate of fire in burst mode of 1200 rounds per minute.

Karl Mirjana was a serious man, which suited Bolan just fine. The Executioner was serious himself.

The sentry stepped back from the vehicle. "Follow road past the main house to left, *ja?* You drive all the way through the property to lodge where Mr. Mirjana meets clients. Do not get out of car. Security meet you at lodge. Go."

The man stepped back inside the gatehouse and worked a button on his console. With the hum of powerful electric motors the gate unlatched and began to swing open. Bolan waited until the gate was fully open before driving through.

He did not wave at the man as he drove past.

WHILE BOLAN DROVE into the estate Calvin James circumvented the property and approached it from the rear. The going was tough. The woods were thick and the terrain steep. A former Navy SEAL, James had been in uncompromising physical condition before coming to Stony Man and still followed a grueling fitness program.

Despite his level of fitness, James sweated freely in the commercial camouflage suit. He scrambled up hillsides thick with brush and weeds, making his way around Mirjana's estate toward the rear. He swept up the incline, sticking to patches of deep woods and using game trails so that as he made his final approach he was coming downhill toward Mirjana's property.

As he neared the back of the estate James was forced to slow his approach. From his earlier reconnaissance he knew that a line of wild brambles and blackberry shrubs marked the beginning of Mirjana's property line, set well before the wall that encircled the estate. The ex-Navy SEAL made his approach toward the brambles with trepidation.

Just beyond the brambles Mirjana's security consisted of an array of spike microphones. Anyone thrashing through the brambles would be picked up on the hidden mikes and trigger an alarm response. Because of that James knew he would have to leave behind the relative invisibility offered by the ghillie suit.

James sank to the forest floor and quietly removed the camouflage. The loose patches and swathes of fabric that were so effective in breaking up the outline of a human body would only serve to snag and catch on the brambles and thorny blackberry branches.

Moving carefully, he crawled into the thicket on his elbows and knees, picking up thick vines and sliding under them, carefully dragging his weapon with the stock folded down behind him. He pulled a pair of garden clippers from a cargo pocket and carefully began to cut out a path.

Though he had purposefully chosen a section of bramble thicket that was in his opinion less dense than some other areas, it was still painstaking work. Every movement he made had the potential to be detected by the electronic sensors positioned on the other side.

Sweat rolled down his face. He pressed down slowly and steadily with the clippers to avoid the snipping sound common to his activity. Beyond the thicket and across a strip of tall grass Mirjana's wall rose in an imposing barrier.

One thing at a time, James told himself. One thing at a time.

RAFAEL ENCIZO PURGED his regulator and slipped into the Sava river without disturbing the surface. The closed-system rebreather eliminated the telltale exhaust noise and bubble trail left by conventional Scuba gear and provided for a more silent diving experience.

Encizo felt the current of the deep river catch him up

and sweep him along toward his target as he descended into the chilly darkness. His load-bearing harness was front-loaded, and the Phoenix Force commando compensated by adjusting buoyancy for that and the gear attached in oilskin to his back. He settled slowly down through the murky water and began to check his analog and digital displays. He would use the bottom to ensure depth consistency and a built-in pace counter to indicate the distance he swam.

Encizo kicked out gently with his swim fins, using the current to push him along and conserve energy. His breath echoed slightly behind his mask and visibility was less than an arm's length in the polluted river water.

The little Cuban took in calm, even breaths, conserving his energy and executing his movements with a maximum of efficiency. Occasionally he was forced to dodge underwater obstacles like dead trees or bits of garbage, which required that his concentration remain sharp.

He checked his watch and cross-indexed the time he had swum with the distance his pace indicator displayed as traveled. When he calculated that with what he believed was the appropriate figure, Encizo began to rise, kicking forcibly for the surface. It was imperative that he not overshoot his target and miss Mirjana's quay.

He rose up from the depths, and his head broke the surface of the water. He kicked against the current, slowing his drift with the river until he could get his bearings. Fifty yards down he saw the wall of boulders Mirjana had used to construct his quay-pier.

The yacht, which sat in the protective lee of the quay, was almost eighty-five-feet long, and Encizo recognized it as a Princess 25m motor yacht, powered by Twin Caterpillar 1570hp engines. Despite himself the mariner in Encizo was impressed.

How Mirjana had earned that beautiful three-level craft turned the Cuban freedom fighter's stomach. The craft itself was a thing of perfection. Capable of being manned by two to five crewmembers, the Princess 25m had port and starboard guest berths in addition to the owner's salon. When Mirjana cruised the Sava he obviously did so in style.

Encizo allowed himself to drift in toward the big yacht, his predator senses alive. He floated into the wall of stacked boulders and grasped them firmly, allowing the current to gently pull him along the wall of rock as he watched the boat for any sign of movement. The flying bridge, with its sweeping arch housing the communications antennas, was empty.

Through the heavily tinted windows around the forward salon Encizo could see the flickering distortion of what could only be a large-screen TV. Someone was on board. He submerged and floated until he came to the end of the jetty wall.

He swam into the open mouth of the quay, which faced south, away from the river current. Kicking deeper, he entered the pocket of water protected from the pull and ebb of the current. The water was calm there, like a gloomy pool, and Encizo floated.

He broke the surface at the rear of the yacht as he had intended, very near the flat extension of the tender deck. A Yamaha wetbike was secured to one side of the dive platform. A swim ladder extended over the edge and dipped down into the water.

Encizo's eyes searched the back of the boat. He could hear the sounds of the television coming muted through the closed doors. The yacht was immaculate, and for the first time Encizo could see the name on its side: *Djodan*.

Deep in his zone of predator awareness, Encizo reached out for the ladder and prepared to board Karl Mirjana's yacht.

BOLAN CRUISED through the estate at a sedate 15 mph, eyeing the layout and gathering his bearings as he moved past the main house and through the outbuildings. The grounds were well tended and the main house loomed in an imposing manner that brought to mind Southern plantations.

The mansion was three stories high and had three separate wings. It blazed with lights, and Bolan hoped extraneous servants and family members remained out of his way. The life Karl Mirjana had made for a wife and children or a mistress had been built on a shaky foundation, and Bolan had come to this place to blow his house down.

As Bolan drove up, a man in blue coveralls and a pistol belt stood at the head of a circular drive that looped off the main estate avenue and ran past the massive front doors. The man was broad-shouldered, with a narrow waist and close-cropped hair. The sentry waved Bolan past the turnoff to the mansion and up the road as efficiently and bored as any construction flagger or traffic cop.

Bolan drove along a line of evergreens and the hunting lodge came into view. The "lodge" was a two-story, three-thousand square-foot A-frame log house. It was a temple to conceit, arrogance and corruption.

As the soldier slowed the SUV, two men dressed in subdued uniforms of jeans and blue blazers, unlike the typical coveralls he'd seen so far, stepped off the lodge porch. One of the men carried a handheld metal detector wand shaped like a long narrow paddle. The second man was simply huge. Bolan turned off the engine and stepped out of the vehicle. The giant on the right watched Bolan with slow-witted pig eyes. The security technician approached Bolan, indicating for him to lift his arms.

"Mr. Mirjana is expecting you inside," the man said. "This is merely a formality, you understand, but times are trying for a man in Mr. Mirjana's line of work. I'm sure you understand." His English was clipped and precise.

"Of course," Bolan allowed, playing his role. "Austrian?" he inquired as the security tech ran the wand across his body.

"Swiss," the man answered.

"Your English is very good," Bolan said as the man finished the check.

"I attended the U.S. Air Force Academy in Boulder, Colorado," he replied. "Mr. Mirjana will see you now."

Stepping forward, Bolan moved past the silent giant who scrutinized him. Closer up now, the soldier could see the man had at least six inches in height and more than a hundred pounds of body weight on him. His thick hands were as big as shovel blades.

Bolan climbed the broad steps leading up to the porch. The deck itself was a low veranda covered by an extension of the roof and surrounded by an intricate, hand-carved railing. Two massive oak pillars supported the overhang, one on each side of the two heavy doors leading inside the lodge.

He entered the building, noting that he was indeed moving past a walk-through metal detector much like those used at airports. Behind him the two security techs circumvented the detector to avoid setting it off. He found himself in a long, high-ceilinged hallway lined with three doors on each side, leading to other rooms.

Bolan moved down the hall and past a large closet with a sliding door. Paintings hung on the wall, mostly of scenes that seemed inspired by Wagnerian operas. The decor was unabashedly masculine and reeked of privilege.

At the end of the hallway Bolan walked into a large open room. Against the north wall a wide balcony overlooked the sprawling living area, which was framed by couches and comfortable divans. An onyx and black-oak wet bar took up one wall and a immense stone fireplace with a fire burning in the hearth stood directly in front of Bolan. Ornamental andirons were set permanently into the stone and on a wooden end table between one couch and the bar sat a lamp of heavy, burnished brass.

A Kodiak bearskin rug was splayed across the floor at Bolan's feet. The interior of the lodge was burnished wood with darker wainscoting. Stuffed heads from a variety of wild game were mounted on the wall. It was obvious that the unpopularity of trophy hunting brought about by political correctness and legitimate conservation concerns had failed to convert Karl Mirjana.

Big bay windows on either side of the fireplace showed the heavily wooded slopes of the mountains beyond the brick wall that encircled the estate. Bolan turned slowly, taking in everything. He noted exits and passages, setting the building's layout firmly in his mind in case he was forced to navigate it under pressure or in the dark.

Behind him the two security techs entered the room and took up unobtrusive positions against the wall, their hands folded carefully in front of them.

A door just off the great area swung open and Karl Mirjana entered the room.

CHAPTER TEN

As Mack Bolan turned to meet Karl Mirjana, Calvin James cut his way through the last bit of brambles separating him from the grass strip surrounding the northern estate wall. In the area beyond the thorny bushes cheat grass waved slightly in the breeze that came down off the mountain slope.

The Phoenix Force commando halted and slowly scanned the area, spotting the back gate to the estate to his left. Despite the temptation offered by the dirt track leading to the rear entrance, he had avoided the egress point for his approach as being a focal center for the security system.

His reconnaissance during his meet with Mirjana and on his previous soft probes had revealed the pattern for the estate defenses. That had dictated his infiltration pattern.

There were trip indicators, cameras and armed guards. Trip indicators had been placed around the general perimeter with CCTV camera networks on the gates and building exteriors. A trip indicator would alert a system controller in the main house, who would then either maneuver the camera pods off the gates and toward the source of the trip, or dispatch personnel to the site. Inside the wall, guards patrolled at night and manned unobtrusive posts during the day.

By moving slowly and avoiding the CCTV camera pod clusters, James hoped to circumvent the eyes-on areas of the system. The problem was that Mirjana's trip indicators were good. Pedestrian compared to some of the laser fences utilized on facilities with less foot traffic, but dependable.

Moving carefully, James entered the cheat grass. He kept low, parting the tall stalks with his hands then slowly penetrating forward into the field beyond the brambles, which was filled with spike microphones. Every few yards James was forced into an awkward two-step to avoid another one of the trip indicators. He was sure his sound signature was being picked up by the system controller, but he hoped by moving slowly the disruption of rhythm would prompt the technician to dismiss the sound fluctuations as wind causing the tall grass to rub on the microphones.

The ground surveillance system had been created and initially utilized by military intelligence programs to help pinpoint unsuspecting troop movements along trails and a lone operator already aware of the presence of the devices had a good chance of cat-dancing past the spike microphones.

James exercised his self-discipline, squashed the trepidation he felt at being so exposed and forced himself to continue moving slowly. There would be little indication when the defenses hidden among the tall grass

changed from passive to active. Alertness was para-
mount.

Rifle slung over his shoulder, James sank to his
knees. He slowly felt out in front of him, moving even
slower now as his proximity to the wall increased. As
he parted the grass, his touch became a gentle caress.

His fingers found the tripwire.

James carefully raised his hand and focused his eyes
on the threat. He followed the line of the wire to where
it disappeared into the clumps of tall grass. Slowly he
eased himself forward, following the trip line deeper
into the minefield. Fifteen harrowing feet later, James
came up to the mine.

A phalange circle of trip prongs stuck up from a metal
bottleneck buried in the ground. James recognized the
mine as a PROM-1 bounding antipersonnel mine. The
PROM-1 was a homegrown Yugoslavian product and had
been used prolifically during the Bosnian conflict.

When detonated the mine bounded into the air to a
height of roughly six-yards before it detonated, unleash-
ing steel fragments in a 360-degree arc out to thirty
yards. The shrapnel was propelled by 425 g of Compo-
sition B explosives, making the PROM-1 a highly effective killer. James gave it the respect it deserved. First
he snipped the wire to release the tension on the trigger,
then moved carefully around the antipersonnel mine.

Three more times he was forced to repeat his dangerous game until he reached the estate fence. Finally
the ex-SEAL was flush against the brick wall of the
compound property. He rested momentarily.

James slowly rose out of his crouch. The wall was
ten feet high and made of smooth-fitted red brick.

James unslung his APS-95 assault rifle and undid the black nylon strap from the buttstock attachment point, leaving it still secured at the muzzle under the front sight. Having prepared for this, James took a thick needle from where he had inserted it through the cloth on the cover flap of his cargo pocket.

The Stony Man commando slid the free end of the nylon rifle strap under his belt and pushed the needle, point down, through the two folds of the strap, attaching it to himself quickly and efficiently. Without hesitation he placed the assault rifle against the estate wall and used it like a step ladder, exploiting momentum to keep the ad hoc platform in place.

His hands grasped the top of the wall and he smoothly pulled himself into position, the assault rifle dangling behind him. Once astride the brick wall he leaned low to avoid silhouetting himself, pulled the rifle up and rolled over onto the lawn.

He landed cat-quiet and pulled the needle free, releasing the strap from him. He swept the rifle up and scanned the area quickly, finding no movement, hearing no alarm. With deft fingers he secured the sling to the buttstock swivel and rose.

Like some malevolent ghost, Calvin James penetrated farther into the Mirjana estate.

RAFAEL ENCIZO KICKED OFF his fins and let them drift away into the water before ducking under the surface and peeling off the rebreather kit. From beneath the surface Encizo grasped the yacht's swim ladder with one hand and pulled himself up.

As he rose, the Cuban-born commando removed one

of Karl Mirjana's little treasures. The PB/6P9 pistol had come out of a crate stamped with a Chinese ideogram, but the pistol itself was a Russian Spetsnaz favorite.

The 6P9 was a direct descendant of the Makarov and designed specifically for use with a sound suppressor, though it could be fired under emergency situations with the front half of the suppressor removed. At close-quarter battle range the 9 mm round was more than sufficient for putting men down.

Encizo came out of the water smoothly and slid across the deck. He kept the 6P9 up and ready, as he stalked through the outdoor lounge area with its white couches and toward the door leading into the aft salon. The sound of the television grew louder as Encizo approached the door.

He heard rapid bursts of what he thought was German followed by grunts and high-pitched squeals coming from the surround sound system. He moved through the aft deck in a slight crouch, attempting to present as low a profile as he could manage to avoid being silhouetted through the tinted windows of the passenger salon.

He reached the door and quietly pulled it open. Immediately the level of noise from the television rose, no longer muffled by the barrier. The porno orgy raged on a plasma screen cranked to a generous volume. The video's porn stud grunted and cursed in German and the woman screeched and shrieked with such clichéd enthusiasm that Encizo winced under the sudden auditory assault. Beyond the salon a large galley and dining area were situated before the floor plan tapered up into the helm.

Encizo had checked the blueprints for the yacht on-line while waiting for Bolan to join them in Zagreb. He knew exactly which door led to the staterooms below-decks, and he kept one eye cocked toward the door and the curved stair leading down from the flying bridge as he ghosted farther into the salon.

He tracked slowly with the silenced 6P9 as he moved through the room. He felt confident that if a sentry had been on the flying bridge he would have seen him from the water, so Encizo kept most of his senses keyed toward the door.

Beyond the couch that stood in front of the plasma screen, a heavy coffee table commanded the center of the generous room. On the floor beyond it was a pair of black thong women's panties, wadded up and forgotten. A Monet in a heavy gilded frame had been placed on the coffee table, glass face up. On the protective glass sat several conical heaps of white powder Encizo recognized as not cocaine, but the newer form of heroin that could be insufflated, or snorted. A woman's silver lipstick case sat next to the picture, a matching silver razor blade placed beside it.

He peered into the shadows beyond the galley area to try to pick out a shape or motion from the helm con-cave but found nothing there. He rounded the edge of the couch facing the plasma screen and looked to see if one of Mirjana's employees was laid out on the lavish piece of furniture.

The door leading up from the staterooms burst open and Encizo shifted, snapping the silenced 6P9 around in a two-handed grip. The dark paneled door bounced off the inside wall, and a couple stumbled through it, tangled up in each other's arms. The man wore a rumpled and unzipped pair of the blue coveralls Encizo recognized as Mirjana's generic security uniform. The man held a giggling brunette in one hand and an open magnum of champagne in the other. Huge tuffs of black chest hair spilled out of the partially open zipper, a thick gold chain glittered in the tangled nest.

The woman wore a flimsy but expensive kimono-style bathrobe strained to the limit by generous breasts. She laughed wildly as a second man, behind her, grabbed her buttocks.

She looked up, saw the masked Encizo with pistol drawn and screamed.

The ex-SMJ commando snapped his head up, his laughter dying. He saw the dark figure of death standing in front of him. Behind the intruder mechanical sex pumped out on the plasma TV screen, punctuated by shrieks and gasps. The man dropped his champagne flute and the magnum bottle as he went for his holstered pistol.

The glass magnum struck the carpet and bounced. Champagne bubbled out furiously, like white-water rapids spilling over rocks. The woman screamed again and the man cursed. Encizo's hands were stone steady on the trigger of the Russian pistol.

The 6P9 spit twice with subdued pops as the sound suppressor's muzzle brake bled off the sonic vibrations. The first security guard lost a left eye, and an untidy comma cracked open his forehead. The man went rigid and dropped to the floor, crimson splatter running down the woman's face like ropes of spit.

Still shrieking, she was brutally shoved aside as the

second sentry pushed past her, pulling his Glock 18 free from its holster. Encizo gunned him down with a double tap to the head, as well, and the man dropped to the carpet, dead. He lay there, his cheek caressed by the spilling champagne, his eyes staring wide open and fixed.

The woman turned and saw the second man in her ménage à trois fall dead at her feet. Her hands flew to her blood-splattered face and she sank, screaming, to her knees.

Encizo rushed forward. He was brutal and efficient, operating without pity. He pulled the woman up by her wrist, desperate to stop her screeching before she alerted the entire Mirjana estate to his presence.

He released her, and she stumbled back against the bulkhead but stayed on her feet. Encizo's eyes surveyed her anatomy with precise intentions. The carotid sinus was a network of nerves running along the side of the neck just under the ear. Encizo raised the 6P9 and chopped the butt of the pistol into the nerve cluster along the woman's throat.

Her central nervous system short-circuited, much like someone crossing the polarities on a car battery. Her eyes rolled up, showing whites, and she folded like a house of cards, unconscious. Encizo let her fall and dropped to his knees beside her as he pulled his dive knife from his calf sheath.

He quickly cut the laces from one of the dead security men's boots. Sheathing the knife, Encizo bound the woman's hands and feet behind her then used her own kimono to hood and gag her, tying it off with her silk belt. He picked her up and threw her on the couch.

Tired of the noise, Encizo turned and punched off the power button on the plasma screen with one gloved finger, killing the graphic sex flick. He hoped the woman had enough alcohol and heroin in her system to keep her out. He fisted the 6P9 and cleared the rest of the yacht in as expedient a manner as possible.

Coming up out of the staterooms, Encizo checked once more on the woman. She remained unconscious but breathing, and the Phoenix Force warrior quickly mounted the stairs to the flying bridge.

From the bridge he commanded a good view of Mirjana's estate, including the front and west side of the arms dealer's extravagant hunting lodge. Sitting in the pilot seat, Encizo put the 6P9 away and shrugged out of his oilskin gun carry.

From inside the bag he removed a plastic security case and popped open the snaps. Inside was a Chinese QBU-88 designated marksmen rifle, broken down into its main components. The rifle was of bullpup design and equipped with a flash suppressor, detachable bipod and 4x power scope. Aware of the considerable illumination found from various sources on Mirjana's estate at night, Encizo had chosen not to go with a night sight or Starlite scope.

The 5.8 mm People's Republic of China assault rifle was not a true sniper or match piece, but rather was for those conventional infantry soldiers designated by command elements for engaging targets beyond normal infantry weapon ranges on the battlefield. That made it versatile, sturdy and more than adequate for the ranges Encizo would be called upon to fire across in his security support position.

Encizo inserted the 10-round detachable box magazine and chambered one of the special, heavy load 5.8 x 42mm cartridges. Nestling down behind the scope, He acquired the front door of the cabin and fine-tuned his scope to the range. He exhaled slowly.

"MR. COOPER," MIRJANA SAID in flawless English. "Welcome to my home. I hope your trip was pleasant?"

"Oh, this is a hell of a lot more pleasant than Baghdad," Bolan laughed and held out his hand, playing his role. It was an act he had honed over years of Mafia infiltrations.

Karl Mirjana moved forward and took the offered hand. The Croatian arms dealer was tall and trim with a European metrosexual style that leaned heavily toward machismo. His hair was silver and brushed straight back from a broad, high forehead to hang down past his shirt collar. He wore a stylish if affected Van Dyke beard, and was adorned with heavy gold at his neck, wrist and right earlobe. His watch was the same heavy gold, and his fingers were adorned with thick gold rings.

As he walked toward his guest, Bolan was able to see how the man kept his silk shirt unbuttoned to midchest and note the obscenely tight fit of his tailored Italian slacks. It was not a view Bolan enjoyed. He shook the man's hand firmly anyway and found the Croatian's clasp dry and warm, the shake confident.

"In our business we often find ourselves in unpleasant environments, no?" Mirjana asked.

Bolan nodded as his host ushered him toward the wet bar. "You have to go where the money leads you," he said.

Mirjana laughed. "True. Very true. What can I offer you? I have American bourbon if you wish. I drink gin myself."

"Whatever you're having is good enough for me." Bolan casually noted the Bavarian clock set on the wall. The Stony Man team had cut a fine operational timeline, and he was especially concerned that Calvin James hadn't been given enough leeway. Bolan continued to casually case the room.

"Can Erazmus take your jacket?" Mirjana asked as he poured drinks.

Bolan nodded and slid out of his leather coat. The Swiss security tech stepped forward and took the garment. Bolan watched him open a cedar closet door set on one side of the room. He noted pillowcases and additional sheets for bedding set in the cupboards along with a battery-operated, European-style iron and ironing board in addition to some other coats and rain jackets.

"I trust your associates were happy with the sample equipment I provided?" Mirjana asked, handing Bolan a cut-crystal tumbler. The soldier smelled the pine-needle sent of good gin.

"So far," Bolan allowed, and sipped. "Enough to convince me you were exactly the man I needed to talk to."

Bolan leaned against the bar, apparently at his ease. It was a ploy devised to convince the Croatian gangster that he had no desire to sit in the deep, comfortable seats arrayed in the great room around the massive fireplace.

"That's good to hear." Mirjana seemed accommodating to Bolan's desire to stay by the bar. "Cigar? They're Cubans. I've found my Western clientele enjoy the novelty."

"No, thank you," Bolan said. "Though your offer does provide a convenient segue way for some of my concerns."

"You have concerns?"

"You are aware of the sensitive nature of my contract?" Bolan asked, already aware that Mirjana knew every scrap of cover information provided by Stony Man on North American International.

"In general. I have certain…shall we say services available to me as courteousness from certain aspects of my government."

"Well, yes," Bolan said. "That's really the crux of the matter, isn't it?" He looked up and eyed the giant Croat and Swiss security men standing nearby, pretending they were as deaf as posts and twice as blind, as well.

Mirjana's brow furrowed. "Go on."

"It's just that I had assumed that you worked through RH-Alan and were sanctioned in that matter. Such sanctions are important, what with all the negative media coverage of private military companies lately. I would very much like to know how you come by your weapon stocks."

Mirjana set his glass down slowly. He frowned.

"I enjoy my privacy," he said. "I also extend that thoughtfulness to my clients."

"Do you extend that thoughtfulness to Scimitar?" Bolan asked.

Playtime was officially over.

CHAPTER ELEVEN

Calvin James crossed the lawn at a dead run. Out on the flying bridge of Mirjana's yacht Rafael Encizo saw him emerge from the shadows of the estate wall and began actively covering his movements with the QBU-88 designated marksmen rifle.

James ran with the APS-95 up and in his hands, the stock folded down and the shoulder sling crossing his body. He angled straight toward the lodge, avoiding the large picture windows and approaching from an oblique angle. He'd pinpointed exactly where the breaker box for the hunting lodge was located on his earlier visits, and he made a beeline for it now.

From the flying bridge of the yacht Encizo caught a flash of movement as he swept the 4x power scope across his field of fire. He saw two security men leave the main house from the front door and stroll over to a dark blue Peugeot vehicle. The headlights flared on and the compact SUV pulled out from the main house.

Encizo shifted the muzzle of the QBU-88 as he followed the vehicle's progress. The driver seemed to be in no hurry as he steered the Peugeot up the main estate avenue in the direction of the hunting lodge.

The Cuban kept the approaching security team in his crosshairs.

James reached the edge of the hunting lodge. He dropped to one knee under the breaker box set into a custom-built wooden cabinet around the metal container on the east wall, drew a Gerber fighting knife and slid the blade inside the hinge latch.

He exhaled through his nose and snapped the 440 stainless-steel pry bar down with a sharp motion. The hinge popped off the cabinet with a sharp, audible snap, and the cabinet door swung open under his touch.

James snorted in frustration. Inside the cabinet the breaker box was padlocked closed. The lock was a key-operated Master Lock and as big as a grown man's fist.

Wishing he could just dab some plastique on the wall mount and blow the thing, James removed a lock-pick gun from his gear and opened the padlock. He replaced the gun, removed the open padlock and threw it aside. Reaching up, he worked the latch and revealed the inside of the metal breaker box.

With cool efficiency James followed the electronic diagrams of standard Croatian breaker assemblies Aaron Kurtzman had sent him via secure e-mail and shut off communications and power to the hunting lodge.

Instantly the lodge went black.

The building was protected from the view of the main house and the gate sentries by a stand of evergreen trees placed to give the lodge a feel of isolation. In the moments before the outbuilding went dark the Peugeot

SUV pulled up in front of the lodge and the security teams emerged from the vehicle.

As the lights shut down and blackness settled like a blanket over the structure, the Peugeot driver ducked back through his open door, obviously reaching for a dash-mounted radio. Encizo took up the last bit of slack in the QBU-88's trigger. The rifle cycled and he felt the recoil punch comfortably into his shoulder.

The 5.8 mm round cut flat in its trajectory across the 230 yards and slammed into the throat of the ex-SMJ police commando with sledgehammer force. The glass of the driver's window shattered as the bullet passed through to the man's neck and blood splattered out to spray inside the cab of the SUV.

The second sentry backpedaled in surprise. He turned to identify the shooter, and his hand went to the useless 9 mm Glock 18 pistol on his hip. Encizo put his second bullet center mass and knocked the guard to the ground. The man was tossed flat on his back and Encizo could see the brutal depression in the man's chest where the 5.8 mm round had collapsed his ribs and blown his heart apart.

Encizo pulled his head back from the scope. He saw a sudden motion from the corner of the log hunting lodge and shifted his scope automatically, putting his crosshairs on the figure.

His finger relaxed on the trigger as he recognized his team member. James held a hand up in the direction of the river and yacht and began to cross the porch, heading for the front door.

ERAZMUS AND THE GIANT sensed the sudden tension in their boss at Bolan's question and stepped toward the two men. Mirjana, his face carefully neutral, held up a hand to stop them.

"You are a very impolite man, Mr. Cooper," the arms dealer said. "It matters little that I have no idea who or what this 'Scimitar' is. It only matters that you presume to come into my home and attempt to pump me for information about my private business."

"The only one getting pumped was your mother," Bolan said carefully.

"Punish him!" Mirjana snarled, his face scarlet with outrage.

Instantly the two security operatives sprang into motion. As fast as they were, Bolan quite literally beat them to the punch.

He slid off his bar stool and threw his gin into the sputtering Mirjana's face. The man shrieked in surprise, and his hands flew to his stinging eyes. Bolan reached out and swept the heavy, cut-crystal tumbler down, smashing it over the top of the man's head, driving him to the floor.

Using the momentum of his overhand swing, Bolan turned in a tight circle and scooped up his bar stool. The room layout had caused the onrushing hired muscle to converge as they navigated around a couch to reach Bolan.

The heavy stool struck them in the legs and they both went down in a tangle of limbs, cursing. Bolan shifted and kicked Mirjana in the gut, driving the wind from the man's lungs and putting him down in a heap as he gasped for breath.

Bolan sprang forward and swept up the heavy lamp of burnished brass he'd noted on entering the room. Snatching it under the bulb and yanking the electrical cord free of its socket, he tossed the lamp up like a circus juggler and grasped the cord with both hands. He twisted at the waist and snapped his shoulders, swinging the solid fixture around like a medieval ball-and-chain flail.

He whipped the twenty-pound piece of brass down with all his strength just as the gigantic security man pushed himself up from the ground on arms thick as stone pillars. The lamp made a sickening thunk as it crashed into the man's head, and blood burst onto the hardwood floor along with blue-gray, scrambled egg clumps of brain tissue.

The man sagged like a bag of loose meat. Bolan slid his rear foot back and began to twist the heavy lamp around for a second strike. Erazmus was much faster than his partner. He lunged forward and grabbed Bolan's ankle, snarling with the effort, and then pitched the unbalanced Bolan to the floor.

The soldier and the bloody lamp rolled away. He looked up from his back and saw Erazmus coming for him, hands outstretched and teeth bared. Bolan kicked out and caught the bodyguard across the face and tore his lip, snapping his head back, but the strike was a glancing blow and Erazmus's inertia kept him surging forward.

As he landed on top of Bolan the man lashed out with a wild swing, but missed. The Executioner brought his hands up in boxer's huddle and fended off a second punch, as well. His legs snapped tight around the security man above his waist in a Brazilian jujitsu "guard" position, preventing the nimble fighter from raining blows down from a superior position.

Erazmus leaned back and began throwing left-handed punches as his right hand went for the inside of his blazer jacket. Bolan brought his own right arm up and managed to get his elbow inside the sweep of the man's punches, close into the line of the man's center of gravity.

Bolan tucked his chin down to take the man's blows higher on his head where the skull was thicker, then grabbed Erazmus's wrist as the bodyguard grasped the butt of his holstered pistol. A left-handed punch cracked Bolan in the temple and the soldier saw stars, but his fingers remained like steel bands around the other man's wrist.

The big American flexed his hips and squeezed his legs around the bodyguard to give himself leverage as he sat up, pulling in as close as possible to his enemy. Bolan swept his left arm up in a haymaker roundhouse as Erazmus punched him again and again in the side of the head.

Bolan's thumbnail found the man's eye and slid in behind the eyeball. He hooked his thumb and shoved the digit further into the concave space, thrusting the eyeball to the side like a man digging out grout from between tile flooring.

In the tight lock of Bolan's python grip Erazmus began to scream and thrash as if he were being electrocuted. Blood, sizzling hot, spilled onto Bolan's upturned face and the eyeball squished under his blunt gouging like a grape. Bolan felt the eye come loose and saw it dangle from the optic nerve like a bobber on a fishing line.

He tightened his grip at the guard's wrist and waist, keeping him tight in against his man. Blood spilled across the bodyguard's twisting face. Bolan jerked his arm back and swept it forward, this time driving his thumb into the screaming man's throat behind the bobbing Adam's apple, crushing through cricoid cartilage to collapse the trachea.

The Swiss bodyguard's screams choked off and he shuddered in pain as he fought to breathe. Bolan struck him a third time with a sort of Sumo slap that shoved the spasming man off him. He turned away from the dying man and looked toward Mirjana.

He saw the Croat kingpin pulling himself up by the lip of the wet bar. Liquor and blood streamed off his face from where Bolan had shattered the glass tumbler over his head. The soldier posted on his left hand and twisted his body around.

He lashed out with his right leg and hammered his heel into Mirjana's knee. The Croat buckled but clung to the bar top to keep from going fully to the floor. Bolan kicked the man in the kidney with his steel toe and the Croat arced his back under the impact, moaning with the piercing pain.

Mirjana gasped and slid down to the floor where he curled into a ball. A stream of saliva and frothy spittle ran out of his working mouth, stained bright with blood, and dribbled onto the floor. Bolan got to his feet.

The lights went out.

THROUGH HIS SCOPE Rafael Encizo watched Calvin James reach the front door of the lodge. The ex-SEAL pulled his AN/PVS-8 night-vision goggles into place, and then moved quickly into the interior of the dark building. Encizo shifted his point of aim and began to sweep the estate for signs of movement or alert from the rest of Mirjana's security team.

Inside the building the green illumination and distorted depth perception of the AN/PVS-8's single, cyclopedian goggle lit James's way as he entered the lodge, his APS-95 up and ready. He heard no gunfire or sounds of struggle as he moved down the entrance hall and he resisted the urge to call out to Bolan as he entered.

If the Executioner had handled the situation as his bold plan called for, he would be expecting James's entry. If Bolan had been subdued, then it was the greatest folly for the Phoenix Force commando to announce his presence to potential enemies. A fire burned in a stone hearth at the far end of the hall and in James's night goggles it made the great room as bright as noon.

James crept down the hall, the muzzle of his weapon tracking with every turn of his head. He stepped out of the hallway and into the great room and automatically swept the line of the balcony before dragging his weapon muzzle across the sectors of the wide space.

He saw Bolan standing in the middle of a pile of warmly glowing but inert bodies, his hands up to quickly soothe the Phoenix Force interloper. James swept off his goggles and surveyed the Executioner's handiwork. He saw Karl Mirjana huddled against the lee of the bar and handed his APS-95 to Bolan. The Croat seemed unsurprised to see the black American executive from North American International. Perhaps it was the fugue of shock.

"Nice work," James said. "Rafe's in place. He popped two guards as I was coming in."

"Good, let's get this guy talking," Bolan answered.

James opened a pouch on his web belt and removed a little gray canvas bundle and some plastic riot cuffs. When Mirjana saw them his eyes grew wide and his fugue snapped. He tried to stand, stuttering protests.

James snatched him by his shirtfront and hauled him to his feet. He turned the man and bent him over the wet bar, pressing his face hard into the wood as he reached out and yanked the arms dealer's hands behind his back. James zipped Mirjana's wrists together, then repeated the process with his ankles. Bolan stepped forward and grabbed the Croat under his elbows and threw him down into a deep chair, causing him to wince in pain as his body weight crushed his bound hands uncomfortably.

"I won't tell you anything," Mirjana said, his voice low. "If I tell you, I'm dead anyway. They'll kill my family."

"You've had a hand in a whole lot of families getting killed, so don't start getting soft now just because it's your own," Bolan snapped.

James picked up the little gray canvas packet he had set on the bar and pulled the end table in front of where Mirjana was tied up. The arms dealer watched with terrified eyes as James removed a 3 cc hypodermic needle from a protective case and prepped it for use.

"What's that?" Mirjana demanded.

James ignored him as he tapped the chamber clear of bubbles. The firelight cast shadows across his face. Bolan moved to the closet, grabbed his jacket and slipped it on, slinging the APS-95 as he pulled the iron and ironing board out of the cedar linen closest.

James leaned forward and snatched Mirjana's shirt loose at the shoulder, ripping out the stitching.

"Don't stick me with that!" Mirjana begged.

Then he saw Bolan setting up the ironing board, and he watched in horror as the Executioner turned on the iron's environmentally friendly battery pack. There was a click as the battery powered up and a little orange light bulb glowed in the handle.

"Oh, God no," Mirjana begged.

"What?" Bolan cocked an eyebrow. "You dry clean only?"

"Please, please, I'll talk."

James, holding the hypodermic, looked at Bolan. The Executioner's face was carved in stone.

"Give him the drugs," Bolan ordered. "We can't risk him lying. It's not like this is Camp X-ray and we can just interrogate him again if his information proves false."

"Look at me," James told Mirjana. "Look at me goddamn it!" The terrified arms dealer forced his gaze off the cold visage of the Executioner and onto James's.

"This is a mixture of scopolamine and Valium. It won't kill you by itself. I'm telling you this so you won't fight me as I inject into your arm. If you fight me, I'll climb onto your legs like a lap dancer and jam it into your jugular. Understand?"

The iron hissed and Bolan picked it up and spit on it. His saliva sizzled like lava, and Mirjana looked back toward the grim-faced man standing to the side of him. James reached out and grabbed Mirjana by his face, pulling his head back around until their eyes locked.

"Son of a bitch, I asked you if you understood me."

"I understand," Mirjana gasped. "I understand you."

"Good, then hold still." With deft, practiced motions, James inserted the hypodermic needle into a vein in Mirjana's forearm and smoothly injected the truth serum cocktail. Mirjana's own frantic, pounding heart dispersed the drugs throughout his system with rapid efficiency.

James pressed two fingers to Mirjana's carotid artery when he had finished and noted the pulse. He looked up at Bolan.

"He's terrified," James said.

"Smart boy." Bolan looked at the Croat. "Two questions."

Mirjana looked up at him, and even Bolan was surprised by how quickly the man's eyes had become glassy. The arms dealer swallowed hard and his tongue was coated with spittle. Bolan could literally see the man becoming more relaxed by the moment.

"That worked fast," Bolan said, impressed despite himself.

"My own concoction. I read how the old KGB used pure alcohol to disorientate their prisoners. I put a little in with the scopolamine and Valium. Seems to have had a synergistic effect."

"Good. Maybe we won't have to use the iron then, huh, Mirjana?"

The arms dealer's head sagged on the end of his neck. His rapid, shallow breathing visibly slowed and deepened as Bolan knelt beside him. The soldier gently slapped the man, calling Mirjana's attention back to himself. Over the next ten minutes as the pharmaceutical cocktail began to reach peak levels in the man's system, Bolan and James softened the arms dealer up through the use of verbal ruses and the constant threat of painful violence.

Soon the Croat had little left in the way of coherent resistance.

"Mirjana," Bolan said. "Two questions. Scimitar and your arms. We'll go with your supplies first. How do you get your guns?"

Mirjana tried to shake his head no. Bolan uncoiled like a snake. He pressed the man's head back so that his face was twisted up to within inches of Bolan's own. Mirjana's jaw hung slack.

"You calling my bluff, Mirjana?"

"The same," Mirjana muttered.

"The same? What do you mean?"

"Scimitar and weapons the same."

"How do you mean? How are they the same? You sell arms to Scimitar. Do you know who Scimitar is?"

"No. There is no Scimitar." Mirjana's head shook in Bolan's grip. "Scimitar came to me. They have taken over all my Arab contacts and the East African ones, as well. Muscled in. Everything I used to do with al-Kassar is theirs now. Then they started selling cheap arms to me, out of Azerbaijan. Cheaper than I got from RH-Alan or out of Russia."

Bolan let Mirjana's head droop. He looked over and met James's look. One of the numbers gotten from the Syrian diplomat's son had been to a Syrian airline office in Azerbaijan. Coincidences did not exist in Bolan's world. Pieces of the puzzle clicked together.

"What else?" He shook Mirjana by the hair. "What else?"

"Nothing else. Scimitar uses Armenian mafia mercenaries to secure the shipments to the Black Sea. My network takes it from there. That's all I know. What contracts they've left me with are more profitable now because they've reduced my procurement price by over thirty percent."

"They? You keep saying 'they,' Mirjana," James snapped. "What 'they'? How do you get in touch with Scimitar?"

"They, they!" Mirjana repeated, frustrated. His voice was slurred. "They're all Scimitar. Every greedy, threatening Arab motherfucker who takes *my* business and holds me up for more money. All of them have been Scimitar. There is no *him* it is all *they*." Even the slurring couldn't disguise the Croat's bitterness, and understanding snapped into place in Bolan's mind like a light bulb being turned on. "If they're not stealing my contacts, they're trying to exploit my contacts with SZUP," Mirjana finished.

Bolan recognized the name of the Croat secret service.

"SZUP? About what?"

"Not what, who. Ma Ning-tan."

"Chinese?"

"Yes. Wanted to know where this guy was, I don't know why. But they figured my intelligence contacts would be able to find him. They wanted him 'punished,' that's all they would say."

"Did you find out?" Bolan demanded. "You point the hit man in his direction?"

Mirjana nodded. The movement was sloppy and he burped. His tongue kept working hard to moisten his lips. He looked like a snake sensing the air for stimulus. "What was I going to do? He's in Kuwait City, on the coast. An agricultural assistant to a company closely tied to the Beijing consul. My people had it from the Syrians he's taking orders from Tehran."

"How long ago?"

Mirjana shrugged. "Yesterday, day before, I don't know. It got those bastards out of my hair. What more do I care about?"

"Yeah, screw poor Ning-tan," Bolan said, his voice as dry as desert wind.

Mirjana shrugged. "Better him than me."

Bolan turned to James. "C-4 in place?" he asked.

"I placed the charges after I took out the breaker," James replied.

"Let's go. We have what we need. Scimitar contacts him, he doesn't contact Scimitar."

James rose and Bolan handed the ex-SEAL his assault rifle. Mirjana slumped in the chair. The Croat arms dealer was conscious but completely sedated. His eyelids slid down into heavy hoods and his face muscles relaxed until they drooped. He seemed to take a breath only once a minute, and any trace of anxiety was long gone.

James gathered his equipment and the two commandos left the lodge. Bolan opened the back of his SUV, ignoring the dead security men on the lawn. James hopped into the back compartment and crouched. When Bolan slammed the rear hatch closed, the Phoenix Force commando was invisible behind the deep window tinting.

Bolan climbed behind the wheel of the Excursion

and turned the engine over. He smoothly pulled out and headed toward the front gate, keeping to a sedate pace.

He powered down his window at the gate and waved to the guard who dutifully powered the electronic locks open and held his hand up as the black Ford Excursion cruised by. Bolan drove down the long winding drive until he reached the turn-off for the highway.

A mile and a half down the road James climbed into the front seat next to Bolan and blew the charges, decimating the hunting lodge. The explosion was easily heard by both men as they fled the scene to make their rendezvous with Rafael Encizo.

CHAPTER TWELVE

After blowing the late Karl Mirjana's warehouse near the rail yards in southern Zagreb, the Stony Man team quickly formed a plan of operation designed to exploit their intelligence. James and Encizo would go on ahead to Amman, Jordan, to follow up on the number taken from the young Syrian's cell phone.

Barbara Price, through the efforts of Carmen Delahunt and Aaron Kurtzman, had managed to attach a physical address and a possible name to the number— Yazid Marwan, a former Saddam loyalist who had gone to live with relatives in Amman after the former dictator's capture by the Americans.

It would be the responsibility of James and Encizo to acquire a cutout agent to serve as a translator and to guide and help them prepare the initial surveillance operations on Marwan, before Bolan arrived and they made contact as a unit.

While the prep work in Jordan was being carried out, Bolan would head into Kuwait. He would try to make contact with the Chinese assistant consul, Ning-tan and convince him his life was in danger. Hopefully the man would be able to provide information that would help the Stony Man team piece together the jigsaw puzzle that was Scimitar before they entered the lion's den of Baghdad.

They left the Ford Excursion in airport short-term parking, unlocked, with the ignition key placed under the back bumper. Encizo then initiated a security cleaning protocol, and the vehicle was picked up by a team of agents stationed in Zagreb who spirited the vehicle to a warehouse on the Sava River where it was sterilized and shipped by rail to Split for reintroduction into the government fleet.

Bolan was on a plane in two hours.

AARON KURTZMAN HAD COME UP with a near dead end on Ma Ning-tan. According to DIA and CIA profiles stored in the Directorate for National Intelligence, Ning-tan was the son of a minor bureaucrat in the Beijing cabinet. Schooled in Russia, he had entered the intelligence wing of the military upon completing college. Married with one young son, Ning-tan had been a rising star, promoted out of the People's Army and into the Central Control of Information agency, first as an analyst and then as an operations officer. Most reports had him involved in southwest Asia, Taliban-controlled Afghanistan, influence peddling in Asiatic former Soviet republics, and Iran. Then, two years after the U.S. entered Iraq, the star had fallen.

He had been "promoted" out of the CCI into the broader umbrella of the Foreign Affairs Ministry. He had been assigned, without his family, to Kuwait where he worked to oversee the use of Chinese donations to relief projects in southern Iraq through the use of cut-out charities.

Because of the confused situation on the ground his exact location in Iraq was ambiguous. Both Price and Bolan had decided that on such short notice a direct attempt at subterfuge might provide the biggest potential payoff.

Bolan would become Mike McKay, freelance journalist, one more time. He would proceed to the small Chinese consult office on Diplomat Row in Kuwait City and attempt to secure an interview for a left-leaning news magazine out of Canada, one that had a history of being sympathetic to Chinese attempts to balance the "predatory influence of western capitalist elites in developing nations."

A State Department courier had been dispatched ahead of Bolan to Kuwait City where the necessary documents had been left at the concierge desk of the JW Marriott Hotel in a sealed pouch and Bolan, under the name McKay, had been booked a room by personnel posing as staff workers for the liberal magazine.

The city of Al-Kuwait, the capital of the nation of Kuwait, was a Persian Gulf seaport, and as Bolan descended into the Kuwait International Airport he was amused that such an important world commerce center only held a population of under 50,000 people, though the metropolitan area held a larger number. It was in sharp contrast to Hong Kong in almost every way.

He had changed the currency of his travel money in Zagreb, and now he paid for a taxi to take him from the busy airport to the popular Marriott hotel. Once there he gathered his pouch of documents along with his key card and proceeded to his hotel room where he took a shower, ate a room-service meal and tried to catch a nap until he could get to the Chinese consulate in the morning.

He could only hope Encizo and James were having as smooth a setup to their wing of the operation.

BOLAN WOKE EARLY. He dressed casual and ate breakfast before catching a taxi provided by the hotel to Yarmouk, Block 4, Street 1, Villa 82, in the city. He showed his press credentials and was ushered into a cramped office where a harried Chinese man of middle age with a short, whispery mustache agreed to see freelance journalist Mike McKay. The consulate official introduced himself as Ko Lung and his female assistant as Mai Li-Aa.

The sharp-eyed young woman in modest dress and aggressive manners served as an English interpreter. Her small smile never reached her dark, almond-shaped eyes and she openly scrutinized the western reporter. Bolan pegged her immediately as Security Services despite the deference she showed the consulate agricultural attaché.

Bolan made the right sounds. He spoke of highlighting the efforts of civilized nations to undo the damage wrought in Iraq by an overly belligerent administration and xenophobic voting demographics. He stressed how important such a story could be in presenting the true story of post-Saddam Iraq to the worldwide readership of his magazine.

If only some photographs of the operations currently

in play and some "hands-on" facilitator interviews could be arranged, he was sure the generosity of the People's Republic could be shown in a favorable light. Bolan hinted that such a story and photos could go a long way toward undoing some of the misconceptions caused by the "troubles in Tibet."

Forty minutes later Bolan had a cell-phone number and address to Ma Ning-tan as well as a letter of introduction on Chinese consulate stationery. He feigned surprise to learn that an interpreter would not be necessary, as Ning-tan spoke English. Bolan left quickly and swung into action as he suspected his photograph had been taken during the meeting. While it was unlikely that he was on file, the possibility always remained given his comprehensive experience with Chinese affairs. He'd ask Kurtzman to hack into the system and delete the photograph, if, indeed, it existed.

He took a ferry from Kuwait City into the port town of Umm Qasr, which was linked by the Shatt al Arab waterway to Basra. In Basra the Chinese consulate, under the direction of former CCI officer Ma Ning-tan, had enlisted the aid of local nongovernmental relief agencies to dispense agricultural aid, knowledge and equipment to Shiite farmers in the region.

Bolan gave the address to a teenage cabdriver who operated out of a battered yellow Oldsmobile Delta 88 converted to service as a taxi. Considering what the price of gas was, Bolan was amazed that the youth could make enough to even keep the monstrous thing running, let alone make a profit. He tipped the youth well when they finally made it to a rather shabby, single-wide mobile home on the outskirts of Basra.

To get there they had gone through three separate checkpoints, one each for British army forces, the Iraqi National Guard and the Iraqi police. The British waved them through after seeing Bolan in the backseat. At the Iraqi army security post, soldiers opened Bolan's bags and looked at his laptop, Nikon camera and cell phone. They didn't search him personally, however, and seemed content after the driver opened his car trunk. Only at the IP checkpoint was it necessary for Bolan to slip a few bank notes with his passport.

Despite rising sectarian violence in the north and west, the clerics and mullahs of Basra had managed to keep their city fairly stable, even in the face of deliberate attempts by foreign jihadists to instigate a spread of the Sunni on Shi'a civil war in the area.

As Bolan rode along, he saw the ravages of war amid the struggle of a people to rebuild in the face of adversity. Rubble lay everywhere, and streets remained lined with the burned-out wrecks of cars. Gaping holes left by tank rounds and the zigzag periods of machine-gun fire pockmarked walls and buildings.

At one intersection a ragtag group of children poked the bloated corpse of a dog with sticks as it floated in an open sewer. The difference in temperature between Basra and Zagreb was staggering.

Hal Brognola had arranged for Bolan to acquire a weapon through a Joint Special Operations Command soldier working undercover as a private military contractor outside of the ferry station in Umm Qasr. He received a .40-caliber Beretta M-96 and two additional extended-round magazines. Even carrying a handgun was a serious blow to his cover as a member of the international press corps, but Bolan wasn't going anywhere in Iraq unarmed.

If it had been Baghdad instead of Basra, he wouldn't have settled for anything less than a submachine-gun.

As it was, Bolan felt distinctly underarmed as the taxicab pulled away from the dirt lot housing the mobile home where the People's Republic of China's agricultural assistant attaché stayed when he wasn't in the field. Bolan surveyed the rundown trailer, noting it had no air-conditioning unit. He walked around back and used a credit card in the name of Mike McKay to force the simple, flimsy lock on the trailer's back door.

Inside the heat was stifling. Flies buzzed lazily, and the stink of the Shatt al Arab waterway just permeated the little dwelling. Despite the primitive conditions Bolan found himself impressed with how neat Ma Ning-tan kept the cramped living quarters. He found no alcohol in either the rickety little refrigerator or the cheap wooden cabinets built into the trailer walls.

He found what could only be black market—the labels were in French—sleeping pills in the medicine cabinets. Bolan supposed he might have been tempted to use something to help him sleep if he had been shunted off to this corner of the world by an ungrateful government, but filed the information away for possible exploitation just the same.

Bolan prowled the little trailer as he waited for Ma Ning-tan to return from his fieldwork. He looked in drawers and cabinets, searched under mattresses and cushions then rummaged through clothing pockets. Knowing Ma Ning-tan's history with Chinese military intelligence and the CCI, Bolan began a more systematic area search after he had shaken down the more obvious locations of inspection.

Finally, under a loose board in the claustrophobic bedroom, Bolan found a handwritten letter on commercial stationery. He scanned the page, which was written in Chinese. He had come prepared for this eventuality. He used the camera in his cell phone to snap a picture of the pages then sent the image to his laptop. He opened the boosted wireless computer and fed the photo of the page into translation software provided to Stony Man through the Justice Department by the NSA.

In rapid time the page had been translated and Bolan returned the sheets to their hiding place before reading the translated version on his computer screen. What he read peaked his interest intensely and he prepped the message for Stony Man when he was done.

Honored Father. If something should become of me I have asked Mr. Dui to send this letter to you. I write you my deepest devotion and faithfulness to the People's Republic. I send also my great pride in my service, no matter the form it takes. I want you to know that there is no shame upon me, Father. It was the right of my superiors to strip me of my rank and office, as it was their right to send me here. Though I greatly miss my son, Ki, I will not offer complaint on these matters. Know this, I write this letter that depends on our family relationship for a reason. No matter what you might have heard whispered in your offices, Father, I hold that Director Li was in the right and that I was correct to stand at his side in support as I always stand in support of China in the manner in which you taught me. Accepting this assignment without protest has only made my position the more obvious.

General Soh is an adventurist and no friend of the Chinese people. His policy of arming the Azerbaijan extremists and the Iraqi killers through the use of the gangster Liu can only serve to further isolate our great country and bring danger to it. Such activity in the backyard of Russia will only undo the fragile ties built up through our mutual support of the antiwestern nations of Syria and Iran and their cutout, al-Kassar.

I fear the allies of Soh do not trust my discipline in keeping my silence from the Americans. In this they are wrong and I hope my devotion to duty in this backward place will prove that my loyalty remains to China and her people. Still, I have trafficked with desperate men in my service and nothing is guaranteed. If this letter finds you, tell my son I was not without honor and give it to my wife, my Cherry Blossom so that, if you find you cannot help, she may present it to the proper people in Beijing.

Your son, Ma

Bolan sat in the chair at the kitchen table. The Beretta 96 was heavy in the waistband at his back, and he pulled it clear and set it on the table. He felt like a man who had been told he'd been using a telescope backward. When he turned it around everything obscure and distant came sharply into focus.

According to Karl Mirjana, "desperate men" did indeed question Ning-tan's discipline, and his superiors at the CCI had conveniently placed him easily within their reach during the political purge that had caused his banishment to Basra, Iraq. Bolan picked up the Beretta 96 and checked the safety. Ning-tan didn't know it, but he had a guardian angel. Bolan turned to his laptop and began to write a communiqué for Barbara Price to deliver to Hal Brognola.

IT WAS DARK before Ma Ning-tan returned to his home. The former intelligence officer pulled his white Kia Sophia into the gravel lot well after his usual dinnertime. Bolan watched through the cheap venetian blinds on the kitchen window as Ning-tan got out of his car. The Chinese spy turned bureaucrat wore black boots and tan pants held up by a leather belt. He was dressed in a button-down, short-sleeved shirt left open at the collar. His armpits were stained from his exposure to Iraqi weather. The Chinese administrator tucked several file folders under his arm and carried a battered black leather satchel stuffed with paperwork in his other hand as he approached the trailer door.

Bolan slid away from the window and positioned himself behind the front door as Ning-tan used his key on the lock. Ma entered the trailer and felt for the battery-operated lantern on the table next to the door, as he was not hooked up to electricity.

He clicked on the lantern and dropped his files and attaché case in a wooden chair. He turned toward the kitchen, and Bolan unfolded from the wall like a ghost rising from the grave. He grasped Ning-tan around the neck and spun him, shoving him face-first up against the wall.

Bolan put the .40-caliber muzzle of the Beretta 96 hard against the back of the Chinese agent's head.

"I bet you're good, Ma," Bolan said, "but don't try it."

"You are American," Ma said, his voice calm.

Bolan ran his hand across Ma's body, looking for a holdout piece he was fairly sure he wouldn't find. When he had finished, he placed his left hand between Ning-tan's shoulder blades and pressed the man against the wall as he backed away.

"Turn around," Bolan said. Ning-tan slowly turned, arms still raised. "Put your hands down, sit in the chair."

Ning-tan did as he was instructed and Bolan met his eyes as he looked up. The soldier tucked the Beretta 96 behind his back and slowly sank into the kitchen chair.

"You're a long way from Beijing. You must miss your wife and son, Ki."

Ning-tan blinked once, sharply, at Bolan's unsubtle mention of the man's family. In the stark light of the tabletop lantern Ning-tan look tired and drawn.

"You seem to know a bit about me."

"I know this 'promotion' out of the CCI wasn't exactly a reward. Why don't you explain to me how it happened."

"Why would you be concerned with the troubles of one so humble as myself?"

"Scimitar."

Ning-tan remained still.

"I do not understand why Scimitar had to use Karl Mirjana's connections with Croat intelligence to find you if your own government wants you dead. They send you to what has to be, hands-down, the easiest place on the earth at the moment to do away with someone and cover it up, then they don't give your stringers the information they need? Doesn't make sense."

"It does if the left hand doesn't know what the right hand is doing," Ma Ning-tan replied.

"You're saying Scimitar operations are the result of an internal Beijing power struggle?"

"I'm not saying anything. I am not a disloyal man."

"Zagreb pegged your location two days ago. Mirjana thinks it was through Syrian intelligence, maybe through al-Kassar. Scimitar is coming to get you. Two days, Ma," Bolan said. He leaned forward. "The clock has run out. I'm the only one who can get you out of Basra. Hell, I'm the only one who even cares. Once you're gone, in disgrace, what will happen to your wife? To your son?"

"My father will protect them."

"Maybe so." Bolan paused then played another card, a long shot based on the letter Ma had written. "But how long will he be able to protect them from General Soh?"

The shot was a bull's-eye; Bolan had touched a nerve. Ning-tan's eyes lit up and he half rose from his chair before he caught himself and regained his composure. "Soh would not dare."

"Soh arms criminals like Scimitar and makes men like Karl Mirjana and the Syrian, al-Kassar, rich. If he would do something like that, then why wouldn't he use every means at his disposal to make an example of your disobedience by hurting your family?"

"Soh wants to keep the West bogged down, to kill them with the death of a thousand cuts by dragging out the action in Iraq as happened to you in Vietnam and the Soviets in Afghanistan." Ning-tan spit in a rush. "I disagree with his methods, but I do not think that means he is a psychopath."

"Fine," Bolan said, leaning back. "You're a patriot. But let's not bullshit ourselves. Scimitar is coming to get you. I know it and you know it, or you wouldn't have written that goodbye letter under that loose board."

Ning-tan sat very still and Bolan pressed on.

"You die, you die. Even if your father's influence helps your wife and son live, they live in shame because Soh's story will be the only one out there. You're dead. Remember what Ki looks like? Do you? Good, because if I walk out of here, you'll never see him again. He grows up without a father and believing a lie.

"Come with me and you live. Come with me, and I swear I'll help get your wife and son out. As long as you are alive, there is hope. If you let me walk out that door tonight, hope dies right along with you."

Bolan was compelling. He wasn't selling the Chinese agent a pack of lies or some political spin. He felt the conviction of what he was saying to his core. It was that utter, simple conviction, rather than the words themselves that seemed to convince Ning-tan that fate had sent him a celestial guardian in this grim-eyed Westerner.

The former spy looked down. Bolan saw him set his jaw in a stubborn line, then the muscles of his face relaxed and when he looked up again he nodded once to Bolan. Relief flooded the soldier in a sudden wash, and he stood.

He heard car tires crunch across gravel and the race

of a vehicle engine outside. Bolan crossed quickly to the window beside the trailer's front door and parted the blinds. Outside a dented and grimy Nissan pickup with its lights off pulled to a stop in a short slide, raising a cloud of dust.

Hooded men leaped from the back of the truck wearing red headbands adorned with Arabic script. Bolan counted four men plus a driver and passenger in the front seat. He saw an RPG-7 and an RPK machine-gun standing out among the thicket of AKM barrels.

"Get down!" Bolan barked, and Ning-tan jumped to obey without question.

Hell had rendezvoused with the Executioner one more time.

CHAPTER THIRTEEN

Bolan realized he and Ning-tan would never make it to the back door in time to save themselves if the death squad was allowed to unfold its trap as it had undoubtedly choreographed.

Bolan would need to put a monkey wrench in their well-oiled machinery if he wanted to live.

The Executioner drew the Beretta 96 and shoved the pistol through the cheap glass of the narrow window set beside the front door of the mobile home. He was already firing as he thrust the pistol through, the .40-caliber slugs ripping out hard one after the other.

The man with the RPG-7 went down as a double tap struck him center mass. The hit squad responded instinctively to the ambush fire and scattered, swinging up their weapons, but their singled-minded purpose had been disrupted by Bolan's aggressive actions.

The soldier kept pulling the trigger as he swept the belching muzzle of the pistol around to the hooded killer trying to bring the RPK machine-gun to bear. Bolan hit him in the shoulder and then skipped two more rounds past him and into the hood of the Nissan pickup.

An AKM assault rifle opened up from the squad, and 7.62 mm rounds burned through the stamped metal and plastic reinforced faux-wood of the trailer door. Slugs whizzed into the tight living room; and then the RPK opened up. Bolan dived to the floor and scrambled down the short, narrow hallway running from living area-kitchen to the single back bedroom.

Just ahead of him Ma Ning-tan crawled along the floor as well, headed for the very back door Bolan had jimmied to enter when he'd first arrived. A fusillade of metal-jacketed bullets tore in through the fragile trailer. Glass shattered as wood and plastic housing materials were shredded under the onslaught. Ning-tan's black attaché case was ripped apart and papers exploded into the air like ragged confetti. The furniture disintegrated as more heavy-caliber main battle rifles joined the barrage.

The RPK cut loose in long, distinct bursts of fire as the machine-gunner dragged the weapon along the length of the trailer. Ning-tan's little refrigerator was knocked apart as rounds passed through the trailer wall behind it. Bolan's own case, still resting on the kitchen table, was ravaged in a relentless cross fire and the expensive electronics were pounded into useless, unrecognizable pieces. The machine-gun severed the door from its hinges and the perforated structure blew inward.

A green tracer round struck a cushion and ignited it so that a small fire started on the ratty couch. The lantern was shattered, and another WARSAW tracer round sliced through the flimsy curtains like a hot knife and set them on fire as well.

In the hall Bolan scrambled to his knees as Ning-tan reached up and opened the back door. The soldier's ears were ringing from the furious din, and he knew it would be only moments before another gunman in the death squad retrieved the fallen RPG-7 antitank weapon and turned it on the mobile home.

Ning-tan pushed the back door open and jumped out of the trailer and onto the ground, with Bolan close behind. What happened next unfolded too quickly for Bolan to consider. He merely reacted on instincts so finely honed by continuous exposure to violence that they were nearly preternatural in capability.

The death squad was smoothly professional and had placed a security gunner on the rear door in a textbook setup. It was the same methodology used by U.S. infantrymen when they cleared a bunker. Bolan saw the muzzle-flash come from a hooded killer lying in a shallow depression beside an old metal trash barrel. He had an impression of the burst hitting Ning-tan, and the Chinese man shuddering under the onslaught. He heard the sound of the gunfire and was already twisting in midair. Bolan's feet hit the ground, and as he sank into a crouch to absorb the impact he triggered the pistol three times.

The sniper's head jerked beneath the black hood and the red headband with its scroll of Arabic characters went spinning off into the brush. Bolan's feet pounded against the gravel as he sprinted the fifteen yards to the downed fighter.

The Executioner slid into place beside the corpse

and from behind him the trailer rocked on its axles as an RPG-7 warhead exploded inside. Jets of flame erupted from shattered windows and the open door. Oily smoke poured into the night sky and a wash of heat rolled into Bolan like a furnace blast. He felt the sting of a piercing wound on the big muscles of his shoulder and a distant part of his mind cataloged the shrapnel wound.

He reached down with his left hand and snatched the bloody terrorist corpse up by a limp arm, then rolled the dead man over as he slid the still smoking Beretta 96 into his rear waistband. He grabbed the AKM used to gun down Ning-tan, then pulled a Soviet grenade from the web belt cinched around the dead man's long black shirt.

The canister-shaped device was an RG-42 antipersonnel hand grenade. The deadly little bomb had a blast radius of seventy-five feet, and Bolan hefted the explosive with authority. He jerked the pin from the hand grenade, then rose, the fingers on his left hand holding down the safety level on the RG-42 grenade. He felt the blood from his shoulder wound roll down his back, sticking his shirt to his skin.

Bolan realized speed and aggression were his only allies now. He broke into a jog and headed toward the corner of the burning trailer. As he reached the front of the structure, he released the grenade's lever and the tightly depressed spring shot the metal strip out into the air away from him. The soldier slowed to a walk and peeked once around the final corner, the numbers counting down.

The death squad approached the door of the burning

mobile home, their formation in an inverted V like geese flying south for the winter. The driver of the Nissan pickup remained behind the wheel of the running vehicle.

The Executioner tossed the grenade toward the death squad. It bounced once and rolled toward them like a can of soda, spinning off a desk and across the floor. One of the gunmen caught the motion and turned, his AKM coming up and seeking a target.

Bolan snapped his hand onto the front stock of his own AKM as he pulled the weapon's trigger. He scythed the man to the ground, then peeled back around the corner of the mobile home. Men screamed in warning, then the grenade blast silenced them.

Angry hornets of shrapnel rattled into the ruined trailer and buzzed through the smoky air. Bolan rolled back around the corner of the house, snuggling the AKM into the crook of his shoulder like a man hugging an old friend.

The hit squad lay on the ground. Some tried to sit up while others reached frantically for weapons knocked clear by the blast. Bolan opened up on them with sustained fire, hosing them down. Spent shell casings arced out of his weapon until it cycled dry.

Bolan threw the hot, smoking assault rifle from him and reached for the Beretta 96 secured behind his back. He spun toward the pickup, falling into a modified, two-fisted Weaver.

The driver had thrown open his door and jumped from behind the wheel. But, like the rest of the death squad, the man had brought an AKM assault rifle to the fight, and the long weapon banged against the steering wheel, then the side of the cab as he tried to yank it free and bring it to bear.

Bolan put four rounds through the gap of open vehicle door and windshield in less than a second. All four .40-caliber rounds found their mark and the man staggered back, dropping the rifle so that it clattered off the truck and onto the ground. Blood rushed in a river from a ruined throat and jaw as the terrorist spun. His feet tangled up in themselves and he went down hard.

Bolan, senses amped to a peak level by adrenaline, heard a moan at his feet and turned without thinking. He dropped his pistol muzzle and put a round in the man lying there then started toward the still running Nissan pickup. He dropped the Beretta's magazine from the butt grip and slammed in one of his backups. His finger found the catch release and the handgun shuddered in his hand as the bolt slid home and chambered a round.

Having climbed into the pickup, Bolan slammed the door closed, stood on the gas and cranked the wheel hard, turning the truck in a tight circle. As he straightened the nose of the pickup back toward the road his front tire rolled over the body of the driver he'd killed with the 9 mm pistol.

With the wheels trailing blood, Bolan sped away into the night.

TEN MINUTES LATER the Executioner ditched the Nissan outside the Basra hospital and walked across the parking lot under the watchful eyes of British army machine-gunners.

He entered the emergency room after showing his

press credentials, telling the British army lieutenant in charge of security that he had been out with an Iraqi patrol that had been hit by an IED and that the Red Crescent ambulances had claimed he wasn't injured enough to ride with them.

The man accepted his story after a perfunctory check of his credentials and allowed Bolan to leave his Beretta with a nearby sergeant. Bolan explained he'd taken it from a dead Iraqi and no longer felt safe without it as he was traveling alone. Guns were a dime a dozen in Iraq, even in the south and both soldiers were nonplussed by the declaration.

Bolan traded several U.S. dollars for some 4x4 bandages, surgical tape and a bottle of hydrogen peroxide. He paid many times their value, called it a donation and the harried-looking nurse seemed grateful for the cash.

The big American left the busy triage area and entered a crowded washroom where he pushed his way up to a dirty sink and stripped off his blood-soaked shirt. He washed his hands as best he could, then poured the disinfectant over the ugly avulsion in his shoulder and taped a bandage into place. The wound was on the opposite arm the Chinese 426 thug had cut open with his knife in Hong Kong.

When he was finished, Bolan put his bloody shirt back on and walked out of the hospital. He retrieved the Beretta from the bored-looking British sergeant who seemed more interested in finding out if Bolan happened to know the European football standings than in how he'd been wounded. The man dismissed Bolan from his mind after the American admitted he didn't know any scores.

Bolan walked across the street and slid into a waiting taxi, managing to stay awake during the ride to Umm Qasr. When he got there he realized there wouldn't be a ferry across to Kuwait until morning so he had the driver take him to the border where he crossed on foot.

He told his story about being a reporter struck by a roadside bomb to the Kuwaiti border guard and made it across without difficulty, though he was forced to throw the pistol in a trash can outside a burned-out restaurant on the Iraqi side of the border.

He wasted little time flagging another taxi on the Kuwait side and directed the man toward the Marriott Hotel.

THE HOTEL WAS subdued. A few tired-looking travelers, luggage in tow, stood at the marble-topped counter checking in. Knowing how he looked, Bolan headed straight for the elevator and rode up to his room. He walked down the hall and pulled his key card from his pocket.

He was bone-tired from his hectic pace and exhausted by adrenaline bleed off. He wanted to take a shower, change clothes and get on to the next plane to Amman. He didn't blame himself for Ning-tan's death; he was too pragmatic for that. Bolan put the blame right where it belonged—on the man's killers.

The soldier inserted the key card into the electronic lock and opened his door. He walked into the hotel room and snapped on the light. The door swung closed behind him and the spring-loaded dead bolt snapped shut. He began to unbutton his shirt as he started toward the bathroom, his thoughts on a hot shower.

The waiting assassin stepped out of the shadows behind the door of his hotel room and sprang into action.

Bolan caught the motion at the last possible instant and thrust his arm up in front of his face. A piano wire garrote looped around his neck, and Bolan felt a hard knee shoved into the middle of his back as the man yanked the wire back in an attempt to decapitate him.

The soldier's left arm was up in time, and it was slammed against his face by the force of the assassin's combination garrote and knee strike. The wire bit deep into the muscles of his forearm and blood splashed out as the white-hot laceration carved through his skin and muscle. He grunted in pain and staggered back.

He shifted his shoulder to the right so that he was at an angle to the attacker and caught a glimpse of a three-piece business suit and a balaclava mask. Bolan smashed the heel of his right foot onto the man's toes through his fashionable dress loafers. The assassin grunted and snatched his foot back.

Bolan used the shift to slam his elbow into the man's gut, pushing outward against the piano wire even as it cut deeper into his arm. Blood poured down the front of his clothes, soaking him further. He struck out with his elbow again and this time caught the man in the solar plexus, which was indefensible.

The assassin sagged as his breath was forced from him in a gasp and Bolan managed to turn fully and shove him backward. The man staggered, and the soldier saw that the eyes behind the balaclava were Asian. He knew instantly that Mai Li-Aa had discovered his identity as a western agent, more than likely from the footage on Jigsaw Liu's CCTV cameras.

The man struck the wall, fighting for position despite the disabling blow. He blocked a roundhouse Bolan aimed at the side of his head, but was unable to return a blow in answer. Unable to use his left arm, which continued gushing blood, the Executioner fired off a snap kick.

The man used his shin to block the kick, and a knife appeared in his fist. Bolan danced back and finished shimmying out of his bloody shirt as the man lunged forward. The soldier darted to one side to avoid a hard slash. The man shifted angle smoothly and stabbed out again with the knife.

Bolan caught the blade with a wild flail of his shirt and jerked. The man held on to the hilt of his knife and pulled back. Bolan let go of the shirt and suddenly lunged forward. He kicked once and struck the man in the wrist, driving it back against his body and knocking the straight-bladed knife from the man's hand. He forced him back up against the wall for a second time. The man blocked one kick and Bolan shot another, breathing hard with the exertion.

The attacker turned a thigh and absorbed the strike, then came off the wall in a rush. He threw a series of vertical fist strikes in the whirling, machine-gun motion common with Wing Chun style kung fu. Bolan took four blows to the chest and a glancing one off the point of his chin.

He staggered back and the assailant pursued. The angry eyes behind the balaclava narrowed in concentration as the man pressed his advantage. He bore into Bolan, driving him back and onto the hotel bed. The Executioner struck the mattress with the backs of his knees and went down on his back. The Asian killer dropped his right arm and brought it around in an overhand hammer strike aimed for the big American's vulnerable throat.

Bolan swept up his legs and locked them around the man's narrow waist like the jaws of a trap snapping closed. His ankles locked above the man's buttocks, and the soldier twisted hard at the hips, throwing his upper body into the roll and shoving off the mattress with his good arm.

Startled, the overextended killer fell as Bolan rolled off the bed and swept him to the floor. The man thrashed as they struck the ground in front of the nightstand, but Bolan hung on like a rodeo rider. He leaned in and threw two elbows into his attacker's face that shook the man so hard Bolan felt the force shivering down through the assassin's body.

The man launched a heel-of-the-palm blow into Bolan's floating rib. The angle was wrong and the bone did not snap. Bolan snarled at the pain and punched down with his nearly useless arm, striking again and again. The man easily fended off the blows, causing the soldier more pain with every successful block.

The left-handed attacks were purely diversionary. Bolan snatched the phone off the nightstand and rammed it into the assassin's upturned face twice, the blunt force trauma crushing the man's nose and knocking several teeth loose. The assassin didn't move.

Bolan staggered to his feet. He moved to the door and threw the second dead bolt. Every minute counted. He was obviously under surveillance, and his actions in Hong Kong seemed to have earned him a death warrant from Chinese intelligence.

Despite that, he couldn't very well go running out covered in the blood of another man or while bleeding so profusely. He slid a chair under the doorknob. He went to the bed and yanked the linen cover from a pillow then retrieved the medical supplies he had purchased from the Basra hospital.

He poured the last of the hydrogen peroxide over the nasty laceration left by the piano wire garrote, keeping the window curtains drawn and the lights off as he worked in case the Chinese had a backup team outside with long weapons.

Wrapping the pillowcase around his bleeding wound, he held it in place until blood had seeped through the linen and stuck it to the wound. Bolan let go and began to quickly wind white surgical tape around the makeshift bandage. He used the tape to seal the wound and reduce blood flow to the area, further helping the wound to clot. It was crude but effective. It would have to do until he could get to Calvin James.

He moved to his luggage and began to rip out the lining of his suitcase, pulling out the soles on the shoes he had packed as part of his checked luggage.

In four minutes he had put together a Glock 19 compact pistol out of its mostly plastic assembly pieces. He racked the slide and chambered a 9 mm round. Armed with his holdout, Bolan stripped down and turned the shower on full-force.

Holding his bandaged arm clear, Bolan slid under the hot needles of water and quickly washed down. The wound on his shoulder had clotted nicely and he tore off the bandage. His injured arm throbbed with pain but it kept him alert against his exhaustion. Once he was rinsed clean Bolan dressed quickly and searched the corpse lying on the floor by his bed.

He found a second knife and about one thousand dollars in Kuwaiti currency as well as a "skeleton" key card the hitter had used to enter Bolan's room, but no identification. The Chinese man had dressed in an upscale business suit and raised no suspicions as he penetrated hotel security. Once in Bolan's room he'd pulled the balaclava from the pocket of his tailored suit jacket and waited for the western agent's return to unleash his strike with the silent garrote.

Absentmindedly Bolan touched his crude bandage. Like many before him, the assassin had come damn close.

Bolan prepared to leave. He wouldn't take his luggage to avoid tipping off any surveillance teams as to his intentions. That would leave him until noon tomorrow's checkout time before maids discovered the mess in the room. He would be long gone by then.

The soldier opened the wall safe and pulled out the pouch containing his travel documents and identification. It was time to retire Mike McKay, freelance journalist for a good long while. Mr. McKay would now be wanted in connection with at least one, and possibly two, murders. Bolan was confident that given time Brognola could expunge the record, but for now it was too risky.

Mike McKay had entered Kuwait, but Matt Cooper would be flying out.

Bolan went to the wall and turned up the air conditioning to max to slow decomposition of the corpse. He crossed the room, double-checking the Glock 19. He slid it behind his coat and smoothed the fit. His arm hurt badly, but he kept his expression neutral as he removed the chair, chain and dead bolts before opening the door to his room.

Bolan stepped out into the hallway, every nerve alive as he searched for hidden killers. The hall was quiet, the lighting muted and tasteful. He checked the time on his watch and fixed his cuff against the bulge of surgical tape sealing his wound.

It was time to roll.

CHAPTER FOURTEEN

Bolan moved down the hall toward the bank of elevators. He thought briefly about taking the service elevator and slipping out the kitchen at the back of the hotel, but then discarded the idea.

If a backup team was waiting, then all the exits would be covered. It was better to stay in the public eye. Intelligence agents were not terrorists, for the most part and they preferred anonymity to splashy scenes of indiscriminant civilian casualties. If they were waiting for him, then his most dangerous time of exposure would be in the taxicab on the way to the airport.

The elevator to the lobby opened with a ding and Bolan stepped inside. He turned and the doors closed behind him. He pushed the lobby button, and after a short ride the elevator doors slid open. Bolan scanned the lobby carefully before stepping out. He was more worried about a surveillance team at the moment, but he was prepared to react to whatever the Chinese might throw at him. He crossed the lobby and gold-gilded automatic doors whispered open in response to invisible sensors as he approached.

A uniformed valet raised an eyebrow as Bolan walked out. The soldier gestured toward the short line of cabs waiting at the curb despite the late hour, and the man put a narrow whistle to his lip and called one over. Bolan got in the cab and said, "Airport." The taxi drove out into the street and began the short cruise toward the Al-Kuwaiti terminal.

The backup team didn't wait long.

The taxicab driver, a chain-smoking Filipino man with pictures of his wife and eight children taped on the dash of his cab, stopped the vehicle at an intersection. Bolan automatically surveyed the area, looking around and behind him. Looking over his shoulder out the back of the cab he saw the powerful Yamaha 1200 motorbike, riding double, race from around a corner.

Bolan's Glock 19 was out and in his hand before his heart had beaten twice. He jerked open the rear door and bailed out of the cab, yelling for the driver to go.

The motorcycle rider, who wore a black helmet with its tinted face visor down, saw Bolan bail out of the taxi and hit his brakes. The rear tire on the Yamaha locked up and swung around, leaving a half-moon arc of rubber on the pavement.

The second rider lifted a Skorpion vz. 83 machine pistol. The weapon was inaccurate, but so cheap it was as common as silverware in some parts of the world, making it a good throwaway weapon for hits. In addition, though poorly made and inaccurate, it had a high cyclic rate of fire and an acceptable man-killing caliber in 9 mm.

Bolan leaned forward and fired his Glock quickly across the trunk of the cab but his rounds flew wide as the Filipino driver screamed in fear at the sudden violence and stomped on the gas. Bolan knew the man would be on his radio to his dispatch and Kuwaiti cops, hypervigilant to the threat of terrorists, would soon arrive. Their arrival could save his life, but Bolan could no more afford to be taken into custody by them than the Chinese hit squad. The difference was that Bolan would never fire on the police to facilitate his escape.

As the taxi raced away, Bolan threw himself flat in the middle of the street and took the compact Glock19 in both his hands. He fired the trigger in a rapid series of smooth squeezes, and the handgun roared in his grip even as the Skorpion sputtered its own mechanical dirge.

Sparks skipped off the street as the 9 mm rounds deflected and ricocheted around Bolan, some landing so close they sent chips of asphalt stinging into his face.

His first round took the motorcycle driver in the knee and he heard the man scream at the sudden pain. The wounded motorcycle rider goosed the big bike.

The Yamaha lurched forward, nearly unseating the gunner sitting pillion. The maneuver caused his weapon to swing up and off target, probably saving Bolan's life. The soldier put the next two rounds through the gunner's helmet visor.

Reinforced safety plastic shattered under the impact of the 9 mm slugs as they punched the gunner in his face, opening bloody cavities and knocking the man to the ground. Seeing his partner down, the Chinese agent did not flee.

With the engine still running, the man dumped the bike and scrambled for the Skorpion machine pistol.

Feeling a grudging admiration for the man's devotion to duty, Bolan pulled down on him. The driver spun his back to the Executioner and scooped up the machine-gun before pitching over his right shoulder as he sought to twist into position.

Bolan helped him complete his somersault by putting a second bullet into the agent, just below his left shoulder blade. Knocked off his zenith, the man sprawled across the street and the big American fired a coup de grâce to finish off the threat. The 9 mm round traveled under the helmet and tore through the soft flesh behind the assassin's ear before mushrooming outward to scramble his brain.

Blood pumped out in spreading pools along the street. It looked as black as ink in the soft illumination of streetlights. Bolan leaped up and jogged toward the still purring Yamaha. He realized he was in a race for time as he slid his semiautomatic pistol into his waistband.

In the distance he heard the screeching of high-pitched sirens in the abrupt disjointed beat of European police rather than the longer wails of American-style vehicle sirens. The police response was impressive, Bolan thought as he muscled the Yamaha motorcycle up off the ground.

He swung his leg over, ignoring the pain in his wounded arm. So far the heavy wrapping of surgical tape had done the trick of preventing his wounds from tearing open again, but he knew he was going to need stitches, and quite a few, for the healing process to truly start working.

He turned the motorbike in a tight circle as lights

began to come on in the windows above the street. He used his toe to coax the Yamaha into gear and gunned the 1200 cc engine wide open. He tore down the road like a man strapped to a rocket and despite himself he felt exhilarated.

He had missed riding motorcycles he realized.

USING HIS NEW PASSPORT Bolan managed to get out of Kuwait. He ditched the Glock 19 and flew into Maro, as it was the destination of the next available flight leaving al-Kuwait, and he spent the night there. After changing identities, he then flew into Amman, Jordan, in the morning. It would have been easier to have a dedicated pilot, but not necessarily better. A lone plane was easier to trace than a man hopping from one international airport to the next. Not all of the countries he moved through were prepped to overlook covert air activity and many did not even contain a U.S. military presence. Even in cases where there were American air assets, Bolan's activities could have served to raise uncomfortable questions.

Plausible deniability was the lifeblood of Stony Man, and its operatives were expected to take the risks associated with that. If they didn't like the rules, they could play a different game. The trade-off was unprecedented freedom to wage results-orientated warfare in whatever manner they deemed necessary. It was a Congressional Oversight Committee's worst nightmare, inexcusable in an age of hypermedia exposure and all the more efficient because of that.

Bolan's beard had grown in fully by the time he flew into Jordan. The painkiller wasn't easing the pain from the wound in his arm but had managed to knock his fever down. In Maro he'd stripped off the surgical tape and treated his wound with supplies he'd purchased at the airport pharmacy, using pictures on the packaging to pick out what he needed as he couldn't read the script. The wound hadn't appeared infected, but it was healing in an ugly manner and Bolan had enough experience to know that he'd just added a rather significant souvenir to his trophy case of scars.

He hoped that in Calvin James's hands the scarring would be greatly reduced once he reached Amman. Scars could serve to identify him as easily as fingerprints.

Amman, Jordon—along with Islamabad, Pakistan—had become a hotbed of modern espionage activity where both sides in the global conflict could operate in a fairly efficient manner. Western intelligence enjoyed the alternatively tacit and enthusiastic support of the Jordanian monarchy while enough Whabbist madrassas and Shiite clerics linked to Hezbollah and the Muslim Brotherhood existed that the street remained an open ground for those opposed to Western ideals.

There were plenty of Amman neighborhoods that did not suffer an infidel lightly, and the predominantly Sunni Muslim Jordan had been the homeland of the leader of al Qaeda in Iraq, Abu Musab al-Zarqawi. Despite this, enough hotels and businesses, along with government bodies, had been sympathetic enough to the anti-Saddam cause that Zarqwi had seen fit to perpetrate acts of terrorism in his own country. Mostly notably in the Radisson hotel where his suicide bombers had slaughtered a Jordanian wedding party consisting of fellow Muslims.

In some quarters of the city the slain terror leader was still seen as a martyr because of his struggle against the Western influences that ran counter to his radical interpretation of the Quran.

Mack Bolan had a few radical interpretations of his own when his back was forced against the wall.

He was held up in customs for a while because he fit a suspicious profile. He'd been forced to purchase a one-way ticket in cash and had no checked luggage. His cover story was in place and a tight fit, so after about two hours he was able to leave and catch a taxi to where James and Encizo were waiting for him.

It was early morning, and the streets were stirring as market bazaars and shops began to open up in the neighborhood away from the international district. Traffic was increasing, and groups of people lined the street on their way to work or school. Traditional Arab dress was not an uncommon sight in the metropolitan crowds.

Bolan scratched at his beard. He had dressed in khaki trousers, a button-down, short-sleeved shirt and sturdy tan shoes with a thick tread. The soldier preferred solid-colored-shirts, but the one he wore now was striped with multicolored check patterns after the fashion taste more common on the Arab street.

He had stopped chewing gum, something he did to help his ears pop on airplane flights, eschewed sunglasses and replaced his Rolex Submariner watch with a cheaper Egyptian model with a leather band. He needed his phone, but he kept it buried in his pocket and had turned the ringer to vibrate. He made every attempt to downplay his Western profile.

Due to a traditionally large minority of people from Circassian descent—former natives of the Russian steppes moved south during the reign of the Ottomans—and Chechen immigrants, Caucasian features were not unknown among the citizens of Jordan. Bolan hoped that fact would bolster his ability to move without suspicion through the streets, though his lack of language skills would instantly mark him as a foreigner no matter how he was dressed.

The taxi took Bolan away from the more affluent West Amman and into the poorer neighborhoods of East Amman, far from the Hyatt hotel, American Embassy and the giant Safeway grocery store. Here Palestinian refugees formed a strong minority, completely dominating some neighborhoods stacked with poorly constructed tenements and scattered with small shops.

That fact was pointed out to Bolan by his driver, a man named Omar, who spoke serviceable, if broken, English. At one point he noted to Bolan that they had entered an area exclusive to Palestinians, a tent city from 1948 that had grown up into a labyrinth of winding, narrow streets separating concrete apartment buildings and one-room shops of every description.

After fifteen minutes of travel through the hilly capital city, the taxi entered another Palestinian enclave and stopped in front of a four-story apartment building. Standing on the street, waiting for him, was Rafael Encizo dressed in traditional Arabic garb of a red-and-white checkered headdress and white robe. The Cuban-American had grown a thick circle beard which stood out jet-black against his olive-skinned complexion.

Bolan paid the driver and got out of the cab. Encizo was holding open a steel door and he nodded and smiled in greeting.

"¿Que pasa, hefe?" he said, letting Bolan through the gate into a small courtyard and then the building itself. The big American nodded a greeting and began to ask the Phoenix Force commando a question. Encizo shook his head and whispered, "upstairs."

The soldier followed Encizo as they climbed four stories up a narrow, bare concrete staircase. At each landing a large, square window opened to the outside. On the fourth floor the two men entered a stark, poorly lit hallway. At the end of the hall Bolan saw a woman in a traditional dark robe duck into a door to avoid them.

Calvin James, obviously waiting for them, opened the door to the apartment. Bolan entered the room, shaking James's hand once he was inside. Encizo shut the door behind them and flipped closed a series of dead bolts.

Immediately upon entering the apartment, Bolan saw that a short, alcove-style hall to the left led to an open closet and the bathroom. A Claymore antipersonnel mine was set up in the entranceway, angled at the door so the back blast would be funneled into the alcove. The ignition cord trailed down the hall, taped to the ground to avoid tripping anyone and leading around a corner.

"What's up?" Bolan asked. "Didn't want anyone hearing us speak English?"

"I want to avoid it as much as possible," Encizo said, nodding. "Cal and I might fit in better than David or T.J.

would, but nobody around here's really fooled. English is pretty common, but it shouts 'outsider' in a way that makes me nervous in these Palestinian hoods."

"It's like in my neighborhood on the south side of Chicago when I was growing up," James added. "Everybody knows who belongs in the hood. Cops try to send in a black officer in plain clothes and he was always spotted. The gangs know if a guy comes from three streets over, let alone from out of town. That's why we're wearing traditional garb even though Western dress is so prevalent here. I'm hoping it makes us look like the Jordanian version of country bumpkins come to the big city, as long as we don't open our mouths."

"It's only going to get worse in Baghdad," Bolan observed.

James shrugged. "Like Rafe said, he and I are better than David or T.J., and in crowded markets or just out and about we'll move easier. We knew it was going to be tough."

"Barbara needs to send someone to language school and get some Stony members speaking Arabic or Farsi. Too much is going on in this part of the world for us to overlook those skills," Bolan said, and Encizo nodded.

They led Bolan farther into the cramped, four-room apartment. The walls and floor were of the same bare concrete as the staircase. Bolan realized there would be no insulation, though the windows at least had glass in them.

"Plumbing okay?" he asked.

"Toilet and shower are weak but working. Don't drink the water," James answered.

"How's it going?" Bolan asked, meaning the surveillance operation.

James led him to the large common area at the rear of the apartment. Bolan saw a battered old futon couch next to a kerosene stove and several battery-operated lanterns. Encizo and James had put down foam mattresses and sleeping bags on the concrete. There was an additional one for Bolan.

A Soviet 7.62 mm Dragunov sniper rifle with the standard PSO-1 scope mount was set up on a tripod in the middle of the room. Three AK-104 Kalashnikov carbines leaned against the wall. On a card table near the couch and weapons sat a VINCENT sat-com unit, a laptop, two Nikon cameras—one digital and one 35 mm—as well as a satellite phone.

"The Agency set us up good," James said. "Your wish list for weapons and equipment was waiting for us when we got here. They got us Jordanian pistols instead of the more generic Makarovs, but since they're Jordanian army I didn't bitch."

Bolan grunted. The Viper JAWS—Jordanian Arms and Weapon System—had a great reputation for a 9 mm pistol, especially when compared to the older Soviet Makarov and Tokarev, and was the product of a joint American-Jordanian effort. He supposed that with them going into service with the Royal Jordanian Army it was feasible that some would have made it out onto the black market.

"Good enough. What about our good Yazid Marwan?" Bolan asked.

"Take a look for yourself," Encizo said, and indicated the Dragunov.

The designated infantry support weapon was set up on the ground on a foam shooter's pad. It was pointed out a sliding-glass door that opened up on a railing around a patio that only extended about six inches out. The glass door opened up on a narrow alley and James and Encizo had hung drapes, keeping them only open a few inches, to avoid being seen by anyone across the way.

Bolan settled into position. The PSO-1 scope was angled through the wide-set, wrought-iron bars of the balcony and out toward the mouth of the alley, which opened up on a busy avenue. The crosshairs of the sniper rifle were focused on a balcony across that street, the fifth one up from the bottom and two over from the left edge of the target building. The balcony there was as narrow and unadorned as the one attached to the Stony Man team's own safehouse.

Inside the apartment Bolan could clearly distinguish the front door through his sniper scope. A battered old television with rabbit-ear antennas played what Bolan took to be a local soap opera. He had a clear image of the back of a large, balding head facing away from the open balcony.

"Looks like our guy," Bolan said.

"Got him?" James asked. "Good. Now come here. I want to show you our little glitch."

"There's always a glitch," Bolan muttered as he stood.

James led Bolan to the edge of the drapes covering all but two inches of their apartment balcony. The soldier stood at the edge of the curtain and looked out. He heard the sounds of the street, smelled exhaust fumes from the cars. In the distance he heard the familiar call to prayer, broadcast five times a day across the city. Persian carpets aired out over balconies. Clotheslines filled the space above the street between buildings, dripping with laundry.

On the street women in *abayas* hustled by on errands while men in dirty jeans and battered sandals rode in threes and fours in the open backs of pickups down the narrow avenue. He saw street vendors selling vegetables and cutting meat from hanging carcasses.

The unemployed lounged in little clusters and argued and laughed with animated hand gestures. School-age children kicked grimy soccer balls in the gutter. Rebar struts stuck out from the unfinished corners of old buildings.

"Look down, against the wall, across the alley. See him?"

Bolan looked down. He saw what appeared to be a vagrant dressed in filthy western shirt and pants under a grimy *thobe*. His beard was patchy, almost mangy, and the man's overall appearance was completely unkempt. Bolan narrowed his eyes. There were two empty bottles of the potent Jordanian beer lying empty beside the man, who clutched a brown paper bag.

Bolan frowned. "A drunk? In the open?"

"Exactly. Not in Jordan, he smelled the first time I laid eyes on him. And I'm not talking about BO," James said. "Here." He handed Bolan a compact pair of Zeiss binoculars. "Check out his right ear under the headdress."

Bolan took the offered binoculars and zeroed in on the lounging man. A small earpiece was fitted into the man's ear. Bolan grunted at the wireless communications tech. "Pretty upscale for a gutter drunk. Our boy

Yazid is being watched. I'm guessing not by Jordanian security, either, considering how the observer's screwing it up."

"Probably rules out any Middle Eastern agency, including Israel," Encizo said.

"Hell," James snorted. "Pretending to be a drunk, in Jordan? I think that rules out any first tier western operators, as well."

As an Arabic nation Jordan was technically "dry." Nightclubs flourished in the upscale West end of the city, and alcohol was served in the open. However, there was still such a great social taboo on public drunkenness and alcoholism that displays considered common in American or European neighborhoods were rare in Jordan.

"Ex-Soviet republics? The Asian ones maybe?" Bolan offered. He took in how the man's hawk nose was more pronounced from having obviously been broken more than once.

"Sure, maybe," James allowed. "Maybe the ones whose intel guys came up in the Interior Ministry or the GRU military intelligence instead of the former KGB. They'd have the tech expertise, but their surveillance experience would all be internal police actions, not covert foreign ops. All I know is that he showed up in the morning after we got here. I don't know how long he's been out there."

"You don't think he's on to us?" Bolan handed James back the binoculars. "What happens when Yazid leaves his apartment? That guy tail him?"

"No," Encizo replied. "Another guy, taller and thinner, tails him in a white Celica. They're definitely following our man. I followed him following Yazid shopping one day. I could have sliced his throat at any time. He was positively asleep, real tunnel vision." The Phoenix Force knife expert mimed drawing a finger across his neck. "I took some photos instead. Besides, what's the range on a wireless earpiece like that? Even with the receiver in the bag? We're clean for bugs in here and he'd be set up differently if he was using a parabolic mike. They must already have a bug in Marwan's apartment."

"I assume you got film on that jackass down there, as well?" Bolan asked.

"Yep." James nodded. "Sent it off to Aaron. He said he'll get back to us. That was this morning."

"We have to know who they are before we roll," Bolan said. "The Syrians could have tipped someone off after Toronto and sent a team hoping to ambush anyone who checks out Yazid Marwan. Whoever they are, they've just made number one on our list of priorities," Bolan decided. "What happens at night?" Bolan asked.

"Third man," Encizo answered. "Yazid isn't exactly a playboy. They keep the indigent in place until dark, then they have a night shift guy, different from the daytime shadow, in a late-model Ford V8 van. He parks in the alley, crawls into the back and pulls the curtain. Must have a sibling transceiver to the one used by our Mr. Bum-by-day down there."

"He goes first, then," Bolan said. "Let's move out."

CHAPTER FIFTEEN

The Stony Man commandos settled in to wait.

Bolan took one of the 9 mm Viper pistols and stuck it in his waistband. He changed into a *thobe* and checkered, red-and-white *shumagh* headdress. With his darkly tanned complexion and full beard he didn't particularly stand out, but he knew better than to think he could pull off any complicated subterfuge.

They made strong coffee and took turns behind the PSO-1 scope, watching Yazid Marwan's apartment. The former member of the Iraqi Special Republican Guard led a fairly sedate life. The spook in the alley outside whiled away the time with a patience that Bolan had to admit was professional.

While Encizo took watch behind the sniper scope, Calvin James inspected Bolan's garrote wound.

"Nasty piece of business," James said. He carefully unwrapped and cleaned the laceration before smearing it with iodine. He peppered the gash lightly with antibiotic powder and began to stitch the wound closed.

"Yeah. That agent at the consulate was able to run my face from the Hong Kong incident."

"Bound to happen to us," James said. The former SEAL medic's eyes never left his task as he spoke. "Too many urban ops, too many cameras. You can't infiltrate in balaclavas every time. Still, the Chinese know you're a player, but they don't know how or who. Could be worse."

Bolan grunted as James pulled the surgical thread through the flesh of his forearm. It wasn't the first time in his bloody career that his face had become a potential liability, but there was a limit to how many times he could have it changed. He didn't want to end up looking like one of those tired celebrities in the supermarket tabloids, long past their prime with the mannequin look of too much plastic surgery. He put it out of his mind for now.

Thirty minutes after James had bandaged the wound the sat phone on the card table next to the laptop buzzed. James picked it up. "Go."

He listened for a minute, and Bolan could almost hear the smile in his voice when he answered. "Nice, Bear, nice."

While Bolan watched, James moved to the laptop and nudged the touch pad to disrupt the screen saver. A rectangle graph showing an incoming download appeared. Once it hit 100% Download Complete, James said, "Got it. Striker will call as we move forward. Out."

He hung up the phone and clicked on the download icon. Instantly Interpol photos with accompanying text appeared on the screen. Bolan came in close and studied the screen.

"Got a match on FBI Russian mafia files. Cross-hit

in Interpol. These guys are Armenian mob freelancers." Bolan read.

"Armenians?" James mused. "Mirjana said it was Armenians who coordinated Scimitar weapon shipments in Azerbaijan. Either way, Mirjana or Scimitar, it's a funny coincidence."

"No such thing." Bolan grunted. "They're here because the opposition is afraid someone is running Yazid Marwan down. If they were a hit team, they'd have taken him out by now."

"Jesus," Encizo said from behind the rifle. "They're Armenian. They would have blown up the whole damn building or gone in and chewed him up with a chain saw in front of his family by now if they'd been paid to take him out."

"So we take them out?" James asked Bolan.

"We can't have them on our six when we go in after Yazid," Bolan said, thoughtful.

"We take them out, then whoever called in the shadow will know we're in Jordan and onto Yazid," Encizo pointed out.

"Toronto cell hit. Jigsaw Liu, dead. Karl Mirjana, dead. The hit team going after Ma Ning-tan, dead." Bolan ticked off his points on his fingers, one by one. "This op is wet already. Scimitar and sponsors know we're onto them. Subterfuge will only take us so far. Speed and aggression is our key now, just like always."

Encizo and James nodded.

"So we take 'em out before we interview Yazid," James stated.

"Yes," Bolan replied. "But I want to make sure I get every last one of them possible. Not just the point men."

"Find the nest?" Encizo said.

"And clean it out," Bolan finished.

"Problem," James said, looking at the screen. "Not one of these assholes speaks English."

"I knew this was going to happen sooner or later," Bolan said. "We can follow them home, take them out, but we won't be able to verify who put them on Yazid's tail."

"Yazid speaks English, right?" James said.

"Yeah, went to Oxford back in the days when Saddam was chummy with Thatcher and everyone hated Tehran," Bolan replied.

"Maybe he's all we need," Encizo said.

"Maybe," Bolan agreed. "The clock's ticking. We need to interview Yazid. We can't do it with that surveillance and I'm not predisposed to letting Armenian hit men run around at will if I can have anything to do with it."

"I think we have an understanding," James said. "We go in, shoot and loot. At best we get some paperwork, a hard drive and/or some cell phones. Otherwise we simply put some bad operators out of business."

"Win-win situation," Bolan said.

"THEY'RE ON THE FIFTH FLOOR," Encizo said. "Room 519. There's at least three of them in there, but I think more like twice that."

"Building materials?" James asked.

"Reinforced concrete for load-bearing structural, but only plasterboard covered by wood between rooms. The doors have a lock, a single dead bolt and a security chain."

"Windows?"

"Commercial variety. Set in the wall with no balcony. They open inward with a metal clasp-locking mechanism. The glass is set into four even quadrants of windowpane around standard molding and wood frames. High quality but not security level."

"Wall penetration will be a problem with our weapons. Even the 9 mm," Bolan said.

"C-4 breaching charges on the door and shotguns with buckshot or breach-shot for the takedown?" James suggested.

"What's security like in the hotel?"

"They have Jordanian police out front armed with a pistol and submachine-gun each. They liaison with hotel private security who have a heavy presence in the lobby and restaurant area. They make hourly passes through the guestroom halls. They carry 9 mm sidearms," Encizo answered. "I think we could get in and do the takedown. It's getting out without slugging through security forces I'm doubtful of."

"Position to snipe on the window?" James asked.

"Negative. The Mecca Mall is across the street. Ninety-five thousand square feet. No defilade and no angle other than up trajectory. Lousy for shooting."

"That kind of exposure rules out rappelling down the outside, even if we could get to the roof." Bolan rubbed at his beard, thoughtful.

"Bait and switch followed by a bum rush?" Encizo suggested.

"How do we get out?" James countered.

"I think I 'SPIE' a way." Bolan smiled. "Rafe, I'll need you to find us a good covert LZ on the edge of

Amman, out toward the desert, and pinpoint the GPS reading."

"That'll work. Depends on how fast Stony Man can get us a bird. This'll have to be black from CENTCOM, and even from Jordanian intelligence. And fast. Very goddamn fast," James said.

"Barb hasn't let us down yet," Bolan stated.

ENCIZO WALKED OUT of the hotel and dodged traffic as he crossed the busy street. James pulled out from the curb and met him as he crossed the meridian. Encizo opened the passenger-side door and slid into the seat.

"It's a go," he said.

"Good," Bolan replied from the backseat. "Let's do it."

Driving quickly, the Stony Man team circumnavigated the luxury hotel and pulled into the parking lot of the Mecca Mall, quickly losing themselves in the enormous parking lot, which could hold 3,500 vehicles. A State Department courier with no association to the mission would pick up the vehicle ten minutes after the commandos left the area.

Over the horizon, in the hot Jordan night, Charlie Mott was already inbound in a AH-6J Little Bird attack helicopter. The numbers had already started to fall. Dressed in their flowing white robes and headdresses, the Stony Man commandos moved quickly toward their objective.

The hotel loomed above them as they crossed the street. Bolan felt his frustration rising over the broken jigsaw that was the international web in play around the enigmatic Scimitar. A cell in Toronto, penetrated by the most feared unit of Syrian intelligence, had opened up a convoluted plot with the fingerprints of malignant puppet masters in Beijing all over it: a triad gangster with CCI ties using his opium and heroin networks to move weapons into the hands of Armenian mobsters working on contract for a Croatian arms dealer being coerced and intimidated by a terror network, apparently gone criminally commercial, operating out of Iraq; a former CCI agent gunned down by a terror cell hit squad in Basra and Armenian mobsters showing up in Jordan, running an operation against a former member of Saddam Hussein's Special Republican Guard; obtuse clues about the identity of Scimitar leading back to Syrian and Chinese patrons and sponsors. And, behind it all, the shadow of the death merchant al-Kassar.

Bolan intended to seize the chance to vent his frustrations in righteous wrath against violent, international criminals. It was a relief, a short-lived blessing.

Walking fast, the Stony Man commandos moved onto the sidewalk behind the hotel. Dressed in black nightsuits and body armor under their robes with various weapons and tools attached for instant use once the dynamic entry began, they approached their target. The ornate wall ringing the hotel was broken by a gate opening up on the loading dock where deliveries were made.

Jordan was a security conscious nation in a volatile region. Yet its problems were minor compared to other neighboring states and the well-developed sense of paranoia evident in Lebanon, Israel or Iraq was largely missing despite sporadic terrorist attacks. As such, its security was as capable of being exploited as those in other, more violent nations.

They reached the back gate, hands sliding into black

driving gloves of kid leather. As one, the three men reached up and swept their headdresses to one side. The checkered red-and-white clothes tumbled forgotten to the ground. The black balaclavas were pulled into place, obscuring the commandos' faces from internal CCTV cameras. Encizo pulled a pair of short-handled bolt cutters from under his robe as James grabbed the chain and padlock looped around the chain link fence gate and offered it up.

Encizo cut through the chain in one easy motion. His Phoenix Force teammate pushed the gate open as the Cuban dropped the bolt cutters next to the discarded headdresses on the ground. The Stony Man team rushed through the opening, Encizo taking the lead. The three commandos stripped off their robes on the run, leaving them behind on the ground.

Each man carried the 9 mm Viper at either shoulder or hip, and all three wielded Saiga-12K Russian .12-gauge assault shotguns with folding stocks and shortened barrels. The 8-round box magazines went into a weapon designed on the AK-74M paratrooper carbine. Loaded with No.1 buckshot of 16 pellets of .30-caliber diameter, the rounds were considered effective man-stoppers. They were also considered generally more efficient at causing blunt trauma through protective vests, or even in general, to the more widely touted antipersonnel fléchettes round loads.

The first two rounds in Encizo's shotgun were breaching rounds designed to penetrate the civilian locks on interior doors. The outer fire door was made of metal, reducing the effectiveness of the rounds and potentially signaling the team's presence before they had fully exploited their surprise advantage.

As they reached the fire door, James allowed his combat shotgun to hang from its strap across his torso. He pulled up a titanium, two-foot-long crowbar fitted with rubber grips at the end from a carabiner holster on his rappel harness. While Bolan and Encizo covered him, shotguns at port arms, James went to work.

Without preamble James wedged the comma-shaped end of the crowbar under the overlapping lip of the steel fire door. Throwing one big boot up on the other door, he grabbed the crowbar in both of his gloved hands and yanked back sharply.

There was a screech of metal and then a loud pop as the door snapped open. A fire alarm began to wail. James dropped the crowbar and grabbed the door with one hand as he scooped up the pistol grip of his Saiga with the other. Bolan went through the door, shotgun high, followed hard by Encizo.

Once inside the hotel, James stepped through, letting the fire door swing closed. The Stony Man team took the stairs in a rapid, leap-frog pattern. The stairs themselves were metal and set into the wall with a three-rail guard running along the outside edge. The staircase ran up in a squared spiral with a flat landing at each level where doors opened off onto the guest hallways. The cacophony of the midnight fire alarm was deafening.

Bolan bounded up to the second floor, then covered the area as Encizo and James raced past him, the pounding of their boots echoing up and down the vertical shaft. They continued on until the fifth floor, where Bolan stepped onto the landing and off to the left as Encizo rushed forward. The Cuban snatched open the door leading to the hallway.

The Executioner rushed through, shotgun up and ready, his teammates hard on his heels. A few hotel guests, eyes sleepy and hair mussed, had opened their doors and stuck their heads outside in response to the fire alarm. At the sight of the night-suited and masked intruders they screamed or shouted in terror and slammed their doors shut.

Bolan knew that security, already alerted by the fire alarm, would now have guest reports to guide their response protocols. He began to race faster down the hall.

The occupants of Room 519 hadn't opened their door in response to the alarm. Bolan streaked past the room, ducking under the spy hole set at eye-level in the muted wood of the door. He spun and put his back to the wall on the handle side of the room door. Encizo ran up and halted in the middle of the hall at a sharp angle to the door as James slid into position on the other side of the door.

Encizo's shotgun roared. The breaching shot slammed into the door just behind the handle. A saucer-size crater punched through the solid wood. The Phoenix Force warrior shifted the combat shotgun's muzzle and fired his weapon again, blowing out the dead bolt.

The Stony Man hitters had been inside the hotel for less than three minutes.

CHAPTER SIXTEEN

The door shivered under the twin impacts of the special rounds, then shook open, trailing splinters of wood and loose pieces of stamped metal. Encizo stepped forward and kicked the door wide before peeling back.

James pumped two loads of buckshot around the corner, aiming high for covering fire as Bolan squatted and let his flash-bang grenade roll across the threshold. The canister-shaped grenade bounced into the room as Bolan swung upright and pressed himself against the wall of the hallway.

A flash of light like a star going supernova followed the deafening concussion of the grenade. Bolan swung through the door, Saiga shotgun leveled at hip height. James followed him as Encizo brought up the rear.

The Executioner saw an opening to his left and covered it with his shotgun. It was a door to the bathroom. He caught a glimpse of a shoeless man in trousers and a white cotton tanktop T-shirt staggering against the sink. A Skorpion machine pistol lay on the tile by the European-style toilet.

A blast from Bolan's shotgun punched the Armenian mercenary in the chest and cracked open his sternum. The man was knocked across the bathroom counter, and blood splattered the mirror and sizzled on the light bulbs.

According to the hotel's Web site the room was a luxury suite, with two big bedrooms opening up on a common living area and bar. James, second in the file, raced past the engaged Bolan and peeled off to the left. Encizo sidestepped to the right.

A wet bar and service sink took up the front part of the suite while toward the far wall three couches had been set up in a U-shape around a large-screen television. Whoever was footing the bill for the Armenian cell's logistical support hadn't skimped. Three men in various stages of undress were in the room, attempting to scramble back up to their feet and recover various submachine-guns.

James took the man on the left. The Armenian wore a huge gold hoop in his ear, and his long hair was swept back in a tight ponytail. He wore silk boxers and a stunned expression on his face as he looked up into the cavernous muzzle of James's combat shotgun. James pulled the trigger and suddenly the man no longer possessed enough of a face to wear any kind of expression.

Still firing from the hip, James swiveled as the second man rose, fumbling to bring his H&K MP-5 into play. A trickle of blood flowed from the broken drum of his right ear and splashed the bare skin of his shoulder. James's point-blank shot knocked him back to the carpet.

The third Armenian in the room lifted his Skorpion

and turned it toward the killer who had just gunned down his cell members. The blast from Encizo's shotgun hit the man with sledgehammer force in the neck and left shoulder, folding the gunner at the knees so that he flopped like a fish to the floor.

The muzzle of a second MP-5 thrust around the door of the left bedroom. Encizo fired a blast from the hip, tearing through the wood jamb and wainscoting around the door. Bolan sidestepped between James and Encizo, firing a blast of harassing fire as he charged the bedroom. James moved to cover him as the Executioner entered the doorway. The Saiga bucked hard in Bolan's hands as he stood in the entrance. He shifted and fired twice more into the room.

Encizo moved quickly to the door of the second bedroom. He kicked it open and entered the room. He fired a blast through the closet, then checked under the bed, finding nothing.

"Clear!" he shouted in Spanish.

Since all three of the men shared different levels of fluency in that common language they had opted to use it on the ambush raid to confuse anyone overhearing them and reduce any sense of an "American fingerprint" on the operation.

"Clear!" Bolan answered in the same language from the far side of the suite.

The Stony Man hit team folded back into the room. A haze of gun smoke hung in the air and trailed from the barrels of their shotguns. Cordite stink was a bitter perfume and the metallic scent of blood was pungent.

"Let's shake it down," Bolan said. "Rafe, cover the door."

Encizo was already in motion as James and Bolan began looking for paperwork, cell phones and laptops. They had discovered nothing other than two unattended cell phones when Encizo alerted them from the room door.

"Company. Security," he said. "Time to roll."

"Which side?" Bolan demanded.

Encizo dropped his box magazine from the Saiga. "Elevators," he replied. "Two, with pistols and radios." He slammed a fresh 8-round magazine with a short strip of green tape on one side into the shotgun.

"We go out to the right. Let's roll," Bolan ordered as both he and James replaced the magazines in their own assault shotguns.

Encizo thrust his weapon around the corner of the door and unleashed three blasts. Hard-packed, nonlethal beanbags spread out down the hall and knocked the startled security officers to the carpet like drunks under a bouncer's haymaker.

The Cuban rolled back around the door and James stepped past him, tossing a grenade. The force of the concussion assaulted the commandos ears as they raced out of the area of operation and headed for the staircase.

As Bolan and James sprinted down the hallway, Encizo fired his shotgun twice more, and the brutal smacks of the riot load beanbags as they struck flesh was audible over the blaring fire alarm.

Bolan kicked open the fire door and pressed it open against the wall as James went through. Encizo caught up, and they raced up the staircase. When the sound of angry voices from below reached them, the Executioner leaned over the railing and triggered a double blast of his shotgun, hoping the thunderous sound would discourage anyone following them.

Encizo yanked the pin on a flash-bang grenade and let it drop down the spiral well. It fell three floors and detonated, using the echo chamber effect of the stairwell shaft to redouble its impact on the security forces below the Stony Man team.

They reached the top floor forty-five seconds later, then burst through the access door and out onto the roof.

The lights of nighttime Amman blazed around them and they could hear the cars and horns of late commuters. Police sirens rushed closer, sharper and more disconnected in rhythm than the blaring fire alarm. Bolan pulled a flare from a web belt pouch, popped it and tossed it through the air ahead of him.

It fell on the roof, burning intensely. James pulled a spring-loaded door wedge from a pocket and dropped it down in front of the access door. He kicked it into place and triggered the spring. Instantly a v-shaped wedge of hard rubber locked into place, jamming the door shut.

From overhead they heard the whir of rotor blades as a helicopter swept. They looked up as the Little Bird arrived to hover above them. A long, thick rope uncoiled and hit the ground. Loops of canvas had been sewn into the rope and the three commandos moved forward and hooked on at two points with their D-ring carabiners.

The technique was called SPIE, or Special Patrol Infiltration/Extraction and was common among recon troops and special operations forces. Bolan gave the signal once Encizo and James showed him a thumbs-up, and the chopper shot straight up out of its hover. The three men went into the arms spread position to avoid spinning.

The helicopter pilot, Stony Man's Charlie Mott, swung the nose of the chopper around and pointed it toward the northeast. The tail rotor elevated above the main blades as it sped off toward the LZ whose GPS coordinates had been programmed earlier by Encizo.

THE STONY MAN WARRIORS stealthily approached the late-model Ford van parked in the alley behind their safehouse.

Calvin James approached from the front while Bolan and Encizo vectored in from the rear. All three were wearing traditional Arab attire. Bolan walked up to the back bumper and stopped, then looked over at Encizo who nodded back. He cocked an eyebrow toward Calvin James who stood by the driver's door.

Bolan nodded at Encizo, who then drifted up the side of the van and took up a position next to the passenger-side door. The former anti-Castro guerrilla drew his Viper 9 mm pistol. He could see the closed curtains separating the back of the van from the front cab. At the rear of the vehicle Bolan slid out at an angle to avoid opening himself up to crossfire from either Encizo or James and covered the rear doors of the blocky vehicle.

James reached into his sleeve and removed a long, thin piece of metal. Working smoothly, he inserted it between the window and the door and, with one swift pop, manipulated the control arm on the vehicle lock, forcing it open. James left the piece of metal in place and used his left hand to open the van door as his right pulled the Viper from its hidden holster.

As the door swung open the black cylinder of an MP-5 equipped with a SD-3 sound suppressor slipped between the part in the curtain. James saw the action and rolled clear, at too awkward an angle to fire around the opening door. The silencer muzzle angled toward the ex-SEAL with deadly promise.

Encizo unloaded his weapon.

The black curtain jumped and danced under the impacts as the 9 mm manglers slipped through the cloth like burning needles. The exposed sound suppressor of the silenced MP-5 jerked and pivoted toward the roof, as two random bursts sent six subsonic rounds into the ceiling of the van. The metal roof tinged as the bullets clawed their way clear.

On the other side of the van James lunged through the open door and snatched the curtain back. An Armenian hardcase looked up at him with a stunned expression, blood leaking from a triumvirate of holes in his upper abdomen. A black receiver stuck from his ear under an unruly shock of dark wavy hair.

The enforcer gasped for breath and his eyes narrowed as he tried to focus in on Calvin James. He made an ineffectual gesture with the MP-5, trying to bring up the weapon. James shot him once in the forehead and the Armenian hitter slumped over backward.

"Let's go," Bolan hissed in Spanish.

James slid into the van behind the wheel. Encizo reached in through the shattered passenger window and popped the lock before opening his door. He clambered in and jumped over the front seat into the rear of

the van. In the driver's seat James took a flathead
screwdriver out and, without preamble, slammed it into
the 1970s vehicle's ignition slot. He grunted with the
effort, ignoring the ugly sound made by the invading
metal.

Bolan jumped into the van on the passenger side and
slammed the door closed. James turned the handle of
the screwdriver and the V8 engine roared to life. He
flipped the gearshift, throwing it out of Park and into
Drive.

Coolly, James eased the van out of the alley and into
the street before turning left and heading away from
Yazid Marwan's neighborhood. Bolan turned in the seat
and swept the curtain back so he could get a look at Encizo as the man searched the back of the vehicle.

"What'd he have?" Bolan asked.

"Wireless receiver. The bug must be in Marwan's
apartment for sure because he doesn't have a parabolic
mike set up, either. Unlike the day man, this guy was
set up to record. Got a plastic bottle half full of piss and
a couple dozen skin magazines."

"No Koran?" Bolan asked, deadly serious.

Encizo shook his head. "No. These guys were hired
guns through-and-through, most definitely not fanatics."

"Send the bill to Interpol," James said, his voice arid.

"Let's dump this van and make contact with Marwan," Bolan said grimly. "The pieces are starting to fall
right into place, but I have a hunch he holds more than
a few answers in that bald head of his."

BOLAN ENTERED THE HALL on Yazid Marwan's floor in
the tenement building. Like much of the East Amman

architecture Bolan had already seen, it was a stark concrete shaft, its length broken up by flimsy wooden doors and illuminated by a bare, open window frame at either end of the hallway. The former officer of the Special Republican Guard had fled Iraq to live in a harsh poverty.

Bolan led Encizo and James down the hall until they stopped in front of the apartment door. The Executioner looked at the other two commandos, then shrugged. There was nothing left but to make contact. Bolan kept his hands free while James held his 9 mm Viper hidden in the fold of his robe. Encizo carried a battered leather briefcase with dull, gold clasps.

Yazid Marwan was a potentially very important asset, and Bolan intended to give the man respect. If he could exploit the man's knowledge to kill his enemy he would. If he couldn't…then he'd have to see.

Bolan looked into the black eyehole bored into the center of the apartment door above the unit numbers. He reached a hand inside his robe and felt the package he had secreted there. Resigned, he lifted one big fist and pounded three times.

In response a gruff voice called out a challenge from the other side of the door, speaking Arabic.

"Opportunity," Bolan answered in English, guessing at the man's question out of common sense. He pulled his left hand out of his robe and held the bundle of U.S. twenty-dollar bills in front of the spy hole.

"Americans?" The man spoke smooth English with just a hint of British accent.

"The money is," Bolan answered. "So why the hell not us?"

"What do you want?" Marwan sounded cagey.

"I want to give you one hundred, twenty-dollar bills," Bolan said. "That's two thousand dollars just to open your door and hear us out."

"Hear you out about what?"

"I won't say more until you open this door, Marwan." Bolan snapped, his voice low. "I killed five men to make sure I got this chance to talk to you, but I won't say another word until I find the microphone-bug those Armenians hid in your place."

There was silence from the other side of the door. After a second Bolan heard a string of Arabic curses being muttered. Then there was a loud sigh and Bolan knew he had the old man.

"Armenians?" Marwan's voice was resigned.

"That's right," Bolan acknowledged. "Armenians. Know anybody who might send Armenian mercs to shadow you?"

"Wait," Marwan said.

Bolan lowered the hand holding up the money. The three Stony Man commandos heard a series of dead bolts being thrown back. James drifted off a little to his left, prepared to swing the Viper into action. Bolan stood without moving, his expression neutral.

The door opened an inch to the end of a security chain. Bolan saw a brown eye, bloodshot and yellowed under a bushy, gray-haired eyebrow, peering out at him. Suspicion was a tangible glint there.

"Are you armed?" Marwan demanded, his voice gruff.

"Bet your ass I'm armed," Bolan retorted. "But if I'd wanted to kill you, I would have pulled the trigger on the sniper rifle I had trained on the back of your head while you watched *Almal Walbanoun*," Bolan said, referencing the popular Egyptian soap opera James and Encizo swore the man never seemed to miss an episode of.

Yazid spit a foul curse in frustration, then closed the door. Bolan heard him snap the chain clear, then the door swung open wide, admitting them.

"Come in quickly before someone hears you speaking English," he snapped.

CHAPTER SEVENTEEN

Bolan slapped the two-thousand-dollar bundle into the soft expanse of Marwan's gut, where it stretched the stained and filthy cotton fabric of the man's T-shirt. As Marwan stepped back, hands flying to the money, Bolan entered the apartment.

Encizo, carrying the briefcase, entered behind him and James brought up the rear. Marwan looked up from counting the money, and his gaze narrowed as they went from Encizo's briefcase to James's 9 mm pistol. He was experienced enough to understand their implication.

The carrot and the stick.

"Sit down," the man said.

Bolan looked around the room. It was poor but immaculately clean, with comfortable rugs thrown here and there on the floor. The couch was old and decorated with brilliantly patterned silk throw pillows.

"I'll stand," James said, falling into a security position beside the door.

"Rafe," Bolan said, "find that bug and see if the rest of the place is clean."

"Sí," Encizo replied as he sat the briefcase on the long, low end table in front of the worn couch.

Marwan's eyes were pulled to it like lodestones. Encizo pulled a black plastic wand shaped roughly like a paddle from a side pocket in the briefcase, and it chirped as he powered on the device.

"We all alone?" Bolan asked.

Marwan pulled his gaze off the lucrative promise of the briefcase and met the big American's eyes. He nodded once and swallowed so hard Bolan could see his Adam's apple bounce with the effort under his double chins.

"Yes. We're alone. My nephew is at work. His wife goes to help in her father's shop during the day after she drops the boy off at school."

"Sit down," Bolan said.

Marwan looked at James standing by the door with his pistol drawn, while Encizo moved his bug detector around the apartment. He swallowed and lowered himself into a chair, then put the two thousand in cash on the table. Sweat beaded the broad sweep of his forehead, and he rubbed his hands on his trousers to dry them.

Bolan sat on the couch across from him. He saw a dark-red pack of cigarettes next to a heavy glass ashtray. He gestured to the pack.

"Smoke," he said. "I'm here to bribe you, Marwan, not torture you. Baksheesh. Not that stuff you Special Republican Guard types used to pull on the Kurds and Shiites."

Marwan's eyes flicked back toward the pistol in James's hand. He reached out and picked up the pack of smokes and lit one. Bolan watched him, relaxed. From behind them they heard an electronic chirping that signaled Encizo's success at searching for the bug.

"Got it," Encizo said. "It was here, near the telephone." He worked for a minute, then held up the minuscule device. He turned it over in his hands, dropped it on the floor and crushed it under his heel. "Pretty generic. Ex-Soviet. You can pick them up at the military-intelligence bazaars in the former republics cheap. A lot of cutout stringers are being fed them by big nation agencies. Could still be straight mercenary tech, as well."

"I guess we both know who uses Armenians, Marwan," Bolan said.

"Mirjana's dead." Marwan took a long drag on his cigarette and blew a cloud of gray smoke toward a fan slowly turning overhead. It was obvious he was still connected.

"The people who use him aren't," Bolan replied.

Marwan shrugged and leaned forward to stub out his cigarette in the ashtray, then he lit another one and settled back into the chair.

"Our friend from Zagreb is like the Safeway store in West Amman, you know. Everyone who can afford to shop there does."

Bolan leaned forward. "I heard he wasn't calling his own shots there at the end. I heard he was taking orders from Baghdad. Maybe Damascus, and maybe Beijing behind it all, but he was taking orders from Baghdad."

Marwan looked down at his lap. The cigarette burned in his fingers, the ash growing longer in his silence. Finally the former Special Republican Guard spoke, his voice quiet.

"Scimitar," he said.

"Scimitar," Bolan repeated. "There's ten thousand U.S. dollars in that case. Tell us what we need to know and the money is yours. If we find out you lied, we'll come back. This time we don't bring money. In case you're confused about what I mean, think about what your friends in the Fedayeen used to do to the Shiites."

"I was an officer of Saddam," Yazid said fiercely. "I was Special Republican Guard. The Fedayeen were Uday's, and Qusay's after that. I was a soldier charged with protecting my commander! The Fedayeen were…something else."

"Scimitar is Fedayeen. Who? Or how many who's?" Bolan asked.

"Neither. Both," Marwan sighed. "Scimitar was set up to be a name, a persona. By having an entire organization be one man that man could become a supernatural demon, killing in Tikirt one hour and then again twenty minutes later in Basra. A boogeyman."

"How many?"

"Only a handful of us knew about the Scimitar initiative. It began after the first Gulf War. The Shi had been emboldened, and there were fortunes to be made smuggling around the UN restrictions. You know oil-for-food, yes? Extortion and criminal enterprise were sewn there. Six cell leaders operating under Qusay's nose. Each one a captain of his own cell so that Scimitar represented a 'battalion' of soldiers."

"So they were never extremists? Never jihadists?"

"No, never. They were loyal to Saddam and therefore baathists, which means atheists. Maybe they talk the Koran now, but it means nothing to them, these aren't the Taliban or the Muslim Brotherhood."

"You know names?" Bolan asked. He watched Marwan stamp out the butt of his second cigarette.

"Yes. I know names. I know names by rumor. I was told to investigate this Scimitar Qusay was hearing so much about. He was always on the lookout about what Uday was up to. He never trusted his brother. I checked them. I found them."

"What did Qusay and Saddam do about members of his personal death squad going off the reservation?"

"Do?" Marwan snorted and lit a cigarette. "He didn't do a thing. I went to Scimitar and told them what I knew. Then I offered to work for them, for a price."

Bolan looked around. "They don't seem to have paid well."

"I had a million dollars in francs in the wall of my kitchen when I left Baghdad. The neighborhood was filled with former Republican Guardsmen. It was flattened to rubble and burned by the time Saddam was killed. Hell, by the time Uday and Qusay were killed."

"So six men, then. Kill six men and the Scimitar falls apart?"

"Yes. This isn't a fluid organization like the Russian syndicates. Everything is divided into cells with Scimitar providing communication between those cells. Without the network the cells become local problems. The Scimitar plan is simple. They operate in Iraqi-controlled areas and buy the local politicians and mosques. They keep violence down and export destabilizing forces to keep everyone's attention focused elsewhere. They live like warlords in the Shan states of the Golden Triangle. They provide money to the jihadists to keep things in turmoil. From the eye of the storm they make themselves rich."

"So they're organizers. Administrators?"

"Yes and no." Marwan shook his head. "They keep their cells disparate, as I've said. Because of that they handle some internal security and foreign operations themselves, to keep the other cells in the dark. You're lucky, someone has already done part of your work for you."

"How so?" Bolan asked.

"There was recently a matter of, let's say 'international significance' just handled by two of the six personally. A former ally in Basra with a foreign government. They went to execute him just a few days ago and he put up a fight. The hit team was wiped out."

Bolan kept his face expressionless.

"I need the names."

"Let me see the money." Sweat streamed down Marwan's face. "I pass on information for them here. I cannot get other work. These damned Jordanians embraced the Palestinians, but they treat us Iraqis like untouchables. Scimitar pays me to shuffle certain things back and forth, to translate the occasional document. It is the only money I can get to help my nephew. Syria gives me money to let certain foreigners stay in my nephew's house as they move around the region. I am a very poor man."

"That's a real sad story, Marwan," Bolan said.

He had a hunch that this was a man Stony Man could use in the future. Information was as viable and valuable as hard currency in Bolan's world, and here was a man positioned to be of help. Bolan leaned over and worked the worn gold clasps on the briefcase.

He opened the carry-all and revealed the neat rows of stacked bills. Marwan's eyes went to the cash. His tongue worked at the corners of his lips. He looked up from the money toward Bolan, then back at the money.

"You play it straight and there's more money down the road. You lie, and you'll fry, understand?"

Marwan nodded. He began to talk quickly, his cigarette bobbing like the fulcrum of an oil derrick as he spoke.

"Uday was caught funneling weapons from the Republican Guard to the Fedayeen without permission. The Fedayeen were given to Qusay after that, understand? Uday was running certain parts of the Fedayeen operations out of the building where the administration for the Olympic Committee was housed. That changed when Qusay took over. The original files were left there. The Fedayeen made sure it wasn't looted in the riots after Saddam fell, but when they moved to Al-Ramadi and then toward the Jordanian and Syrian borders they left it. No one cared, and the building was forgotten. Now the Iraqi soccer team is administered out of there instead of the Green Zone. No one wants to hurt the soccer players, but the man in charge there was a Fedayeen bureaucrat before the Americans came. He still knows where the paper skeletons are kept in the closet. Go there."

Bolan nodded. He leaned forward and pulled out a yellow legal pad and pen from the side pouch on the briefcase. He threw them on the table in front of the Iraqi.

"Get writing, Marwan," Bolan said. "I want that man's name. I want the names and profiles of the Scimitar captains. Don't leave anything out. I don't like surprises."

Marwan cocked his cigarette up at an angle in the corner of his mouth and reached out to take the pen and tablet. He crossed his legs as he sat back and began to write. He wrote steadily for the next ten minutes in a neat, concise script that filled pages from one margin to the other with a certain geometric precision that revealed his formal academic training.

When he was done Marwan set the tablet on the table. Bolan picked it up and looked it over. He lifted a page, impressed with the man's English. He would have to scan and send a copy of the original to Stony Man. Not only would the information be useful, but a handwriting analysis specialist could ascertain the best methods of approach to use with this new Jordanian asset in the future.

"That is everything I remember. Their names, my memories of their strengths and specialties. Their reputations and such," Marwan said.

Bolan set the tablet down and watched the man light yet another cigarette from the smoking butt of the one he had just finished. He believed the man instinctively. Trust but verify was Bolan's intuition in this case, and he would check out Marwan's story as much as possible. Still, it felt right. He simply didn't understand what a well-connected man like Marwan was doing living on the margin like this, why the man had taken himself out of the game and onto the sidelines.

"Why'd you leave Iraq?" Bolan asked. "Why aren't you living in style in the south like the Scimitar captains?"

Marwan narrowed his eyes, obviously surprised by the question. He worked his cigarette until it puffed like a chimney. He rubbed his nose and looked away from Bolan. Then he shrugged and his whole body seemed to relax.

"Okay, Mr. American, I tell you. But I don't think you will believe me so much, understand?"

It was Bolan's turn to shrug and Marwan pushed on.

"I told you my house was bombed, yes? Well, what I didn't tell you was that I was still in it. My wife, my two sons and my daughter, all of us hiding in the basement while insurgents battled the Marines outside. A group of Egyptians took over the house, used it as a fighting position. They were tough, willing to die for God. The Americans called in an air strike from what I later learned was an A-10. The Warthog, understand?"

Marwan slapped his hands together with a loud, sharp sound, his face an ugly, fierce grimace. He leaned forward and continued his story.

"Everyone dies. Everyone. The Egyptians. My family. Everyone. The roof comes down, fire sweeps through the structure, everyone dies."

"Except you," Bolan said.

Marwan leaned back, scratching the inside of his arm like a junky, leaving long red marks as his nails worked the flesh there. He nodded.

"By the grace of God. You understand? I was not Muslim. I was a Baathist. When you are an atheist there is no such thing as a miracle. But there it was. I was alive, unscratched, while death had struck all around me. It was nothing that could happen except by the will of God. I found my heritage. I found the faith of my people. I renounced violence as the Prophet did. Maybe I translate papers, maybe I pass on a message from one man to another, but I do not kill. I do not fight.

"The captains of Scimitar are atheists, offensive to God, Arab betrayers of the Prophet. I take their money because I must make my pilgrimage to Mecca as the Koran commands. How else will I, an Iraqi in Jordan, do so?"

Marwan held up his hands, helpless by the logic of his moral compromise.

"But I will help you," he continued. "I will help you destroy this enemy of God. I will take your money and I will go to Mecca."

Bolan stood to go. "'The enemy of my enemy is my friend,'" Bolan quoted, and held out his hand.

Marwan took it.

CHAPTER EIGHTEEN

Once on board the plane, Bolan forced himself to relax.

He pulled out the tablet with Marwan's notes on it and read his report yet again, working to commit the names and biographies written there to his memory, searching them carefully for insight to help him take them down.

He sat in a Royal Jordanian Fokker F-28 jet with forty-eight other passengers, leaving Amman for Baghdad International Airport. He'd carefully examined his fellow passengers when he'd first entered the cabin, noting Iraqi officials in expensive dark suits and clipped facial hair. Mixing easily with them were Western faces, the private military contractors and security consultants dressed more casually.

There were a cluster of nuns obviously involved with international relief efforts, journalists with rolled shirtsleeves and a few visiting dignitaries or corporate representatives.

The soldier returned his attention to the tablet, ignoring even the flight attendants as they moved back and forth up the narrow center aisle.

Wadi Haddad—A Sunni of Kurdish origins, noted for his skill in tracking and outdoor survival.

Said al-Nasr—This unassuming fellow has the face of a choirboy but excels at the most brutal forms of hand-to-hand combat. Al-Nasr has a knack for silent movement.

Ghaleb Awwali—Awwali is a native Russian. He serves as the group's expert on electronics, explosives and other technological items. He came as a military adviser after first Gulf War and stayed.

Hanadi Jaradat—Jaradat came from southern Iraq, and seems almost Oriental in appearance. She speaks fluent Chinese and spent the years 1979-1981 on liaison with the embassy of the People's Republic of China. Jaradat knows numerous languages and is good with foreign cultures. (KIA in Basra)

Zuheir Mohsen—Mohsen is an excellent marksman, with a passion for things military. He shuns the company of others.

Jamal Othman—Othman serves as the leader of the cell for field operations. He has a cunning mind and a taste for cruelty. He wears a drooping mustache and was favorite of Uday. (KIA in Basra)

Bolan idly wondered which of the masked and headband-wearing killers outside of Ma Ning-tan's trailer Othman and Jaradat had been. He felt a grim satisfaction knowing he was a third of the way through his operation already.

Bolan settled back into the seat. It didn't escape his attention that the two Scimitar captains killed had been a field leader and the one with the most experience in dealing with the Chinese. Everything about this nest of snakes pointed toward a Beijing power struggle. Certain elements wanted the West bled to death much the same way America had used Afghanistan as proxy against the Soviets in the 1980s or the Soviets had used Vietnam against the Americans twenty years earlier, just as Ning-tan had said. The information Bolan was uncovering was leaving the Oval Office with some stark, unpleasant truths.

But obviously not everyone was on board in China. Ma Ning-tan had been only a foot soldier in the bureaucratic struggle. He'd had bosses, and his bosses had bosses. Someone didn't like the game of brinkmanship during this time of heightened tensions over the rogue state of North Korea. Not with most favorable trade status the big prize being left on the diplomatic table.

Bolan closed the tablet and rubbed his eyes. Perhaps there was a way to exploit this. Perhaps not. He'd follow the trail of Scimitar breadcrumbs and see where it took him.

Then there was the matter of Musa Marzook, Marwan's contact inside the old Olympic building offices.

Baghdad was a brutal place of savage ambushes and frequent betrayals. The Stony Man team's cover as reporters willing to pay for a story could open them up to as many dangers as going in surreptitiously or on a hard probe. The problem was that searching for Scimitar files inside the Olympic building would be like looking for a needle in a haystack.

They needed help, so they had to try to contact Marzook to see if he was willing to play. Despite the danger, the clock was ticking. On top of that there was the logistical nightmare of moving through Baghdad itself. Basra had been bad enough, but it was like a stroll through Central Park compared to the Iraqi capital. Death could come at any instant, and be completely unrelated to the mission at hand.

"How you feeling, Striker?" James asked quietly.

"Good enough. Charlie Mott's ready at Baghdad International Airport. We have a trailer along with some military contractors in Camp Slayer, so we'll be ready to roll with gear and vehicles as soon as we hit the ground. It's going to all come down to how Marzook greets us."

"We'll watch our backs, keep our heads up," James said. "If Rafe there doesn't jump ship on us."

Bolan followed James's gesture as the ex-SEAL jerked his thumb toward Rafael Encizo. The man was sitting two seats up on the aisle. The Phoenix Force commando was chatting up a pretty flight attendant. She laughed and let her slim, manicured hand rest on Encizo's broad shoulder.

"That beats the hell out of some Baghdad shootout," Bolan admitted.

CHARLIE MOTT MET THEM outside the airport, in his usual battered brown leather jacket and green baseball cap. He grinned as he took in the Stony Man team's beards. Bolan reached out and shook his hand as they met in the parking lot outside the terminal.

"That was nice flying over Amman," Bolan said.

Mott shook hands all around. "I aim to please. Cutting the border over the desert into Iraq was the worst, but I flew so low I was dodging Bedouins and it all worked out okay. I made it into Camp Korean Village just fine."

"What have you got set up for us, Charlie?" Calvin James asked.

"Full spectrum. As far as Army and contractors know, you guys are high-speed VIP protection with a State Department contract. You've got contractor numbers and operations IDs to match your passports. You'll roll in and out of Camps Slayer and Victory without problem. We've got rooms in Camp Slayer on one of Saddam's old artificial lakes. The guest house used to belong to his palace complex and is a freaking decorator's nightmare, garish as hell but filled with civilian security experts so no one will give you a second glance. You need intelligence or air travel vectored in then you have a Special Access Program that piggybacks right out of CENTCOM and onto Joint Special Operation Command's network. The left hand never knows what the right hand is doing."

"How about a translator?" Encizo asked.

"That's bad news," Mott said, his face grave. "You know how short we are for those, especially people who know the Baghdad scene. We had you one on loan from the DIA, but he was killed today coming out of Gate Three of the Green Zone in a drive-by shooting. It appears unrelated to your mission, just Iraq as usual. Barbara said she's scrambling, but with things being the way they are…" Mott let his words trail off and he shrugged.

"How are we set for rides?" Bolan asked.

"That we had no problem with. Chevy Suburbans,

up-armored with blackout windows, solid tires and gun slits. You can roll hot in that or we got some ugly-looking white Kia minivans with V12 engines dropped into them. They look like every other thing on the road, but you'll go twice as fast. Kevlar drapes inside and diplomatic windows."

"How's travel?"

"Route Irish is looking better these days, but no wagers. You get off main patrol routes in the wrong neighborhood, and no one can promise you anything," Mott said.

He used the term "Route Irish," which was the U.S. Army's designation of the road linking the Baghdad International Airport to the Green Zone. The same road was referred to as the "Highway of Death" by most of the world's press and the Iraqi people, though it had become comparatively safer of late.

"I searched an online map of the old Olympic Annex," Bolan said. "I know how to get there. Problem is, when I overlaid the route with sitreps from the DNI briefs, it shows us crossing three separate militia zones."

Mott shrugged, helpless. "Welcome to Baghdad, Mack." He stuck his hands in the pockets of his leather jacket, which he wore despite the warm temperature. "I'll fly you in a heartbeat. Say the word. I'll roll overwatch if you want, as well, of course."

Bolan shook his head. "No. We'll try rolling low profile, guns in. With my letter of introduction from Yazid Marwan, I'm really going to try to milk the whole reporter thing."

"That's your call. I got both your vehicles outfitted with positioning transceivers so I'll follow you the whole way," Mott said. "If things go south I'll put the chopper into the air."

The group climbed into the black Chevy Suburban and Mott started it up. The big engine growled as the vehicle headed across the parking lot toward the security gates. In fifteen minutes the Stony Man team had suited up under robes and headdresses once again and were pulling out of Checkpoint 1 and onto Route Irish.

Pulling out onto the Highway of Death.

THE FIRST PART OF THE TRIP was almost anticlimactic. Concrete construction barriers lined the road like the ramparts of a medieval fortress. Checkpoints secured every intersection and military vehicles patrolled incessantly. Dust was in the air like a curtain and the heat was stifling.

Just past the Sunni slum of Amariyah, which bordered Camp Victory, the Stony Man team turned north, heading toward the Abu Ghurayb Expressway, which ran east-west through the northern section of city. It was there, well outside the International Green Zone, that the Olympic Committee Annex was located. According to Marwan, it had never been investigated by Western or Coalition forces.

The Baghdad slums were the worst in the Middle East. Military checkpoints gave way to Iraqi Police checkpoints as they moved deeper into Sunni-controlled neighborhoods. The threat of radical militia infiltration increased tenfold and at any checkpoint, the men of Stony Man knew they could find themselves facing people who wore the blue of Iraqi police but whose allegiance remained tied to local radical clerics.

In which case there was no respite. If Shiite militia thought them Sunni, they were dead. If Sunni thought them Shi, they were dead. If either recognized them as Western—as was bound to happen as soon as they were forced to speak—they were dead. As dangerous as driving through such a gauntlet was, walking would only have been worse.

Both Bolan and James kept their windows rolled down, despite the heat. Having the windows up would have offered only dubious protection from a roadside IED and went a long way toward slowing their return fire should they come under small-arms attack.

In the back Encizo had pushed the Kevlar draping away from a rear window set high in the minivan's back hatch. The factory window had been removed and he operated rear security with an AKM to which he'd attached a drum magazine and an M-203 grenade launcher.

"We're in now," Bolan said after they made it onto the expressway and started speeding west. "No more stopping at checkpoints. It's just too dangerous. We blow by everyone but Iraqi National Army or Western forces. We show our contractor ID to the wrong Iraqi police group and were going to end up on the Internet with our heads being carved off by a machete. Agreed?"

"Agreed," Encizo and James echoed.

Neither man was pleased with the turn of events but complaint or denial didn't change the facts. They were operating in the most unpredictable of environments while completely surrounded by a multitude of forces bent on killing them. If they came under attack there would be no safe haven, no cavalry and no respite. They would be modern warriors trapped in a crumbling, violent city more than four thousand years old, the cradle of civilization. A city of suicide bombers, improvised explosive devices, rampant torture, video taped beheadings, sectarian violence and universal angst. Hope and determination were twin streams running through the barbaric quagmire, but they were weapons of the long term and like a stream of water on stone the changes they made happened over time by erosion and were not dynamic in nature.

For now Fire, with its insatiable appetite, ruled here with Hate, and violence could not be met with understanding. It could only be met with further violence until one side or the other was broken.

Ten minutes later everything began to fall apart for the Stony Man warriors.

CHAPTER NINETEEN

A flash on the horizon caught the eye of Calvin James. He turned his head and squinted hard against the harsh sunlight. A sudden column of rich, black smoke roiled up out of an urban topography of rubble piles, low-rise tenements and apartment buildings off the Expressway.

"What the hell's going on?" James said, catching Bolan's attention.

Though it was daylight it was easy to watch the swiftly progressing wave of power failure spread across the unincorporated sections of the city like a tsunami. Every evidence of power usage clicked dark like dominos falling in a row.

Bolan watched the spreading blackout with unease. He knew generators were common because of these attacks, but gasoline was expensive and such outages always posed a hardship for the millions struggling to lead normal lives in the hellish zone.

"Crap," Bolan said as he drifted through speeding traffic toward the right lane, headed for an off-ramp.

"That outage should make every person with a gun jumpy as hell."

"Including us," James said. "Looks fairly localized, though. Probably a relay station and not a main breaker."

"Thank God for small favors," Encizo said from the back.

"Trouble," Bolan stated.

James looked up as Bolan pulled onto the off-ramp. The soldier worked the brakes immediately. A line of vehicles stretched up the ramp from an Iraqi Police mobile checkpoint set up at the bottom. Two Nissan pickups with RPK machine-guns mounted in the back formed a wedge in the road.

The gunners watched the line of cars with suspicious eyes. Two police officers with AKMs stood off to one side against a concrete embankment, fingers on the grips of their assault rifles as they watched the scene.

On the driver's side of the vehicle line two more police officers worked their way up the row. One held an AKM at the ready while an officer armed only with a pistol asked the drivers of the different vehicles for their paperwork.

Still seven or eight cars back, Bolan reached over to put the Kia van into reverse. A 1980s Volvo station wagon pulled off the expressway and came to a halt inches from his rear bumper. He cursed.

"How do you think they're going to like our hardware?" James asked, eyeing the Iraqi police.

"Not too much," Bolan replied.

"We can get out of line, go up to the next off-ramp then cut back," Encizo offered from the back. "But hurry up, cars are stacking up behind us like SEALs at a Tijuana whorehouse."

James flipped him the bird by way of response.

Bolan eased his foot down on the gas, inching his minivan forward while cranking hard on the steering wheel. He thought there was probably just enough room for him to make it out of the line, but it was going to be tight. He reached over to put the vehicle into Reverse.

The car came out of nowhere. It shot past Bolan on the shoulder, racing down the ramp, and he had only a fleeting impression of primer gray. It hurtled down the line of idling vehicles and made a kamikaze rush straight toward the IP roadblock.

"Down!" Bolan snarled.

Both James and Encizo reacted without question. The Cuban sprawled flat in the back of the minivan as James threw himself between the break in the front seats, landing in the back, as well. Bolan threw himself down across the seats and over James's legs, using the dashboard and engine block as a bulwark against the car bomb.

The vehicle-based improvised explosive device— VBIED—detonated.

The boom was deafening, and even the battle-hardened Bolan hadn't heard an explosion that loud in a good long while. His ears rang painfully in his head, and even seventy-five yards away the minivan was rocked hard on its suspension by the blast concussion. Bolan's driver-side airbag popped open in a rush.

Shrapnel cut through the air like steel rain and shattered the windows of the Kia. Glass shards sprayed through the inside of the van, coating Bolan. Pieces of metal, probably carpenter nails, steel washers or ball bearings added to the VBIED to increase collateral damage, whistled through the inside of the minivan and punched holes through its light metal skin. The airbag was shredded by the deadly missiles.

Black smoke, dust and airborne debris rolled over the ravaged vehicle in a smothering cloud, cutting out sunlight like a death shroud. Bolan began to cough as grit filled the air along with the stink of burning gasoline. And burning bodies.

There was a moment of thunderous silence as if the heat and force had stripped all of the oxygen from the air. Then Bolan's ears popped and he heard stuck automobile horns blare and, as if at a director's cue, the screaming began.

Still shaken from the concussive impact and sudden senseless violence, Bolan pushed himself into place behind the steering wheel and snatched up the AK-104 carbine he had placed between the seat and door.

The front windshield was a jagged-toothed cavity and he coughed harshly again at the smoke and dust in the air. He caught a flash of color and blinked. The front hood of the Kia was splattered with blood and coffee-cup-size chunks of flesh and hair.

Suddenly pieces of metal began to fall out of the sky. A front bumper struck the roof and spun down onto the hood. Bolan flinched instinctively and lifted his arm. A single hubcap bounced off the front of his vehicle, and as the smoke parted he saw the long metal pole of a streetlamp rising straight up from his hood.

There was a sickening splat and Bolan saw a human hand strike the glass-littered plastic of his front dash by the air-conditioning vent. He forced himself to ignore the grisly sight.

"You all right?" he asked over his shoulder.

Encizo and James responded immediately. They rose and armed themselves, James with a second AK-104 and his partner with his drum-magazine-supported AKM. Bolan tried to open his door but found the latch was crumpled inward. He growled in frustration and threw his big shoulder against it. The door popped open with a protesting screech.

"Let's see if we can help," Bolan said.

Encizo and James scrambled out of the back. All three men kept their weapons up as they surveyed the scene in case the ambush had been a complex operation and further attacks were planned.

The hot desert sun was obscured by the smoke and the heat of the day was intensified by the several vehicles burning down the line near the blast center. Bolan looked in that direction and saw both Nissan trucks used by the Iraqi police overturned and burning. One was barely more than a pile of melted metal and a snapped axle in a pool of flaming gas.

Three other cars were burning, and bodies and parts of bodies were spread around like confetti after a ticker-tape parade. Blood stood in pools or dripped in streams off the hoods and roofs of random vehicles. The blaring of broken horns and a strident car alarm created a cacophonous background to the continuous wailing of human beings in agony.

People staggered back and forth, clutching wounds, screaming in agony, and several fell in front of Bolan's eyes. A woman in Western but modest clothes, cradled a bearded man in her lap. The man's eyes were open and staring. He had no arms, and blood pumped in jets from his shoulders like water from a burst fire hydrant.

"Striker!" James yelled. "If authorities show up and see us in these robes they might think we're jihadists."

Bolan nodded and began stripping off his robe. He'd rather risk coming under terrorist fire from a secondary ambush than forced to fight army or police units arriving to help. Encizo and James followed his example.

"I'm going to see what I can do," James said.

Bolan grabbed the medic by his arm. "We can't be taken in for questioning," he warned.

James nodded. "Rafe can cover us. We'll just pull anyone we can clear of the flames and stop the bleeding. When ambulances arrive we'll boogie."

"Do it," Bolan agreed.

A car exploded behind them as its gas tank caught fully and burst into flames. Leaving his weapon dangling from its sling, Bolan began to jog down the off-ramp. He saw a woman in traditional garb trying to pull back a car seat and crawl into the rear of her little sedan. Orange flames licked at the hood, and black smoke poured into the air. The windshield was shattered.

Realizing instantly what was happening, Bolan ran forward. He pushed the ineffectual and hysterically screaming woman out of the way. She fell back and a distant part of his mind recognized that her left eye was an empty, bloody socket.

It felt as though he were moving under water as he bent and found the seat latch. The hot metal scorched his fingers. He could hear the baby screaming now, hear the piercing shrieks reverberating inside his head.

He felt his gorge rise as he smelled the blood and sick sugar smell of burned flesh.

He forced the seat back and shoved his torso into the car. He saw the little girl, a toddler, locked tight in her car seat, chubby little arms and legs flailing as she screeched. He saw the face running from blood where shards of windshield had peppered her cheeks and forehead. He could see the splash of melted vinyl sticking to her neck, searing in there.

Bolan pulled out his tactical folding knife and thumbed it open. The blade made a greasy snick sound as it opened. He lunged forward and slid the serrated blade under the nylon straps securing the child into her safety seat.

Behind him the mother, insane with pain and panic, clawed at him, screaming. Something inside the cooking engine ignited and the crumpled hood of the little compact car popped open in response. Flames shot into the already burning sky, and a wave of heat rushed into the cab of the car.

Bolan was shoved forward as the maddened mother struck him. He could see tendrils of black smoke rising from the baby as the splashed vinyl continued to burn into the toddler's exposed flesh. Bolan yanked his folding knife back and cut the harness above the center clasp.

He dropped the knife as he struggled to pull the baby clear. He grunted in surprise and pain as the woman sank her teeth into his leg just below the knee. He got the little girl free as the front seats burst into flames. He grabbed the toddler and hugged her screaming, burning, bleeding body to his chest, folding her in tight the way a good receiver cradled a football.

He managed to get his left hand around the door frame, and he struggled to pull himself clear of the burning cab. The exposed flesh on the back of his neck tightened in protest at the waves of heat washing over him.

The crazed mother punched him with adrenaline-charged power but Bolan ignored her as he pushed himself up. He turned and lunged away from the car. The woman caught hold of his legs and dragged him down so that he hit the road. As he fell, he turned to protect the baby girl from the impact and absorbed the force on his shoulder.

The woman, screaming something in Arabic, clawed at him, reaching for the child. Bolan reached out with a big hand and shoved her in the throat, pushing her back. She sat up and he rolled onto his back and put his boot against her chest and shoved instead of kicking. The woman stumbled back and the baby squirmed in his arms, reaching out for her mother.

Bolan struggled to his feet and used a corner of the baby's clothes to wipe away the oily smear of the melted vinyl searing her flesh. He turned toward the mother as she rose to her feet. She was filthy and bloody, and the mutilation on the left side of her face was even greater than he'd first realized.

Stunned, the woman looked at him, taking in his Western-style black fatigues for the first time. She lifted her arms and Bolan gave her the screaming, bloody child. The woman clutched the injured child to her and began to sob.

Helpless without further medical supplies, Bolan turned away. He looked up the off-ramp and saw James working frantically, using a leather belt to tie an ad hoc tourniquet around the ragged stump of an old man's leg.

Up the road beyond him Encizo had an unconscious man by the shirt collar and was dragging him clear of a burning Volvo work truck. The Phoenix Force commando held his AKM by its pistol grip as he scanned the roiling smoke for any sign of new attack.

In the distance Bolan heard the sirens and knew security and rescue units were responding. He realized how vulnerable his team was in the situation. He looked toward his minivan and saw for the first time that both of the front tires had been blown to shreds.

Bolan swore. His eyes stung from the polluted smoke and he couldn't shake the image of the one-eyed mother clutching her bloody baby. He saw James rise from beside the old man, the tourniquet now in place. The sirens were closer.

"Let's go!" Bolan shouted.

James nodded and turned back up the ramp. "Rafe, we have to go!"

Encizo pulled the unconscious man in tight to the lee of the concrete construction barrier lining the off-ramp. He took the AKM in both hands and began to jog down the ramp toward his teammates.

Bolan turned as Encizo and James caught up to him and started down toward the avenue intersecting the exit ramp under the overpass. He ignored the mother clutching her baby and the other scenes of tragedy as he jogged past. Help was coming. He had nothing to offer these people without medical supplies. Even a medic as skilled as Calvin James could do little in such a situation with only his bare hands.

Bolan left the ramp and walked onto the neighborhood avenue. Smoke rolled in columns between the buildings, and the cars backed up by the IP roadblock had jammed together in gridlock. Civilians rushed forward to help their fellow Baghdad residents. Two blocks down, stuck behind a tight phalanx of cars, a Red Crescent ambulance with an orange light bar fought to move forward.

The Stony Man warriors struggled through the rushing crowd, weapons out and up and ready, as they made their way down the street and away from the scene. The windows of shops near the off-ramp had shattered and glass littered the street, crunching loudly underfoot.

Bolan kept his eyes on the move, glancing everywhere. The neighborhood reminded him of the East Amman slum, though it was far worse. Shoddily constructed tenements rose above street level beside stores selling everything from rugs to sandals to canned goods. Several stalls had their items scattered like trash across the street.

He saw a preteen boy in a red-and-white striped shirt stealing fresh tomatoes from a wooden stall while the shopkeeper watched the fires. He saw a soccer ball rolling forgotten in an open gutter.

Every building showed the scar of fire or the pockmark stamps of weapon fire. Every third structure was a rubble pile. Smoke from the burning vehicles hung like fog, blunting the hard light of the desert sun. A knot of women in veils and long, dark robes were wailing and clutching at one another.

Bolan was suddenly, viciously thirsty. He turned his head and spit the taste of diesel smoke and burned flesh from his mouth. He looked up and saw several people climbing up on the roofs of the gridlocked cars.

He was only about forty yards from the intersection of the avenue and off-ramp. Something caught his attention, some sense of disquiet he couldn't place at first. He narrowed his eyes, sharpening his focus as he hunted the crowd.

Then he saw the man in the black headband climb up on top of a car in the very middle of the street.

CHAPTER TWENTY

Bolan felt time slow and stretch around him.

His vision sharpened to a laser intensity. He watched the man, about thirty yards away, throw off a thigh-length canvas jacket and saw the explosives ringing his torso in the canvas pouches on the OD green webbing.

The man shouted "Allah Akhbar!"—God is great!—as he turned his body to face the greatest knot of people rushing to help the original victims. The second prong of the attack would be as effective as it was ruthless. Bolan swept his AK-104 to his shoulder but with sickening clarity he realized he'd never make it in time.

He caught a glimpse of a metal plate on the front of the suicide bomber as he put the folding stock of the Kalashnikov into the hollow of his shoulder. Then James hit him from the side and knocked him to the street.

Only the fact the suicide bomber was facing away from them saved the Stony Man warriors. Pinned underneath James, Bolan didn't see the detonation but the explosion rendered him deaf in a split second and the concussive force of the charge rolled into him with a gale-force intensity and he blacked out.

Feeling brutally nauseous, Bolan swam back into consciousness moments later. He pushed at James as the ex-SEAL lay across him. From the dead feel of the big man's weight Bolan realized James had to have been knocked unconscious by the blast, as well.

Bolan sat up and looked around. He surveyed the scene like a man watching a silent film. He worked his jaws to pop his ears, but his hearing refused to return. He saw dozens more people down in the street, saw people's faces stretched to the tearing point as they screamed, but no sound penetrated his quiet bubble.

He rolled his unconscious teammate onto his back and crouched beside him. He saw immediately that the man was breathing easily. James's eyes fluttered, then opened, and Bolan patted him reassuringly before searching out Rafael Encizo. He saw the man lying just feet away.

The Phoenix Force commando was pushing himself to his feet. Then Bolan's ears popped for a second time and he heard the Cuban-American cursing. Or praying.

"—Dios Mios, madre puta!"

The back of Encizo's head was plastered with blood that flowed freely down his neck and soaked his black fatigues. Bolan noted that all three of the Stony Man team were covered with brown-gray dust that stuck to their blood and sweat, them, forming a gritty muck.

Beyond Encizo, Bolan could see what the suicide bomber's tightly packed charged had done to the dense knot of civilians who had run to help with the first attack. There was so much blood that it flowed like a river in the street and the gutter grates were clogged with the ruins of human bodies.

Bolan struggled to stand. He glanced to one side and saw the red-and-white-striped shirt belonging to the preteen boy he had seen stealing vegetables earlier. The boy's arms were twisted out at odd, unnatural angles. Bolan couldn't see the boy's head.

A single tennis shoe sat on the sidewalk, a trail of smoke rising from it in a lazy curl. Shattered glass was scattered everywhere, twice as thick as Bolan had seen on the off-ramp. He reached down and grabbed James by the arm, noting that the veteran soldier hadn't released his grip on the pistol grip of his AK-104.

Bolan hauled James to his feet and they both turned to help Encizo, but the Cuban fighter was already standing. Sirens were everywhere around them now. Bolan saw emergency lights flashing on the off-ramp and two blocks down the avenue a three-vehicle convoy of Iraqi police turned a corner and drove onto the clogged street.

The Executioner indicated a shattered storefront directly in front of them. A wooden door hung off one hinge, and a corpse dangled half into the store amid the ruins of a display window. A haggard, stunned-looking man in a soot-stained white apron staggered outside followed by a teenage girl bleeding from her nose.

"Let's cut through there!" Bolan shouted.

The three Americans stumbled toward the shop as the Iraqi police vehicles drove up onto the sidewalks to try to navigate the obstacles blocking the avenue. Reaching the sidewalk, Bolan hopped over an outflung arm and approached the door. The shopkeeper turned toward them, his eyes wide in terror as he took in their beards and automatic weapons.

Bolan held up his hands to placate the frightened man as the shopkeeper shoved his daughter behind him. From Bolan's left heavy-caliber machine-gun fire opened up from a second-story window of an apartment building outside the blast radius of the suicide bomber's charge.

The sound signature of the weapon was instantly recognizable to Bolan as an American made M-60 machine-gun. The heavy slugs ripped into the thin-skinned Iraqi police vehicles with merciless power and efficiency.

Bolan stopped running in midstride, his eyes drawn toward the tongue of flame spitting from the apartment window like dragon's breath. He saw a hailstorm of 7.62 mm rounds slice into men and vehicles. Two Kalashnikov rifles opened up from the window next to the machine-gun position.

Iraqi policemen, crammed into the open truck beds, jerked and undulated under the impact of the bullets despite their protective armor. The AK fire stopped for a moment even as the M-60 continued to rake the trapped men.

"Harass the window!" Bolan shouted.

Encizo turned and sprinted for the cover of several vehicles stalled in the middle of the street. He slid behind the engine block of a ruined pickup and raised his AKM. As he knelt he felt glass crunch under his knees and his fatigues were instantly soaked with blood from the free-standing pools on the asphalt.

Instinctively Bolan started down the sidewalk toward the apartment building housing the ambushers, James close behind. On their left the Iraqi police were scattering, but the volleys of gunfire found them as they scrambled.

Encizo slid into position and opened up with the AKM on full auto, spraying the window where the M-60 gunner murdered the police. Suddenly a rocket from an RPG-7 whistled out of the window next to the machine-gun nest.

Bolan recognized the threat immediately as the rocket-propelled grenade streaked through the air, trailing dark smoke. He dropped to his knees and turned to face the building. Calvin James knelt beside him.

The RPG explosion seemed small after the VBIED and suicide bomber, but the whomp of a vehicle's gas tank igniting was loud enough hard on the heels of the initial explosion. Bolan heard Encizo's covering fire coming from behind him as he rose but he could discern no additional fire originating from the police vehicles caught in the complex ambush.

Bolan yanked open the front door of the building and charged through. He snapped his rifle muzzle to the right and then up a staircase, while James took the left.

A doorway down the hall just beyond the entranceway opened a crack, and James sprayed the jihadist security element even as the blue steel barrel of the assault rifle emerged. Bolan saw a figure in loose, dark clothes and black headband turn the corner of the staircase to the second floor.

Bolan gunned him down, splashing the shooter's blood on the bare drywall directly behind him. The man tumbled down and his weapon fell, clattering down the steps.

Bolan ran forward and took the stairs two at a time. He stopped, his weapon seeking a target, and James stormed passed him to the top of the stairs. The ex-SEAL dropped to one knee and swept his weapon back and forth as he knelt in the fresh blood beside the ambusher's corpse.

The Executioner continued up to the second-floor landing, his weapon leading the way as James ran up the steps and covered the opposite end. Clear plastic sheeting covered an open window facing the ambush site. Lengths of rebar jutted from crumbling walls.

Bolan could hear the heavy reports as the M-60 continued to fire. He pointed at a wooden door set in the wall just opposite the landing. The sounds of weapons fire clearly came from behind it.

James looked over at Bolan and put his AK-104 to his shoulder, drawing a bead on the door. Bolan nodded and both men triggered their weapons, the 7.62 mm WARSAW hardball rounds chewing through the flimsy doors, tossing splinters into the air like a wood chipper.

As they continued firing, James moved forward, sliding off to the left and angling his fire through the door. Softball-size holes had perforated the structure, and it was possible to get a glimpse through the wood.

Bolan slid forward, as well, at an angle to the right, crossing streams of fire with James. Their fire formed an overall X pattern, converging like a V at the door after which each man's trajectory spread out from the cross stream to saturate the room inside.

Bolan swept the muzzle of his AK-104 downward, his rounds biting into the metal lock and clawing through it. James swept his automatic fire vertically down the side of the door, blasting the hinges apart. The door shuddered under the continuous assault, dancing loose of its moorings once the Stony Man commandos had fired through the lock and hinges, and it fell in three separate pieces to the floor.

Return fire poured out of the room, answering Bolan and James burst for unrelenting burst. The stench of cordite rose in the cramped quarters like incense, inflaming Bolan's senses. He peeled off to the side, rolling away from the door.

He looked over and saw James doing the same. The ex-SEAL dropped the spent magazine from his smoking AK-104 and slammed a fresh banana clip into the well. There was a sharp snap as he released the catch and chambered a round. A continuous hail of bullets poured out of the apartment as Bolan followed the Phoenix Force commando's lead and swapped out magazines, as well.

The two men huddled on either side of the open door until there was a break in the fire. Without hesitation James stuck his weapon around the corner of the door and began to spray inside the room.

Bolan ducked under James's covering fire and rolled onto his stomach, taking a position at an angle to the door and sweeping the room, tracking for specific targets.

He spotted an ambusher positioned behind a low wall of sandbags in the middle of an open room. The man was firing an AKM through an opening in the wall of the sandbags but James's burst caught him while he was changing magazines and the man huddled down behind the cover of his fighting position.

"Cut!" Bolan shouted.

James instantly ceased firing and Bolan leaped to his feet. He slid forward in a sidestepping shuffle, the AK-104 tucked tightly into his shoulder. Rushing forward, walking heel-to-toe to steady his aim, he fired on the trapped ambusher. His rounds tore into the man, who grunted and screamed as he was blown apart.

Bolan threw himself down as the ambusher feeding an ammunition belt to the M-60 gunner jumped up, a 9 mm Beretta 92-F, pistol in his hand. From his position on his back Bolan triggered the AK-104 and slapped the man back down. The Executioner shifted his Kalashnikov to bring it to bear on the machine-gunner who was still trading fire with Encizo and other forces outside the window.

A third ambusher leaped through an open doorway, a 5.56 mm M-4 carbine chattering as he sprayed rounds toward Bolan. Sliding into the room, James shot the terrorist twice in the head, cutting short his screaming rampage.

The machine-gunner ducked a sudden influx of rounds and saw the men behind him for the first time. He twisted at the waist and tried to swing around the M-60.

Bolan and James triggered their weapons simultaneously. Each Stony Man marksmen put two 3-round bursts center mass on the machine-gunner. He staggered backward, chest exploding as the bullets slammed home in rapid succession. Standing silhouetted in the window, he triggered a burst from the M-60 that went into the floor.

Suddenly the man staggered and the front of his face

exploded, spraying blood and brains like slop from a pail toward Bolan and James as rifle fire from outside arced into the room.

The machine-gunner, as cut to ribbons as any of the Iraqi police he had just butchered moments earlier, fell over to the side on the floor where he lay still. Bolan accepted James's hand in help as he rose to his feet.

"Rafe!" James shouted, his voice carrying out through the window in the sudden silence. "It's good, brother," he said in Spanish.

"Let's get out of here," Bolan said.

"There was nothing but civilians on that second blast, the suicide one," James said, breathing heavily. "Nothing tactically to be gained. Those kids and all those people…"

"I know," Bolan said. "But we have to go, Cal."

CHAPTER TWENTY-ONE

In the confusion and fear it was easy enough to slip away, though they drew looks everywhere they went as they cut down alleys and crossed streets. Finally, about five blocks over, they surprised a cabdriver sitting at the curb and slid in to his vehicle.

He started to protest, frightened by their appearance and the stench of death that clung to the three men. Bolan shoved his hand into a pocket of his black fatigues and the taxi driver strangled a scream when he saw the thick sheaf of money Bolan held out. After that the man calmed down immediately.

He had apparently been a computer programmer before the war and spoke good English. He told Bolan his name was Omar and when Bolan commented that his last cabdriver had been named Omar the man shrugged and asked him if he'd ever met more than one person name John.

Bolan grinned by way of reply and rode the rest of the trip in silence. He forced himself to relax, to let the adrenaline bleed off his body like pent-up gases from an emergency-release valve. He concentrated on breathing as his eyes scanned the ruined cityscape for the next sign of trouble.

Images flashed before his eyes, impossible to quell. The one-eyed mother so crazed with panic she fought him even as he tried to save her child from burning to death. The armless man being cradled by his wife. The headless body of the young boy who had stolen tomatoes. The severed hand that had landed on the dashboard of the Kia minivan.

None of the violence had been a part of *his* mission. None of it had brought him closer to his targets. The men he'd killed could have acted for any one of a dozen motivations that seemed pointless or even counterproductive to Bolan.

He didn't care what they believed. They were cannibals of humanity.

He understood rage in the face of tragedy, such feelings had ignited his own War Everlasting. Yet he had never resorted to blind bombings and random violence perpetuated on the innocent to advance his cause.

He thought about the men he was going to investigate now, men who funded and facilitated the kind of violence he had just witnessed to provide a ready vehicle and convenient smoke screen for their personal, criminal ambitions. At least the insane killers he'd just executed had been believers in something beyond their own self-gratification.

These others, these Scimitars, were simply amoral mercenaries and Bolan would have his vengeance upon them. The men he was going to interview had information that would stop others from putting money or explosives or weapons into the hands of men like the ones Bolan had just killed. Information that would help stop the enabling of the slaughter of innocents.

God help them if they didn't want to talk.

THE OLYMPIC COMMITTEE Annex building overlooked the Tigris River.

It was modern and had been quite fashionable before the Shock and Awe bombing campaign prior to the American ground invasion that had blown out the windows and collapsed the west wing. In the days following the fall of Baghdad, elements of the U.S. Marines had battled Fedayeen units holed up inside the building.

An M-1 A-1 main battle tank had put the skirmish to an end, but the damage to the front of the building had been extensive. Using the river to escape, the surviving Fedayeen had melted into the surrounding Sunni neighborhoods. After the looting began, the irregular forces had returned and actually pulled security on the site, preventing its destruction and the pilfering of much of its interior.

Despite this odd behavior, the U.S. forces had left the building unexplored when USMC units had turned the area of operations over to the Army. No fire had ever been taken from the building after the formation of the interim government.

The three commandos stood on the edge of the Tigris in the shadow of a ruined building, hidden from sight of the Annex and the neighborhood at large around them. They watched their target building, positioned three city blocks to the west.

The taxi driver had driven quickly away after depositing the blood-splattered team on the street some ten minutes from their current location. Considering the likelihood of how fast information traveled in this area, the clock was ticking. Encizo put away his tactical radio.

"Charlie's put the bird in the air," he said.

Bolan nodded. He surveyed his approach to the Annex. The low-profile security stance of the Scimitar depot and forward command post left him with multiple options in his approach. The team could travel down an alley running parallel to the Tigris, to within fifty or seventy-five yards of the structure. Beyond that only open field encircled the building except on the river side, and the team obviously wasn't equipped to make an amphibious approach. But if they simply cut across the open area they ran the risk of sniper fire.

Bolan frowned. The area was quiet and had been quiet for so long Army patrols were concentrated in other areas, in hot spots. If the sentries inside the building fired upon every person who approached then the Annex would come under scrutiny, which was what they, above all else, wanted to avoid. Therefore, Bolan figured, they were judicious in their use of deadly force.

"What do you think?" Bolan asked. "No outside security, if they have any at all. Real stuff, I mean."

"They don't need to frighten the locals," Encizo pointed out. "The neighborhood is Sunni. Those guys pay for the clinic. Their contributions to the jihadists keep those guys out of this area and prevent them from becoming an extortion target. They have a representative on the government council. That keeps the Iraqi police out of their hair and between them and any Shi militia death squads. The area is 'pacified,' so that keeps military operations out of the way."

"Seems like they've thought of everything," Bolan mused.

"Us," Encizo replied. "They didn't think about us."

"How do you want to play it then?" James asked. "You want to try to talk our way past anyone who tells us no? Play it subtle?"

"To hell with subtle," Bolan replied. "After what I just saw, I'm not asking nicely, and I'm sure as hell not throwing money at the problem. There is only give and take. They give and I take. No mercy for those who kill women and children and the innocent by design."

"There are those who say we do the same, do it worse," Encizo said.

"Sure, there are plenty who play the hollow logic of moral equivalency," Bolan agreed. "They have no appreciation of the differences between the actions that are accidental or unavoidable and those that are deliberate."

"They think that the dead are only dead."

"I know better. A man drives his car around the bend in the road and his brakes fail, he loses control and kills a family. If it's my family, or any family, I grieve but I can forgive. Same man, same family, only he's fleeing a bank robbery or is blind drunk when he crashes into the innocents. That isn't even the same scenario. To equate the two simply because the family ends up dead is asinine. I know better. You know better."

"Oh, I'm on board," Encizo agreed. "I just like to hear you say it."

"Let's roll," Bolan said.

THE STONY MAN team picked its way through the rubble, feeling vulnerable and exposed in the hot desert sun as they approached the partially demolished building. As they drew closer, the stone masonry structure loomed larger. Once upon a time in Iraq this building had been a monument to architecture, designed as a showpiece to the rest of the world.

It had been a concrete and rebar version of a shell game, a clever application of smoke and mirrors. From halls dedicated to the advancement of international amateur sport and international cooperation, the sons of Saddam had commanded the most feared of secret police units, a death squad so brutal it made other Iraqi state agencies seem civilized in comparison: the Fedayeen Saddam.

The shadow of that feared militia had stretched out past the men who had originally cast it, morphing into a criminal enterprise of savage capability. Its agents were ruthless and clever, master strategists of asymmetrical warfare who fed instability, violence and suffering to stabilize and protect their own drug- and weapons-smuggling empires.

Bolan was unsure of what specific trappings he would discover in the Olympic Committee Annex, only that it would provide him answers, come hell or high water. He had not crossed Baghdad and suffered the reality of that city's daily life only to be denied.

The three Stony Man commandos navigated the rubble of the collapsed wing as they made their way toward the back door. As they circled the building, the street and neighborhood facing the structure's front disappeared from view. Past the rubble they saw a narrow strip of broken parking lot between the rear of the building and the Tigris river.

The area had once been a garden, but now the concrete walls had been knocked into piles and the grass and fauna left to blister and die in the Middle Eastern sun. A sturdy pier, now neglected, ran from the parking lot into the dirty brown water of the river.

Empty cans and plastic bags filled with trash were scattered around, interspersed with old tires and mounds of molding newspaper. Yellow stubble was all that remained of the lawns, and six vehicles were parked haphazardly in the back. One of them a purple BMW X5 SUV and another a silver Mercedes town car.

An Iraqi boy in short white pants and a loose shirt with a soccer ball on the front poked a stick into a trash-filled burn barrel where greasy brown smoke seeped into the air. He looked over as Bolan and his crew approached, his eyes growing wide. A long pink scar ran out of a shock of unruly black hair and trailed down his cheek to end in a starburst pattern.

His gaze shifted off the grim-faced warriors and their weapons toward an entrance set in the middle of an old concrete loading dock next to several roll-up bay doors.

The boy dropped his stick and turned to race for the entrance. Encizo leaped forward, sprinting fast as both Bolan and James spun in opposite directions to cover the scene from any outside interference. The boy was fast but not fast enough.

The boy ducked under Encizo's outstretched arm and leaped onto the concrete loading dock. The Cuban jumped forward and snatched the boy by his shirt collar, spun him around and shoved him against the loading dock.

The boy, who was as wiry as a snake and looked about thirteen, opened his mouth as if to scream a warning. Encizo slapped his hand across the boy's face to smother the cry. The boys eyes were wide as he stared at the grimy, blood-streaked and bearded Rafael Encizo.

"Shh," Encizo whispered.

The Cuban soldier pulled a multicolored fold of bank notes from his pocket. He held it in front the boy's eyes and slowly removed his hand from the kid's mouth. The boy's eyes darted from Encizo's face to the money, then back again. The Phoenix Force warrior nodded and the boy took the money.

"Now, go," Encizo said in the pidgin Arabic he'd picked up on his own.

The boy spun off the wall and sprinted toward the edge of the building.

"How long you think that bought us?" Bolan asked.

"Maybe ten minutes?" Encizo shrugged. "We go in, find the boss, snatch him and get out into the road so Charlie can get us out."

"Easy," James agreed.

"I knew there was a reason I picked you guys," Bolan stated dryly. "It's your optimism."

THE FACADE OF INNOCENCE carefully crafted by the unit utilizing the Olympic Committee Annex was shattered almost immediately upon the Stony Man warriors entering the building. They found themselves in a wide hallway set just off the loading bays. The wall facing the building interior was lined with doors. In one corner, large, floor-model fans moved hot air around in lazy eddies.

A diesel forklift sat unattended in the middle of the open floor and the back hall off the loading bays was lined with pallets. On the pallets cardboard boxes with white bodies and green lids were stacked six feet high.

A red arrow had been spray-painted on the ground and Bolan knew immediately it pointed south, toward Mecca, to guide the faithful in their daily prayers. About twenty prayer mats were lined up on the ground in neat rows. A black flag hung on the wall with large Arabic script written on it in white.

Bolan had attended enough threat assessment briefings to recognize the icon for what it was. "The Shahada," he said quietly.

"'I bear witness that there is no deity other than God and that Mohammed is his servant and messenger,'" Calvin James recited from memory.

"Seems like Scimitar is running a crew of true believers," Encizo said.

"Exploiting a crew of true believers," James contradicted him.

Bolan let his gaze play around the room, slowly taking in the details. His survey fell on the boxes stacked on the pallets against the wall. He frowned as he took in the orderly rows.

Suspicious, Bolan pulled out his straight-blade boot knife. He stabbed the box, wrenched the blade to the side to rip the cardboard and immediately a stream of white powder cascaded to the floor. James stepped forward and stuck his pinky in the flow. He brought the sample to his tongue and tasted it.

"Heroin," he said, and spit. "So clean you can snort it or smoke it. No needle-fear so no stigma, equaling greater recreational usage. More usage equals more profits. More profits then more money to support jihad."

Calvin James's younger sister had died of a drug overdose. "That's it," he muttered. "Let's kill them all."

At that moment a fat man in greasy coveralls with a folding-stock AKS-74 thrown casually over one shoulder opened a door from off the hall and strolled out. His jaw dropped as he took in the three well-armed and blood-splattered men standing around a spilling fountain of his product.

He hurriedly tried to unsling his weapon. A loud crack sounded in the narrow hall. The drug soldier's eyes crossed as they tried to see the sudden hole in his flat, low forehead, then he tumbled to the ground.

"Rafe, set the boxes on fire and let's sweep toward the front," Bolan said, lowering his weapon.

Encizo produced a lighter and lit the cardboard boxes on fire. Once he had a sizable flame the three soldiers began to move down the hall, James covering their six while Bolan led from the front.

He kicked open a door. Encizo covered his motion in one direction while James secured the hall in the opposite sector. An empty office was revealed. He let the door close. From the end of the hallway he heard men shouting in Arabic. A door opened and Bolan sank to one knee on the floor, bringing the AK-104 into target acquisition.

Three men armed with AKM assault rifles charged into the hall. Bolan and Encizo opened up. Their tight, figure-8-patterned bursts scythed into the knot of running gunmen and ripped them apart. They tumbled over one another to fall in a pile on the floor. Blood flowed out in a red flood across the linoleum.

"Let's go!" Bolan said.

The fire team moved quickly down the length of the hall, weapons up until they got to the room the men had charged from. The outflung arm of a dead narcoterrorist held the door open several inches.

Bolan stepped over the mangled corpse and snap kicked the door open before moving inside. Encizo followed him inside, weapon up and tracking as James took up a defensive overwatch to prevent a surprise attack from the rear.

The Executioner stepped inside, covering his vectors with tight motions of his weapon. He paused in the middle of the room and slowly lowered his weapon, taking in the scene. Behind him Encizo cleared behind the door before lowering his own weapon and whispering a curse in Spanish.

The man hung from chains bolted into the wall. Inside the handcuffs attached to the chains the man's fingers stuck out at odd angles, and he had only raw, bloody patches where his fingernails should have been. His mouth had collapsed inward like that of an old man, his cheeks hollow and his lips stained with blood. Most of his teeth had been yanked from his mouth.

A blindfold had been used to cover his eyes and a ball-gag shoved in his mouth. His head hung limply between his outstretched arms. On a tray set on rollers lay a butane torch, a pair of pliers and some bloodstained garden shears. Forgotten on the floor where the man rested on his knees was a three-foot length of black garden hose dripping with crimson.

On a rickety card table set against the wall Bolan saw an unzipped bowling ball bag. Even from his angle Bolan could see it was filled with stacks of U.S. currency. Next to it on the table was a blood-splattered, blue Iraqi police uniform tunic and a Beretta 92-F pistol. Scattered around the table like bloodstained dice, the long root nerves still attached, were the man's yanked teeth.

"They were videotaping it," Encizo gritted. "Look."

Bolan looked up and spotted a minicamcorder set up on a silver-legged tripod. "Take it. They might have been torturing him for information. Whatever they're interested in, I'm interested in."

Encizo collected and secured the camcorder while Bolan moved closer to the man. He leaned in looking for a sign of life. Bolan reached out and put two fingers against the man's neck at the carotid artery, searching for a pulse.

He could find none.

"Let's go," he told Encizo.

As the two warriors headed for the door, gunfire erupted in the hallway.

CHAPTER TWENTY-TWO

Bolan looked out the door of the room and saw Calvin James lying prone on the ground. The ex-SEAL fired his AK-104 in cool bursts, using the dead bodies of the torture masters as a hasty fighting position. The Phoenix Force commando was positioned so that his fire was directed back down the hallway, in the direction from which the team had first penetrated the building.

Bolan threw himself against the right side of the door and angled his weapon to add his fire to Calvin James's. Encizo crouched on the left and swung the barrel of his AKM around the corner. He began triggering long blasts of full-automatic fire as the Stony Man team fought hard to shift the momentum of the battle away from the attackers.

"I can't see them!" Bolan shouted above the roar of the weapons. "How many are there?"

"Four!" James shouted back. "They came in off the loading dock just like we did, I think the boy must have alerted them."

"Rafe," Bolan said. "Check Cal's back."

Encizo stopped firing and repositioned his weapon so that it was articulated in the opposite direction. The Phoenix Force combat veteran threw himself belly-down on the floor and peeked his head around the door jamb to try to cover James's back.

Bolan leaned out of the door and sprayed bullets down the hall. He saw two of the enemy narcoterrorists firing down the hall from positions behind the open doors leading out of the loading bay where the make-shift mosque had been built, smoke from the burning cardboard crates of heroin billowed behind them. They answered the Westerners burst for burst.

James abruptly lifted his AK-104 up at an angle, turning the weapon sideways. Bolan heard the distinctive bloop as the commando triggered the M-203 grenade launcher. The rifle recoiled smoothly into James's shoulder and there was a flash of smoke as the round arced down the hallway.

Instinctively, Bolan turned away as the HE grenade rammed into the wall at the end of the hallway and detonated with a thunderous explosion and flash of light. The crack was sharp and followed by screams. The hallway acted like a chimney, filling with dark smoke from the detonation and funneling it in the team's direction.

Bolan seized the initiative hard on the heels of the grenade explosion. He leaped over the rifle barrels of both Encizo and James and slid across the passage, bounced a shoulder off the wall and centered his weapon down the hallway. He advanced, firing his weapon in tight bursts toward the positions he had witnessed before the explosion.

Behind him James rose to his feet and began to move down the hallway, as well, firing in tandem. Behind them Encizo rolled into position and covered their rear security with his AKM assault rifle.

Bolan caught a silhouette in the smoke and raked it with a Z-pattern burst of 7.62 mm rounds. Bolan's target spilled out onto floor, his chest and throat looking like an animal had clawed it out.

"Magazine!" Bolan warned.

The Executioner hit the magazine release with his finger and dropped his almost-empty clip. His other hand came up with a fresh one and slapped it into place. Bolan's thumb tapped the release and the bolt slid forward with a snap as a round was chambered.

He brought up his weapon, scanning quickly for a target. The smoke from the grenade blast hung in the air, reducing vision. James put a man down, then finished him off with a 3-round burst to the back of the head. Bolan risked a look over his shoulder to quickly check Encizo's status.

Just as Bolan turned he saw the little Cuban come up out of a crouch. The commando lunged toward the open door to the room where he and Bolan had found the tortured man.

"Grenade!" Encizo roared.

Bolan watched as the Phoenix Force commando arched into a dive, his weapon trailing behind him.

Directly under the leaping man's boots Bolan saw the black metal egg bounce once, then get caught on the sprawled-out leg of a corpse. There was a flash of light and suddenly Bolan was slapped down.

His world spun, and he hit the floor hard enough to

see stars. His vision went black for a heartbeat then returned. Once again he had been struck deaf. He lay still for a moment, stunned by the concussive force of the blast. He blinked and the ceiling came into focus.

He saw a dark shape move beside him and turned his head in that direction. The hallway lit up as the muzzle-flash from James's weapon flared like a Roman candle. Bolan saw the ex-SEAL's face twist as he screamed his outrage, but he heard no sound.

Bolan blinked. When he opened his eyes again he saw James roll onto his back and fire the AK-104 back down the hallway from between his sprawled-open legs. With a rush, sensibility rammed into Bolan and snapped him back into the present.

He sat up and his hearing returned instantaneously. He looked down the hall and saw starbursts of yellow light through the fog of smoke as narcoterrorists charged their position. Bolan leaned against the wall before lifting his Kalashnikov and returning fire. He squinted and saw Encizo lying motionless, his legs trailing out from the doorway of the torture room.

Bolan sprayed gunfire down the hallway. He watched his green tracers arc into the debris, dust and smoke, and saw other tracers arc back out at him. Suddenly he caught a muzzle-flash to the right of the hallway, closer than before. He twisted at the hip and fired in response.

A man folded at the waist out of the fog and pitched forward. As he tumbled to the ground, Bolan put another burst into his body. Beside him James rose off the ground, keeping the barrel of his weapon trained down the hall.

The Executioner held his fire for a moment and forced himself to stand. No enemy fire came from the hallway. He took a look behind him, counted the three dead men he and James had shot. The Phoenix Force commando had stated there were four when the ambush had begun.

Bolan took a step down the hallway in that direction, weapon ready, eyeing the crater where James's 40 mm round had impacted and the black scorch patterns spread out from the blast center. A severed arm lay next to a chunk of skull in the hall amid a puddle of blood and he turned back down the hallway, assured that the fourth man had been put down, as well.

James jogged forward. Bolan followed him, his weapon searching for a target through the gloom. The medic reached the motionless Encizo and reached down to pull an enemy corpse off his friend's body. Bolan came even with him as James knelt beside the wounded Phoenix Force commando.

"Rafe!" James shouted. "Rafe, can you hear me, brother?"

At the end of the hallway, through the smoke and haze of dust, Bolan spotted a final door. He advanced quickly and pulled it open. Sinking to a knee, he risked a look around the corner. A long hallway, floored with mosaic tile and painted a creamy-brown, stretched nearly thirty or forty yards toward the front of the building.

A bearded face peeked around a corner at the end of the hallway and Bolan instinctively fired a burst. The head ducked back to safety around the corner. The soldier pulled himself out of the hallway.

"How is he?" he shouted to James.

"Bad."

His voice was flat, lacking inflection. Bolan felt a chill pass through him. Not another brother in arms down, he thought, pulling his tactical radio from his web belt and keying the mike.

"You in our area?" he asked without preamble.

"Affirmative, Striker," Charlie Mott answered. "Doesn't look good for a touchdown except on the main road. Too much debris in those empty lots around you."

"I got a man down, is that the best you can do?" Bolan said. "The front is filled with bad guys.

"There's a dock in the Tigris behind the structure," Mott answered immediately. "I can hover and land one skid on the dock, it'll be tricky but it's workable."

"Copy that, make it happen."

Bolan tucked away his radio and fired a blind burst down the hall as harassing fire.

"We have to go," he said as he turned to James. "Charlie's got the chopper outside."

Before James could answer Bolan heard a loud thump strike the door behind him. Without thought, he leaped forward onto his startled teammate and forced the man down over the mangled and bleeding Encizo.

Behind them the hand grenade went off like a peal of thunder. The door flew off its hinges and went flying into the hallway followed by a billow of smoke. Bolan lifted himself off James and Encizo as debris and dust rained down on the men. He staggered, then shoved hard against the door jamb, forcing himself upright.

He felt like he'd just downed a bottle of tequila and

taken a ride on a Tilt-A-Whirl. He gritted his teeth against the pain and disorientation. He scooped up his AK-104 and moved back to the edge of the hall where he thrust the barrel around the edge of the door and pulled the trigger.

The weapon kicked and bucked in his hand as empty shell casings arced out and spilled across the bloody floor. He fired a sustained burst, burning off half the magazine. Immediately a maelstrom of heavy-caliber bullets sizzled through the blown-open door and hammered the wall behind the Executioner.

"Take him and go!" Bolan shouted. "Get to the river. Charlie's there. I'll hold them off!"

"No good, Striker!" James shouted back. "I have to get a pressure dressing in place or his guts are just going to leak out when I run. He'll die!"

Bolan gritted his teeth, fury rising in him with tornado force. He levered the AK-104 around the corner of the door and fired a burst of harassing fire. He heard the whine of bullets ricocheting off some hard surface and the dull thuds as the rounds burrowed into the hallway walls.

He chanced a quick glance around the corner. What he saw made his heart stop cold. At the end of the hallway a narcoterrorist was inching forward behind the cover of a Level III ballistic shield. Behind the shield-bearer, working in coordinated tandem, shuffled a gunman firing an M-4 carbine in neat 3-round bursts.

The 5.56 mm bullets chewed into the edges of the door frame above Bolan's head, spraying his face with wood splinters. Bolan fired a return burst and saw sparks shower off the shield's gray metal material. Gunmen down the hall started to edge out from behind the corner, emboldened by the shield-bearer's success.

The M-4 gunner ducked as Bolan fired, crouching behind the shield-bearer. His arm arched up and the black metal sphere of another hand grenade flew into the hazy air. Bolan saw the spoon fly off as the bomb arced through the space between them.

Bolan sprayed wildly down the hall, forcing the M-4 gunner to remain crouched behind the ballistic shield. The antipersonnel grenade landed and bounced up. The big American caught the segmented orb in one hand and cocked his arm back. The M-4 gunner held his carbine above his head and fired a wild burst. Bolan dived forward onto the floor and released the grenade.

The fragmentation grenade hit the hallway behind the assault team, bounced once, rolled away from them, then detonated. The explosion was deafening. Shrapnel erupted outward, whizzing through the air, peppering the drywall and plaster across the grenade's forty foot detonation area. Most of the blast and shrapnel was soaked up by the two-man terrorist assault team.

The M-4 gunner was picked up and hurled over the top of the shield man, spinning like a rag doll. He landed hard on the floor of the hall, limbs splayed and head cocked unnaturally.

The shield-bearer was propelled forward by the blast, falling across his shield, which rang with the impacts of metal shrapnel. Bolan lifted his head and saw the man reach weakly for an autopistol on the ground next to him.

Bolan shot him in his upturned face, then ducked back around the corner of the doorway. He dropped the magazine out of his Kalashnikov and inserted another.

He turned to see James working frantically on the wounded and unconscious Rafael Encizo, his blood-soaked hands tying off a knot over his comrade's ripped-open abdomen. Blood was puddled on the ground around the injured man, Calvin James's legs were soaked in it.

Moving fast, James used surgical tape to secure a gauze pad into place. It was instantly stained red.

Machine-gun fire rattled through the open door, punctuated by the slash of green tracers. Bolan turned and fired a burst around the corner. He looked back at James.

"You ready?" he yelled.

James, his face ashen, looked over at Bolan and simply nodded before moving into action.

Letting his Kalashnikov dangle from its strap James bent and pulled Encizo into a sitting position. The Cuban fighter's head lolled on his neck and underneath a shroud of his own blood, the man's skin was deathly white.

James squatted securing his grip on Encizo's shredded clothes. He grunted and lifted straight up, driving with the powerful muscles of his buttocks and thighs. Encizo rose as James did and at the top of the arch James ducked under the limp soldier, shouldering his body weight easily.

Bolan sprayed the hallway through the door without looking. His burst was answered with longer and heavier caliber return fire. James looked toward Bolan.

"Go!" Bolan shouted. "Go, I'm coming."

James nodded once and turned, running down the hall toward the back door through which the Stony Man team had first accessed the building. He slid in the blood splashed across the linoleum but did not go down and Bolan turned his attention back to the interior hall door he held.

Whatever else happened, he had to give the Phoenix Force commandos time to get aboard the helicopter. He would hold off the narcoterrorists located in the front of the building as long as he could, then make his own break for freedom.

Everything had gone to hell in a handbasket in the blink of an eye and all Bolan could try to do now was pick up the pieces. It didn't matter why he had come to this place to begin with, all that mattered was what was happening now.

A burst of machine-gun fire tore down the long hall, then the firing trailed off and Bolan heard the familiar thumping of yet another hand grenade coming his way. He looked down at the threshold and saw the black metal sphere roll into the hall beside him.

He swung his left arm down like a handball player and slapped the grenade back down the corridor. He didn't look to see how far it traveled but instead tucked his head between his arms and rolled away from the opening. There was a boom and he felt the explosive shock waves travel out of the hall and through the doorway to slop over and push hard into his back.

He lifted himself off his belly and twisted back toward the contested door. Standing, he thrust the muzzle of his weapon around the corner and fired until he burned off the last bit of his magazine.

He turned and began to sprint down the back hall of the annex. He dropped the spent magazine on the run and fumbled for another one in his web belt. His combat boot came down on a blue-gray loop of intestine and he went down hard, landing awkwardly on one knee. Pain lanced out from the hinge joint and he gasped in surprise at the intensity of it after all he'd already suffered.

Bolan forced himself up and kept running, leaving the Kalashnikov behind. He reached the open door leading into the loading bay and drew his .44 Desert Eagle from his thigh holster. The silver steel pistol filled his fist with reassuring weight as he raced into the makeshift mosque.

Crossing the wide-open floor, he jumped down the short flight of stairs set just outside the personnel door. As he left the building, he sprinted fully into the glare of sun and was struck light-blind for a second.

He heard the chatter of small-arms fire and blinked the blur of sunlight from his eyes. Weapons fire rang out from his right, to the south where the annex had been collapsed by tank rounds years earlier. He heard answering fire coming from directly in front of him.

His vision returned, and he saw Charlie Mott's helicopter hovering straight in front of him about fifty or sixty yards away. Just as he had in Amman, the expert pilot flew the MH-6J troop carrier version of the Little Bird, its weapons pods replaced by benches that could hold up to six men on either side.

Mott had lowered his helicopter into position over the flowing river, resting one skid on the water-worn wood of the pier and keeping the bird level through fancy flying and sheer determination. As Bolan crossed the broken pavement of the parking lot, he saw Rafael

Encizo sprawled across one bench, a limp and blood-streaked arm dangling over the side.

With one knee resting beside the unconscious man's head and the other leg braced against the helicopter landing skid, Calvin James was firing his AK-104 from the shoulder. Bullets and tracer fire sliced the air around him, and an enemy round struck the bubble front of the Little Bird, starring the glass.

Bolan angled his run to put the vehicles in the parking lot between him and the narcoterrorists firing on the chopper. He slid around the back of the purple BMW X5 SUV and looked toward the sound of enemy gunfire. He saw a bearded man down on one knee, firing tight bursts at the hovering helicopter.

More rounds struck the aircraft and punched through the glass to slam into the empty copilot seat. Bolan drew down on the marksmen across sixty yards, resting across the hood of the silver Mercedes town car. He squeezed the trigger. The 240-grain boattail round slammed into the gunman across the distance and spun him. Blood splattered across the rocks.

One of the narcoterrorists heard the boom of Bolan's hand cannon and saw his fellow cell member go spinning. The man swiveled behind a pile of broken mortar and picked Bolan out. He fired wild in a zigzag pattern with his AKM, screaming over the rattle and roar of his weapon.

Bullets hammered into the Mercedes, and a car alarm blared under the impacts. The smooth, tinted windows shattered, and pockmarks opened up on the sleek lines of the automobile frame. The front tire exploded and bits of rubber flew. A dozen rounds drilled through body and were soaked up by the V12 engine.

Bolan rolled off the hood and hit the ground as 7.62 mm slugs skipped across the vehicle hood. He hit the dirt hard behind the driver-side front tire then rolled out toward the front, underneath the bumper. He took his angle and drew down on the spray-and-pray style gunman. The .44 Desert Eagle roared, and the massive round flew flat and true across the space between the combatants.

The gunman tumbled backward, dragging his weapon with him. Wild rounds chattered out as the man went down then the rifle tumbled from slack fingers and fell silent. Bolan rolled back behind the wheel well of the shot-up Mercedes-Benz.

He put one hand on the ground and pushed up, gathering his feet beneath him like a spring coiling. He rose smoothly and sprinted for the helicopter, which had been forced off its hover by the relentless small-arms fire. Mott spun the nose of the bird around so that the helicopter was between the cluster of gunmen and the wounded Rafael Encizo.

James grabbed the door jamb of the helicopter and fired across the nose, one-handed, as Bolan sprinted forward. Charlie Mott had pulled an H&K MP-5 from the copilot's seat and fired at the attackers, as well.

Mott spotted Bolan and lifted the tail of the helicopter, starting to fly toward the warrior, some six feet off the ground. Bolan holstered the .44 as he ran, leaving his hands free. The helicopter wobbled as Mott skimmed the ground, his skids less than three feet above the broken ground. Rotor wash buffeted into Bolan like high winds.

A wall of grit, dirt and fine debris billowed into Bolan with hurricane intensity, nearly blinding him as the rotor wash kicked up a dust storm. He narrowed his eyes to slits to avoid the painful bits of detritus.

Sparks exploded off the airframe of the helicopter and Mott flinched involuntarily as a bullet struck his aviator headset and tore it off his head. The Little Bird banked slightly to the right, tipping up in the air.

The rotor blades canted at a dangerous angle, kicking up dirt in a line like ocean spray. Bolan leaped forward, landing hard on the bench set above the pilot-side landing skid. Bolan's two-hundred-plus pounds shifted the helicopter out of its tilt and Mott, as graceful as a figure skater cuing off his partner, leveled the chopper out.

The Little Bird righted and Mott went with the momentum, shifting in a tight half circle back toward the Tigris and lifting off from the ground. Bolan gripped a safety strap as the helicopter spun. He lifted his head, fighting the inertia, and looked past Mott to the other side of the helicopter.

On the other side of the MH-6J James sprawled over Encizo, protecting the unconscious, wounded soldier from gunfire with his own body. He hung his AK-104 over the edge and fired it one-handed at the knot of gunmen who sprinted from cover, wildly firing their weapons at the fleeing helicopter.

Mott rose swiftly and began to follow the brown line of the river, quickly pushing the Little Bird toward its maximum cruising speed of 160 mph. As Charlie Mott put the helicopter's tail rotor to the Olympic Committee Annex, Calvin James stopped firing.

Bolan, helpless, turned to his companions and saw James frantically trying to revive his fellow Phoenix

Force commando. The medic's arms were soaked with blood to the elbow as he knelt astride Encizo and performed CPR chest compressions.

Out over the Tigris river, on an emergency flight toward Ibn Sina hospital in the Baghdad Green Zone, the Executioner began to pray for Rafael Encizo.

CHAPTER TWENTY-THREE

The video camera taken out of the torture cell had been in the cargo pocket of Rafael Encizo's black fatigue pants. His legs had protected it from the grenade blast and the information stored in it had been saved. Bolan carried it with him, the camera smeared black with blood.

The Cuban-commando remained in surgery in the Ibn Sina hospital. Once his condition stabilized, if it stabilized, he would be flown to the military hospital at Ramstein AFB in Germany.

If he stabilized.

Bolan had left Calvin James to watch over his teammate and moved quickly to exploit any possible intelligence to be gleaned from the digital recording of the torture session. A ready reactionary force of U.S. Army Rangers in Black Hawk helicopters out of Camp Victory, combined with a motorized company of Iraqi National Guardsmen, had descended on the Olympic Committee Annex as soon as Bolan had given his briefing to the JSOC representative in the Green Zone.

Bolan kept the digital camcorder, and that information went on to Stony Man Farm. Even though he couldn't understand a word of what was said, Bolan had forced himself to watch the torturers at work. He memorized details, cataloged faces.

Now Bolan drank a cold beer out of a long-necked bottle and looked out the window of his comfortable guest house, toward the artificial lake that dominated Camp Slayer's topography. He had spent ten minutes in a hot shower scrubbing the filth and the blood from his body. He had paced back and forth, his mind sliding off the troubling question of whether Rafael Encizo would die in Iraq or not.

He thought about the disparity between that artificial lake outside his window and the brutal deaths he'd witnessed in the Baghdad slums. He kept glancing over at the table where the video conference phone sat, silent.

He wanted to see what Price and Kurtzman could take from the video he'd captured, wanted to see if there would be anything to put him on the trail of the Scimitar puppet masters. Marzook was a lost lead now that the annex penetration had gone so horribly wrong. He did not envy the Stony Man cybernetics team the uncomfortable task of viewing the video. That nameless man had died hard.

Price had chosen to keep word of Rafael Encizo's condition quiet from the rest of Phoenix Force until more concrete information could be obtained. There was nothing the other commandos could do, and their worry could only serve to blunt their focus in a highly dangerous situation of their own. When results were sure, Price would tell her men, but not until then. Until that moment, it was her job to worry and the team's job to perform.

He supposed he should catch a nap while he waited for word, and he should have been dead on his feet from adrenaline bleed-off. The rational part of his mind understood that whether or not he slept would have absolutely zero effect on the outcome of Encizo's surgery. He still couldn't bring himself to do it.

Bolan again looked over at the video conferencer, which remained silent as a tombstone. He finished his beer and set the empty bottle on the table. He eased into the chair and leaned his head back. He felt his exhaustion settle over him like a blanket and he closed his eyes, just for a moment.

THE BUZZING of the video-conferencer woke Bolan.

He blinked, his gaze going to his wristwatch and he realized that he'd been asleep for a little more than two hours. He sat up and punched the connection button on the video-conferencer.

"Go," he growled.

Barbara Price's face clicked into view over the secure channel. She looked cool, poised and unflappable. But she didn't smile, and Bolan knew she'd been shaken by what she'd seen.

"That tape gave us what we needed, Mack. Part of it, anyway."

"You don't know how glad I am to hear you say that," he answered.

"The man being tortured was Colonel Qays al-Mamoury. He had been a sniper in the Republican Guard, then an officer of the Iraqi police. We identified his torturers, all Sunni, all former Saddam loyalists. The problem is that the ones you didn't kill have pretty much been ghosts since the fall of Baghdad. Low-level scuts."

"So a dead end?"

"No. Mr. al-Mamoury got greedy and it got him killed. He was supposed to make a payoff, guarantee delivery of fifty thousand in U.S. to a local sheikh in the Yarmuk neighborhood, a Scimitar captain turned cleric who was placing the down payment on a new Whabbist madrassa."

"Wild guess." Bolan grunted. "The cash came up short?"

"About seven hundred dollars. Al-Mamoury skimmed a few twenties off each stack of cash."

"Less than a grand?" Even the war-weary Bolan was surprised. "They did that to a precinct captain for less than a thousand dollars?"

"It was all on the tape. The sheikh, Omar Mahmoud Abdullah, was there for the first part. You must have missed his eminence by about two hours. The field officer for the annex unit kept apologizing on behalf of Abdullah's 'brothers,' and the sheikh just kept saying 'prove it.' So they did."

"Let me guess," Bolan said. "The only one we have a location on is the cleric."

"That's right." Price's voice was flat, and her eyes looked tired. "We know where the cleric Abdullah is. The sheikh knows where the rest of the Scimitar cell is. That's all we have. The Rangers took down an empty building today. It had been cleaned, booby-trapped and then set on fire. The trail ends there."

Bolan was silent. He was thinking that, technically, the trail ended in Rafael Encizo's hospital room. He felt the awesome responsibility of his mission, his calling, settle on his shoulders like a stone mantle. How much easier it was to fight the battle when the truth was easy and open. But the battle did not stop because the decisions became uncomfortable or murky.

"Send the information," Bolan said. "I'll let you know."

He reached over and shut off the power to the video-conferencer. He leaned back in his seat and wondered how Encizo was doing.

BOLAN READ THE INTELLIGENCE given him by Stony Man. He raided the refrigerator and fed with nearly insatiable hunger before making and drinking a pot of strong, black coffee.

Two hours later, Calvin James entered the guest house. Bolan looked up. The big ex-SEAL shook his head, face grim. "He hasn't woken up and they don't expect him to. You got a lead on someone we can kill?"

Bolan nodded and slid the sheets of information across the table to the Phoenix Force commando.

"I think so."

CHAPTER TWENTY-FOUR

Bolan and James entered Sector 37 North, the military designation for the west Baghdad neighborhood of Yarmuk. In the days before the war it had been filled with two-story, adobe-style homes first constructed in the 1960s for Sunni military officers.

Fourth Street was quiet and dark. Electricity was rationed, and no power flowed into the neighborhood at that time of night. Overhead helicopters hunted the dark on missions of their own. The two Americans had avoided military patrols and slipped into the area driving a battered taxicab and dressed in civilian clothes. The taxi was part of a "gray fleet" kept in various garages by Western special operators and intelligence agents. The 4-cylinder engine had been replaced with a V8 model as well as solid tires, unobtrusive interior armor plating and reinforced window glass.

The two men parked on the street next to the dark windows of closed storefronts, Bolan driving and James seated in the back. Five minutes ago an Iraqi army patrol had been refused entry into the neighborhood by armed local militia. Shi on Sunni violence was the premier threat in Baghdad, and the militias wielded as much power as the government did on the street.

Bolan and James eyed the checkpoint. Four militia guards armed with AKM assault rifles lounged around a now all too familiar white Nissan pickup parked in the middle of the street. They smoked cigarettes and listened to the truck stereo.

Jazzy, upbeat dance sounds floated across the night and invaded the cab of the taxi where Bolan and James surveyed the first obstacle in their path through rolled-down windows.

"See anyone else?" Bolan asked, sliding a sound suppressor onto the muzzle of his folding stock AK-74. The silencer held twelve baffles, eliminated muzzle-flash, reduced recoil to improve accuracy and could operate on fully-auto mode.

"No, just the four," James replied.

His suppressor already in place, James eased his window the rest of the way down. He held up a small laser range finder no larger than a pack of cigarettes.

"What's it say, seventy yards?" Bolan estimated.

"Seventy-two and change. No breeze."

"All right. I'll start on the far side and walk in. You take the man closest to us then the guy next to him."

"Copy."

Bolan eased back from the driver-side window and leveled the compact weapon in his hands. He welded his cheek to the skeletal buttstock of his weapon and acquired his picture through the telescopic sight. He centered the crosshairs on the Sunni militia gunman farthest from his position.

"Good?" Bolan whispered.

"Good," James answered.

Bolan gently took up the slack in his trigger, pulling slowly and evenly. His man went down, the cigarette tumbling from his slack mouth.

Opening his nonshooting eye, the Executioner acquired the second target, who was backing away from the pickup, his mouth gaping and his eyes on his fallen comrade. The man had an Adam's apple as big as a fist under his scraggly beard, and Bolan put his sights on that in the scope.

He squeezed off his second round and the man dropped to the ground, his throat opening up like a fountain under the 5.45 mm round. Bolan lowered his weapon and took in the scene. No militia sentries remained standing. James had put his targets down with equal skill.

The street was still. There were no outcries, no alarms raised. Bolan shifted his gaze to the roofs, but he saw no movement from that elevation, either.

He slid behind the wheel of the cab, his AKS held in his lap at the ready. Putting the car into drive, he gently accelerated out of his parking spot and rolled down the quiet street to where the four neighborhood guards lay dead and bleeding in the street. He pulled the taxi to a stop by the truck and slid out from behind the wheel. James emerged, as well, his weapon up and providing security while Bolan quickly muscled the four corpses into the back of the pickup along with their weapons.

The Executioner surveyed the street. It was quiet, mostly shops with residences set above or behind them.

The target building had been converted from one of the two-story adobe houses typical to the area and was near the burned-out remains of the Rami Institute. The philanthropic initiative, housed in a converted residence, had been seen as too friendly toward occupation forces and bombed sometime after the ratification of the Iraqi constitution.

The cleric Omar Mahmoud Abdullah did not live in or near his mosque. Not a firebrand speaker, he was an organizer and administrator who worked quietly behind the scenes to advance a Whabbist theology among the Sunni insurgency whose ranks were filled with ex-baathists. He ran a successful pharmacy and had taken Coalition money to fill the medicine orders of the Yarmuk Hospital at times.

As part of his administrative duties Abdullah took cash donations, arranged weapons purchases and traded information and intelligence with the Scimitar captains. The man was instrumental in controlling not only the Yarmuk militias, but also the Sunni elements of the local Iraq police units. It had been his money the Iraq precinct captain, al-Mamoury, had attempted to skim and to regain the man's favor Scimitar had tortured the police officer to death.

Abdullah lived in a large, adobe-walled compound just off Fourth Street in Sector 37, north of central Baghdad, just above the Green Zone. During the day, he operated from his storefront office set next to his residence. At night his dwelling sat at the epicenter of a "no-go" zone for any but a chosen few.

Bolan pulled the taxi to a stop in front of the cleric's residence. He and James sat there in front of the gate, engine idling, windows rolled down. Neither man spoke.

After a moment the gate opened a crack and a bearded bodyguard with an AK-47 stuck his head around through the gap. He uttered something harsh, the only part of it Bolan understood was the name Sheikh Abdullah.

"Huh?" Bolan snapped, his voice raspy.

Irked, the man stepped through the door and swung his left hand at the taxi in a dismissive gesture. He repeated his statement in a louder voice. James shot him from a distance of ten yards directly through the heart.

Bolan was rolling out of the taxi even as the man fell, his AKS-74's stock folded down and held at his side. He pulled on a PVS7-3SELA night-vision goggle headset as he moved toward the front of the taxi. James bailed out of the car on the passenger side, keeping his own weapon down, as well.

The Executioner crossed in front of his taxi, which he left running, quite sure no one on the street would molest a vehicle parked in front of Abdullah's residence. He stepped over the glassy-eyed corpse of the bodyguard and pushed through the gate into the courtyard, his weapon up seeking targets as he scanned the darkened courtyard and windows of the house through his night-vision goggles. Behind him, James dragged the dead bodyguard through the open gate and pulled it shut behind him.

Intel had put Abdullah's bedroom on the left, or west side of the residence where it opened up onto a rooftop patio surrounded by a low concrete wall. A circular staircase ran up from the ground beside the garage to the open-air terrace on the second floor.

"Abdar?" a voice on the veranda asked. "Abdar?"

Bolan looked up, his weapon tracking toward the source of the sound. In the greenish glare of his goggles he saw a man holding an AKM in a casual manner. Bolan swept his silenced AKS-74 into target acquisition and triggered a 3-round burst. The man staggered backward under the impact, then dropped to the ground out of sight behind the terrace wall.

"Let's go," Bolan hissed.

James was already on the move. He rushed past Bolan across the tiled courtyard, skirting a small stone fountain before running up the spiraled staircase attached to the outside of the house.

Bolan danced sideways, following James while covering the front doors and windows of the mud-brick house. As soon as James gained the second story, Bolan charged after him, keeping his knees tight and his steps high to avoid tripping with the reduced depth perception caused by his night-vision goggles.

At the top step he paused and took in the second-story patio. He saw the dead bodyguard, low stone benches and tiles of indeterminate color. A second, much smaller fountain gurgled from a stone basin set in a corner. Across the open space, veranda doors led into Abdullah's house.

Bolan jogged across the rooftop deck, avoiding a small lime tree in a ceramic pot. James crossed to the other side and the two infiltrators vectored in on the door. They took up positions on either side of the danger area. In the parlance of SWAT, doors were known as "vertical coffins" and entry was considered the most dangerous point of any mission. Bolan looked toward James and nodded.

The Phoenix Force commando reached across and grabbed the door handle, turned it and opened it smoothly. He held the door wide as Bolan swept through in a tight crouch, his weapon up. A spacious bedroom spread out in front of him. A fan turned overhead, the floor was mosaic tiles under spaced Persian rugs. A robust man in his midfifties slept in a large, comfortable-looking bed. Bolan easily recognized him as Sheikh Omar Mahmoud Abdullah from the digital printouts provided by the Stony Man support teams. Beside the Scimitar captain a raven-haired woman less than half his age slept deeply, snoring slightly.

Bolan pressed the still warm cylinder of his suppressor against the sleeping cleric's head and leaned down hard, driving the man's head into the mattress and pinning him there.

Abdullah came awake terrified. He began to sputter as he struggled to make out the dark shape crouched above him. Bolan bent and slapped a hand across the man's mouth. Like most Iraqi technocrats or intellectuals, the former baathist turned cleric spoke English.

"Shh," Bolan whispered. "Scream and I shoot. I don't want to frighten your children."

The woman stirred next to Abdullah, restless in her sleep. The cleric went to her, then shifted back to the cyborg-looking night stalker who crouched beside his bed. James shifted at the foot of the bed, and the cleric's eyes moved to him.

"Get up slowly," Bolan instructed quietly. "No one has to get hurt in this house. Not your wife, not your children, not your relatives. It is all on you. If you think you're more important than them, then go ahead and struggle. The blood is on your hands."

Slowly, Abdullah nodded. He gradually lifted himself up off the mattress. Bolan kept his rifle muzzle pressed tight against the man's head. The soldier, like a dance partner, shifted his position smoothly as the cleric's bare feet landed on the floor.

The woman stirred. "Omar?" she asked, her voice loud. "Omar, what is it?"

Bolan cursed. He reached out with his left hand and forced the cleric to his feet by the hair, then threw the man up against his bedroom wall and pinned him there with the AKS-74.

Behind Bolan, James moved like a striking snake. He dropped his grip on the AKS and let it hang from his sling. He leaped forward and grabbed Abdullah's wife and pinned her to the mattress. Without preamble he pulled his Beretta 92-F and pressed it against her temple.

"Tell her to be quiet," Bolan grated. "Tell her now, and you can save her." The cleric seemed frozen with indecision and Bolan jabbed him twice, hard, with his rifle muzzle in the back of the head. "Remember how al-Mamoury died? Remember, Omar? Remember what you did? Tell her to be quiet."

"Hanan," the cleric warned, and he told her to be still.

The woman moaned softly into the bed covers. Her protest was a muted whimper low in her throat as James quickly pinned her hands behind her back with a plastic zip tie and then gagged her.

"Look, Omar," Bolan said. He turned the man around, jerking him by the hair. "You see? We keep our word."

The cleric watched as his bound and gagged wife was slid under his bed. Bolan was sure the man's outrage had to be great to see his wife treated in such a matter in his own home, and at the hands of infidels. Bolan was equally sure the cleric had lost no sleep whatsoever at the fate of al-Mamoury's family.

Bolan yanked a balaclava mask on backward over the sheikh's head, blinding him. Then he bound the man's hands behind his back with plastic ties. He moved to one side while James closed in and grasped the man by his left elbow.

The two big men easily manhandled the cleric out of his bedroom and across the patio to the staircase. Bolan let James lead the man quietly down the curving stairs as he kept watch over the garden. Out in the street beyond the courtyard wall Bolan picked out the sound of his idling taxi. A dog barked in the distance and another one, closer by, answered it.

James led the man off the stairs and into the cool shadows of the courtyard, heading toward the front gate. Bolan jogged down the stairs, his weapon at port arms, and crossed around the fountain to open the gate while James held their prisoner still.

Bolan looked out of the gate, then up and down both sides of the street. At the end of the avenue the Nissan truck was silent. The stereo had stopped playing. Walking out through the gate, Bolan crossed to the taxi and opened the trunk.

"Do it," Bolan said.

James came out of the shadowed gate at a brisk walk, shoving the hooded sheikh ahead of him. As soon as he reached the back of the car, Bolan grabbed the man's head and forced it into the trunk while the ex-SEAL simultaneously pushed the rest of the cleric's body inside the compartment.

Abdullah groaned as his head struck the spare tire in the back, then Bolan slammed the trunk lid closed. The two commandos slid into the running taxi. Bolan put the car in gear and they drove away.

CHAPTER TWENTY-FIVE

The warehouse was an anonymous structure in the middle of an empty field. It sat right under the reinforced air traffic control tower serving Baghdad International Airport, and military patrols passed it several times a day, making it an unappetizing location to headquarter insurgents or foreign jihadists.

In the days of Saddam it had served as a morgue. As such, the gloomy structure had a concrete floor equipped with drains, examination tables, coolers and a dedicated sewage and water system. A rolling door led into a bay where ambulances and hearses had dropped off their cargo of human bodies.

James held open the concertina-wired gate and Bolan drove past him. He hit the garage door opener on his visor, and the bay door rolled open as the Phoenix Force commando jogged across the weed-choked lot after him.

Once they were both inside the morgue Bolan hit the button again and the door rolled shut. Once it closed James hit the lights, illuminating the cavernous room.

The furnishings were industrial, spare and austere. There was nothing inviting or comfortable about the chamber. The lights overhead were naked fluorescent, and they glowed with a stark brightness.

Bolan walked around to the back of the taxi as James went to the wall and pulled an ambulance gurney to him, passing a metal table piled with twenty-pound bags of lye. Bolan popped open the trunk on the taxicab and looked down at Abdullah.

The gurney clacked and clanked as its hard rubber wheels rolled across the uneven floor. Bolan reached into the trunk and pulled the cleric up into a sitting position. Without preamble he snatched the backward balaclava from the man's head and threw it on the ground.

Abdullah's eyes remained tightly shut. His lips moved in frantic recitation as he quoted passages of the Koran in prayer. His hair was rumpled and messy, lying flat against one side of his head in some areas and sticking straight out in others.

"Get out of the trunk."

Bolan steadied the shaking Scimitar captain as he unfolded from the back of the trunk. The man moaned when he saw the straps and tie-downs on the gurney beside James. His knees buckled in fear, and it took both Stony Man operators to force him up onto the gurney.

Despite his terror Abdullah kicked and struggled as they secured him to the hospital gurney. They forced the cleric's wrists and ankles into padded straps and secured them to the gurney frame. Then James buckled a strap across the man's chest and his forehead, locking his twisting head into place.

Bolan walked over to a spigot leading up to a showerhead set in the wall above a floor drain. In the past it had been used to rinse the remains of autopsies clear. A mop and bucket on wheels were resting near the wall next to the shower spigot, the mop was stained pink.

The Executioner took a pair of pliers off an examination table and used them to open the spigot's showerhead all the way. Behind him the cleric tried to follow the American's movements with his eyes. Once the showerhead was open Bolan returned the pliers to the table and hit the record button on a blood-smeared digi-corder Abdullah might have recognized if he hadn't been so frightened. Bolan pointed the camera toward the wall so that the instrument would record nothing but audio from the session.

James reached over and gently tapped Abdullah between the man's widespread eyes. The cleric looked back toward the ex-SEAL, took in the bushy, wild beard and deep black skin. James smiled.

"First, Omar," James said, "I would like to apologize to you for any offence I might have caused with my treatment of your wife, Hanan. It was necessary but regrettable, and I can only hope that your cell, Scimitar, takes the same trouble to ensure that innocents are not needlessly killed during their next operation."

Abdullah stared up at James as the man spoke. All the color had drained from his face. White cobwebs of spittle had gathered at the corners of his mouth. His eyes set into hard slits.

"Fuck you, American."

James smiled again. "That's great. I'm not going to lie. I was hoping you'd be a hardass, I really was. But that brings up a point. Lying. I will not lie to you. I will not," James said, his sincerity obvious. "Everything I say to you while you are strapped down and under my care will be the truth."

"Fuck your truth, I am ready for your torture. God gives me strength, and I will tell you nothing."

"That brings us to another point." James nodded, earnest. "I'm not going to torture you. Nor will I give you drugs. Don't get me wrong, this won't be pleasant if you choose not to cooperate, but it isn't torture. And it sure as hell isn't torture compared to what you did to poor al-Mamoury."

Abdullah opened his mouth to speak, his face twisted with rage. James put one long finger against the man's lips. His eyes met Abdullah's, and the cleric looked away and fell silent.

"No talking," James whispered. "No talking. I've no interest in your ninety-nine virgins martyr bullshit. I've got no interest in your tough guy bullshit. None. If you don't have anything to say about Scimitar, then you don't have anything to say."

James removed his finger and pulled his face away from Abdullah's. He crossed his arms over his wide, powerful chest. His body seemed like a spring, pregnant with potential energy.

"Do you have anything to say about Scimitar?" James asked.

Abdullah shook his head.

"Fine, now you listen. 'Cause remember when I told you I wouldn't lie? Well, now I'm going to tell you how you can get out of this without talking. So listen close, you baby-killing motherfucker. I've got the keys to the kingdom."

James wrapped his hands around the metal rails of the gurney and began to slowly push it to where Bolan stood beside the shower spigot. The Executioner was coolly attaching lengths of heavy-duty, OD-green masking tape to a white cleaning rag.

"There's been a lot of talk in the media about water boarding lately," James said. His voice was conversational, and Abdullah had to strain to hear him over the squeaking of the gurney wheels. The lights overhead flashed in the terrorist's eyes, hurting them with their brightness so that he squinted.

"Calling it torture," James went on, "getting it wrong a lot of the time. It sure isn't two SS goons dunking someone in the barrel." James stopped walking, then looked down. "Wait, I apologize. I shouldn't use the SS in that context with you, should I? Hitler's pretty all right with you, isn't he? I mean, that's what you said in that Egyptian university speech you made about six years ago, wasn't it? Denying the holocaust and all that? Never mind, not important.

"The point, Omar, is that I will not really be drowning you. Here's a secret. You'll be able to breath the whole time, isn't that a kicker? In fact, since your lungs will be higher than your nose and mouth at all times, it is a physical impossibility for you *to* drown. Try to remember that, all right, Omar?"

James halted the gurney and walked around to the side and kicked the support legs positioned directly underneath Abdullah's head. The hinge joint on the legs collapsed and the front half of the gurney folded down. Omar moaned at the sudden lurch, and he came to rest with his feet up in the air.

"You will not drown," James continued. "You *cannot* drown. Remember that, and I'll never break you because I will not hurt you, I promise."

Abdullah's face turned bright red as the blood in his body, driven by gravity and his wildly pounding heart, rushed into his head. He began to struggle as he saw Bolan lean over, his frame blocking the harsh light as he placed the cleaning rag across Abdullah's face. The head strap on the gurney kept the Sheikh locked in place, and Bolan was able to secure the cloth with the strips of tape he had peeled off as James had rolled the cleric over to the shower.

James knelt beside the inverted cleric. His voice was a gentle purr in the terrified man's ears, his lips so close to Abdullah's ear that his breath tickled him with repulsive intimacy.

"It's all an illusion, Omar," James whispered. "The water can't hurt you. But it will feel like you can't breathe. It will feel like you are drowning even though you'll be screaming the whole time, and you can't scream if you can't draw breath into your lungs. You brain is fooled into thinking you're drowning, and it creates feelings of anxiety, of panic in you, but it is an illusion, Omar, you can breathe!"

James stood and nodded at Bolan who turned on the water. Abdullah jumped at the sound of the water rushing out and splashing on the floor. He flinched as it struck his face with a light spray.

"Be a man, Omar. I lasted five minutes when the training school instructors did it to me!" James yelled. "I haven't even used plastic wrap!"

Bolan turned up the pressure and the stream of water,

hardly above a drizzle, splashed onto Abdullah's up-turned face. Immediately the terrorist's gag reflex kicked in and he began to squirm and writhe on the gurney. Bolan, remembering al-Mamoury's heat-blistered skin and the collection of yanked teeth on the metal tray, kept the flow of water straight down on the now sobbing man's face.

"Fight it, Omar!" James yelled. "The panic is a lie! You can breathe! Breathe, damn it!"

Abdullah's muscles stood out in vivid relief along his arms and neck as he fought to break the bonds that held him. He was moaning through clenched teeth and suddenly a spreading stain of yellow leaked across his crotch as his bladder let go.

He moaned, then he choked and gasped, sputtered. Then screamed.

Forty-five seconds later he begged them to release him.

James reached down and yanked the soaked rag off Abdullah's face. The man was crying, tears streaming down his face as he gasped again and again for air.

The Phoenix Force commando grabbed the rail of the gurney and yanked Abdullah's inverted head back to level. Then he kicked out the legs at the rear of the gurney so that the terror monger was lying almost vertical with his head higher than his feet.

The man coughed harshly and sucked in huge breaths of air. James watched him, his face neutral. When Abdullah had recaptured his equilibrium James spoke.

"Now we come to another part of the session that has seen much debate in the news around the world. You said you're ready to talk. Okay. People say you'd tell me any lie, anything I want to hear to just get me to stop. God knows al-Mamoury was ready to at the end, right? And I'm inclined to agree with that viewpoint, as far as it goes."

James stepped in close so that he was nose-to-nose with Abdullah. "If I were torturing you to get you to admit something you'd already done, I wouldn't much believe your confession. Not a little bit. A man will admit to anything to get the interrogation to stop. Ergo, they say, rough tactics, even torture, don't work.

"But here's the thing, Omar. I don't want you to admit to a thing. I'm not doing this to punish you, or for fun. I don't want to convict you of some crime you've already done. I couldn't care less right now. I want some information. I want some names. I want some locations. You'll give them to me because you don't want to take another shower. But what happens after that, Omar? What if you give me the wrong information? What if you do, indeed, lie to me?" James finished in a sudden yell, spittle flying from his mouth and landing in flecks on the helpless Abdullah.

The man sobbed and tried to shake his head "no" against the restraints. "I won't lie. I swear, I won't lie."

"I know you won't, Omar," James whispered. "'Cause your ass is gonna be in a cell right here, Omar. If you lie, then I'll know. Then I'll come back here and we'll take another shower and the whole time I'm gone you're gonna be sitting there knowing that when I get back I'm gonna be pissed and that you're going into the water again and the fear of a thing can be just as bad as the thing itself, right? That's why terrorism works, right? 'Cause of the fear? Right? Right, Omar?" James shouted.

Abdullah began to sob and shake, his eyes welling with tears of terror and helpless rage. James laid a gentle hand on the shaking man's shoulder. He gripped him hard, reassuring the cleric.

"You aren't going to lie to me, are you, Omar?"

"No," Abdullah said.

"Good. Then start talking. Speak loudly so the recorder can hear you, and don't leave anything out."

BOLAN PULLED TWO BEERS out of the ice chest and handed one to James. The Executioner stood in the hall outside the bay, his arms folded across his chest as he watched his comrade drink the cold beer from the six-pack they had brought in the little blue cooler. The ex-SEAL drank half the bottle in the first gulp.

"You feel okay about what happened in there?" Bolan asked.

He knew the answer already, but he was trying to present the Stony Man veteran with an opportunity to vent some of the emotion he had built up. James smiled ruefully down at the top of his beer.

"I feel fine. Stony Man was invented to circumvent the things that prevented America from defending itself. I'm not a spy, but I'm not a regular grunt, either. I have to be able to do it all—jump, dive, shoot, communicate, patch wounds, interrogate. I have to do it all and handle it all. That's why I joined Phoenix Force. I don't buy moral equivalency arguments that say if we're rough, then we're just the same as terrorists. They can go to hell on that, okay? But that's as close as I want to come to crossing the line."

Bolan knocked back his beer. "I hear ya."

The Executioner set down his empty beer and slapped James on the back. "I'm glad you're with me. Why don't you go get the vehicle ready while I clean things up."

James looked at Bolan, then nodded and finished his beer. He turned and walked down the hallway. Outside under a tarp behind the building was their upgraded Chevy Suburban SUV.

Bolan watched him go, then turned and headed back to Abdullah.

Outside James stripped the tarp off the big SUV, unlocked the Suburban and climbed in behind the wheel. He started the vehicle but kept the lights off. Sitting behind the steering wheel, he cinched his night-vision goggles into place.

Once the device was securely in place, he checked the loads on his silenced AKS-74 and pistols. Satisfied, he put the Suburban into gear and slowly drove to the gate at the front of the building, got out to unlock it again. Once that was done he got back into the SUV and waited. He methodically chewed a piece of gum, the muscles of his jaw working.

About five minutes later Bolan came out of the morgue building, the camcorder in his hand.

James gently eased the Suburban out through the open gate with Bolan walking alongside. Once the SUV was outside, Bolan closed and locked the gate before climbing into the Suburban's passenger seat. He opened the glove box and pulled out his night-vision goggles, replacing it with the camcorder.

The Phoenix Force warrior smoothly drove them out into the Baghdad night.

CHAPTER TWENTY-SIX

Rafael Encizo lay in the ICU unit of Ibn Sina hospital in the Baghdad Green Zone. He did not regain consciousness and his condition remained too unstable for transport. Upon return to Camp Slayer, with its strange mixture of private contractors, special operators and regular military personnel, Bolan had downloaded the information from the Abdullah interrogation and sent it on to Stony Man.

Now he, Charlie Mott and Calvin James sat around the kitchen table drinking coffee over ice. Barbara Price was on the sat-com video-conferencer, and events were unfolding rapidly.

"We have a convergence of intelligence," Price said. "All thanks to you guys. I've taken it to the director of National Intelligence and he's given Hal the go-ahead to take the lead on this. Some of this you already know because you were there for Abdullah's interrogation, but it blends with our daily 'outsourced' intelligence feeds. So I'll give it you as seamlessly as I can."

Bolan felt a tingling along the back of his neck as he

drank his coffee. It was coming together now. The pieces of the jigsaw had fallen into place and formed a bull's-eye over the final target. He could feel it with cold certainty.

"Al-Rutbah," Price began, her tone clipped, her manner all precision and business, "is a town of about twenty-five thousand people, in Al Anbar province, near the Jordanian and Syrian borders. It is surrounded by sand and more sand, and sits on the Jordan-Baghdad highway. The nearest military base is Camp KV, or Korean Village, home of the First Marine Division Regimental Combat Team Seven. It was out of the H-3 Airfield, Al-Walid Airbase that Charlie Mott flew the SPIE extraction for you in Amman."

"That place is a camel's asshole," Mott said. "There is nothing there but sand, man and more sand, like Barb said."

"Al-Rutbah is quiet. That section of the highway is quiet. Most Marine patrol activities concentrate on the Syrian border to interdict foreign jihadist entering along the 'Baghdad pipeline' starting in Damascus."

"It's quiet because Scimitar wants it quiet," Bolan said. Abdullah had said as much.

"That's right," Price agreed. "They moved out of Al-Ramadi and down to Al-Rutbah. They own the mayor there, the Iraqi police chief and have heavily infiltrated the Iraqi army border post. The arrangement is simple. The border guards are never attacked, the highway stays open and Iraqi-Jordanian convoys with Scimitar drivers are never stopped. No ones dies, at least in Al-Rutbah, and everyone gets a piece of the pie."

"The final three Scimitar captains are confirmed there?" James asked.

"We know they are," Price said. "Ma Ning-tan's replacement just verified it."

"What?" Bolan sat up.

Price smiled. "Ning-tan was killed for his dissent. Before he dissented he was a CCI operative working out of official cover at the Foreign Affairs Office in Beijing."

"Right," Bolan said.

"So on a hunch we coordinated a surveillance investigation on Ning-tan's replacement to that Foreign Office cover post. We got the face, the name and the rap sheet on one Chao Bao. Turns out Mr. Bao had his own file in the DNI computers, courtesy of our friends at the DIA. He was a former special police commando with the People's Armed Police Special Recon Unit. His loyalty is unquestionable and his training impeccable. He served with distinction during the Sino-Vietnamese conflict in 1979. He made his bones as a leader in the subsequent border skirmishes lasting until 1985."

"They gave him the Scimitar support role Ma Ning-tan objected to?" Bolan asked.

Price nodded and continued. "The NSA had a parabolic mike put on him just to cover our bases when that Foreign Affairs job was handed to him. It paid off. First he attempted to contact Karl Mirjana, with predictable results."

Bolan kept his smile in check. He wasn't given to gloating but he liked it when his actions frustrated his enemies. He caught Calvin James's eye and the two men nodded slightly.

"Then he went himself to the Azerbaijan airport,

though that hornet's nest was too secure for us to get people inside. If we ever need to go there, it'll be a hard target takedown," Price said, shaking her head. "It's completely run by the Armenian mafia. It's like a military airbase. We've brought it to the attention of the UN security counsel."

"Don't hold your breath," James snorted. "Someone in France, Germany or Russia, probably Russia, will be getting paid and it'll drag out debate for decades."

"You seem bitter," Price observed.

James shrugged. "I'm a direct action kind of guy."

"Well, putting aside the airport for now, we still have good news. Mr. Bao is apparently going to Damascus. On top of that, fund transfers show that ten first-class tickets were purchased on a Royal Jordanian Airline's flight into Damascus. The tickets were purchased by an account out of the United Arab Emirates linked to payments made to the late Karl Mirjana."

Despite himself Bolan grinned. "Scimitar," he said.

While he represented the action of Stony Man, along with Phoenix Force and Able Team, the truth was that the bulk of the work done to put the action teams into play was performed behind the scenes by Barbara Price and her cybernetics team. Their capabilities kept the Stony Man trains running on time.

"Scimitar," Price agreed. "Bao is upset by what he terms Western disruption of the project he inherited. He is conducting a colloquium hosted by our friend from Toronto, Aram Hadayet's father, who will provide security and the meet location. All at the estate of Monzer al-Kassar."

"It comes a full circle, back to the Toronto contacts." Bolan grunted.

"Damascus will be our coup de grâce," Price said.

"Good. That's my specialty," Bolan replied.

IT WAS WITH GRIM satisfaction that Bolan considered the operation. Suspicion had led to investigation in Toronto, which had set him following a trail of breadcrumbs and what turned out to be disparate threads within a tangled skein. By yanking on the loose threads of the skein he had collapsed the mess into a single Gordian knot to now be severed cleanly.

His rampage of blood and thunder had caused the principals to look to their networks and henchmen. By coming together to do so, Bolan's actions had drawn his enemies into a trap designed to cut the hydra's heads from its body. Chinese, Syrian and Iraqi, each head would roll.

A day of reckoning was drawing close.

DAMASCUS WAS THE OLDEST continuously populated city in the world. To the east of its cosmopolitan towers of modern steel and glass spread the Syrian Desert, one of the most arid wastelands of the Middle East. It extended over much of northern Saudi Arabia, eastern Jordan, southern Syria, and western Iraq. Largely covered by lava flows, the Syrian desert formed a nearly impenetrable barrier between the populated areas of the Levant—traditionally those countries bordering on the eastern Mediterranean from Turkey to Egypt—and the historical civilizations centered in Iraq and Iran, until modern times. Now several major highways and oil pipelines crossed it, facilitating the flows of commerce and people in the region.

Like all centers of commerce and population, it held the potential to become a source for conflict and war. Under Bolan's grim oversight it would reach its full potential. Here, far from the prying eyes of the international community, Syrian Air Force Intelligence, the barbarous IMJ, had arranged for a secure meeting between elements of a global narcoterrorist network.

Informational and operational security meant isolation and isolation was the key factor the Stony Man team intended to use in overcoming locational physical security. The IMJ safehouse was a hard site, but an isolated one. Isolation could be exploited by speed, aggression and firepower.

As always, Bolan's mind turned to questions of logistics, of fuel and equipment and movement across distance. Amateurs thought in terms of tactics, professionals in terms of logistics. Once Bolan put his sights on a target, that target went down, unquestionably. It was the maneuver into that "sights on" position that required the true skill of the modern warrior.

The Syrian desert would require all of Bolan's skills as a flexible strategist. He pored over satellite images of the operational area fed to Stony Man from the National Reconnaissance Office. There were things those cold columns of numbers and precise, factual language could not tell him however and, as always, time was ticking.

Bolan and James worked quickly in the secured Camp Slayer hangar to transform the Little Bird from its MH-6J troop transport version to the AH-6J assault variant. The benches on either side of the fuselage were removed and weapons pods put into place.

The meet was scheduled to take place at the desert residence of Monzer al-Kassar. The Syrian's finger had been in the Scimitar mess from the beginning. The residence itself had been built to obsessively overlook the billionaire's construction and maintenance concerns on the oil and water pipelines in the remote east Syrian desert on Iraq's border.

In reality the palace compound had served as conveniently remote staging area for heroin coming through Iran and Iraq from Afghanistan and on its way to the Bekka Valley in Lebanon before transfer to Europe and points west. It was a place where tons of raw product could be consolidated from multiple supply sources, then redistributed to take advantage of market supply fluctuations.

As long as the heroin was not sold inside Syria, official interest in Monzer al-Kassar was discouraged. In return, money flowed up the political chain of command and Syrian intelligence could piggyback on one of the largest transglobal criminal networks in the world.

Monzer al-Kassar was continuously guarded by former members of the Russian Spetsnaz-trained Al-Sa'iqa regiment of the elite 14th Special Forces Division. Bolan realized the late Karl Mirjana was to Monzer al-Kassar what a slumlord was to Donald Trump, an American real-estate mogul—both traded in real estate, but they weren't in the same universe. Bolan's trail of bloody bread crumbs had led him several notches up on the food chain.

Mott would fly south from Camp Slayer to Al-Walid

airbase just outside Al-Rutbah and stage from the USMC base there, using JSOC approval codes to facilitate CENTCOM channels. Bolan and James would fly from Baghdad to Amman and on to Damascus where documents, electronics and a vehicle would be provided to them by the intelligence support activities operating out of the U.S. Embassy.

From there the two men would travel overland toward the al-Kassar compound in southeastern Syria. At predetermined GPS coordinates and late in the afternoon, they would take possession of an all-terrain-capable Desert Patrol Vehicle they would operate using night-vision devices.

Their strike on the al-Kassar compound would come in the predawn hours when alertness was at its lowest and would be tightly coordinated with Charlie Mott's attack helicopter. Blood and Thunder would replace Shock and Awe. Surprise and violent aggression would overwhelm superior numbers.

In theory.

USING PETTY CASH from their operational funds, Bolan and James purchased Seville Row suits in the Queen Alia International Airport in Amman, Jordan. Then they got manicures, haircuts and shaved their beards before catching their connecting flights.

Bolan had felt that traveling through open source civilian transportation was risky. The Chinese had his face from Jigsaw Liu's, and they were certainly skilled enough to tie in his meeting with Ma Ning-tan as part of the overall assault on Scimitar. However, he had been fully bearded in Kuwait and fairly unshaved while in

Hong Kong. He hoped the change of clothes and the clean shave would be enough to throw off Chinese assets in Amman.

It was the Chinese connections in Syria that worried him.

But again, as always, he was betting his life against a ticking clock. There was a narrow, minute window available to him by which he could strike off the serpent's heads. If he missed that window, then his chances diminished and his enemy grew more capable of defending against his attacks. The Scimitar captains would return to their dens better prepared and informed. Already one Stony Man team member lay at the brink of death.

Relations with Syria were in a "phase of tentative dance" as Hal Brognola had been told by the Executive Office. Al-Kassar's compound would not be taken out by missiles from across borders in this time of détente. If the hit went down, it went down on the ground in close quarters battle.

If he was going to strike he had to strike now. So Bolan accepted the risks.

While waiting in the airport the two men drank coffee and read English newspapers. After about fifteen minutes an attractive, dusky-skinned brunette approached their table and asked to read the entertainment section of their paper. Bolan gave it to her, and she thanked him and left with her coffee. About five minutes later they finished their own drinks and got up, now in possession of a key to a numbered locker in the airport.

Inside the locker they claimed travel documents that

once again set them up with assumed identities as employees of North American International. They proceeded to their flight, landed in Damascus and passed customs smoothly.

Bolan and James claimed their baggage and made their way to the predetermined parking spot in the multilevel garage attached to the Damascus Airport and carefully inspected their vehicle. It was a Toyota FJ Cruiser, a midsize SUV.

James looked at the green Cruiser, openly skeptical. "I was kind of enjoying the Suburban," he grumbled as he removed the keys from a magnetic box under the bumper. He worked the electric locks on the door. The two men threw their carry-ons into the backseat. James slid behind the wheel while Bolan pulled up the carpet in the passenger-side floor and removed their items, mostly navigational and communications equipment.

While Bolan powered the different devices up and checked channels and connections Calvin James quickly assembled, loaded and checked their only armament, two 9 mm Viper JAWS pistols. The 15-round staggered magazines were filled with Hydroshock JHP tipped bullets.

The Hydroshocks consisted of a lead-lined metal jacket around an expansive outer core that framed a steel inner-core central rod to provide for better expansion on impact. In the hands of skilled pistol marksmen like Bolan and James, a double-tap could literally blow the human skull apart.

"If the car was as good as the ammunition," James said, "I wouldn't be bitching."

"It'll be easier to handle in traffic," Bolan pointed out.

"No, there's a tree-hugger in the Damascus office. I'm sure of it."

"Come on," Bolan said with a grin. "We've got a long way to go and a short time to get there."

"Rafe has payback coming," James said. "I'll get us there on time, don't worry."

CHAPTER TWENTY-SEVEN

The Stony Man commandos took the eastern highway out of Damascus. Traffic thinned as the hour grew later and the distance increased from built-up urban areas. The kilometers clicked by with punctual regularity and the two men kept to their time schedule.

Southeast of the city of As-Suwayada they stopped beside the highway to switch places, with Bolan taking the wheel. A massive white pipeline ran above the ground, set over the desert floor on steel triangle supports as thick as a man's leg.

Sand dunes, broken by hard scrabble narrow canyons forming wadis by seasonal flashfloods, swept by them, the landscape blending into itself as they rolled down the long black ribbon of highway. Once they passed a knot of Bedouins standing beside the road with the halters to their camels in their hands. Without thinking Bolan clicked his high beams to low to avoid blinding the desert nomads. They swept past the tiny caravan and continued hurtling through the night. Bolan clicked his high beams back on.

Once they passed a Syrian police sedan traveling in the other direction. It was tense for a moment, but the cop car never turned in pursuit. About 1:00 a.m. the wind picked up and sand began to spill in loose swatches across the tarmac. The hard rubber tires crunched as they rolled over the sand.

At 3:36 a.m. Calvin James looked at his GPS unit and inspected the map.

"All right, Mack," he said. "It's a one mile mark from…now."

"No problem," Bolan acknowledged, eyeing his odometer on the dash and slowing the vehicle slightly.

James began to secure the various piece of communications gear and navigational equipment. He reached down and eased the safety off his Viper pistol. He let the weapon rest in his lap and handed Bolan the AN/PVS-7 from underneath his seat, turning it on.

Bolan slid the night-vision goggles over his head and clicked the Cruiser's headlights off. Night swallowed the racing vehicle.

James slid his own NVD onto his head and adjusted the straps, securing it firmly into place. He clicked a switch and the desert night came into view, the green-tinged illumination giving the whole tableau an otherworldly feel.

Sixty-five seconds later Bolan began to apply the brakes on the vehicle and the ruins of a sandstone-and-mortar building appeared. He guided the Cruiser off the isolated stretch of highway.

Grit and sand scratched across the window, driven by the desert wind. The ruins were thick with shadows. A door frame was set into a crumbling wall and rubble was strewed everywhere. Two windows, like the eye sockets of a skull, showed darkly and the roof had collapsed ages ago.

Bolan eased the FJ Cruiser across the hard scrabble desert floor around toward the back of the ruins. The wind had driven sand against the rear of the building, trapping it against the structure until it had piled up to several feet. A couple of hardy Syrian bean capers, a common weed standing three feet tall, had taken root. Their thick, fleshy leaves spread out in overlapping patterns in the glow of the AN/PVS-7.

Once the compact SUV was out of sight, Bolan brought it to a stop. The two men left their windows up, but cracked their doors open. The 9 mm Viper pistols filled their hands as they surveyed the topography surrounding the ruined building. The wind whistled sharply as soon as the SUV doors opened and the force of its gust pulled at their hands like kites.

Behind the ruins the desert ran for about fifty yards before a line of low hills rose up like broken teeth. A pressure valve and flow meter station set adjacent to the pipeline occupied a square cage of chain-link fence between the two low hills directly behind the ruins.

"You ready?" Bolan asked quietly.

"Absolutely," James answered.

Both men swung their doors open. Bolan had disabled the dome light earlier on the drive down. The desert wind blew into the cab as soon as the doors swung open, and both men felt the sharp grit of sand strike their faces beneath the NVDs.

They exited the vehicle and slowly scanned the desert as the engine idled. Bolan felt the back of his neck crawl with the strange sensation of being watched. Someone was out there, he was sure of it. All that remained to be seen was if it was their contact—or an ambush.

"No more games, pal," Bolan said loudly. "We're here. Either shoot or speak up, but quit jacking me off."

"Don't get your panties in a twist," a voice with a Southern drawl answered from out of the dark.

Bolan shifted slightly. The voice had come from near the oil pipe maintenance station. As James moved toward the rear of the SUV, the Executioner stepped out from the cover of his open door and slid the Viper pistol home in its sling under his left arm.

"Don't worry about my panties," Bolan called back. "You got something for me or not?"

"Parole?" the voice demanded.

"Eleven September," Bolan answered.

"Rolling Proposal," the voice answered in turn.

The man stepped out from the shadow of the oil pipeline behind the hillock. Whatever Bolan had been expecting, this wasn't it. In the AN/PVS-7 the contact looked as wide as he was tall, about six feet in all dimensions.

"Going dark," Bolan warned Calvin James.

"Roger, I got you covered," the ex-SEAL replied.

Bolan reached up and took the NVDs off his head. The contact stepped even closer, his hands held out in an open position. The man's girth was amazing, and Bolan put his weight at more than three hundred pounds. He wore a short-sleeved shirt over tan cargo pant shorts and leather sandals.

Bolan's eyes, already dilated from wearing the low-light goggles, quickly adjusted to the dark. The man was built like a bear, fat but strong-looking with no neck to speak of and wide shoulders over extremely thick arms. As he came closer, Bolan saw that the guy was bald as a billiard ball and sported a thick blond Fu Manchu mustache.

"Oh, you really blend in," Bolan noted dryly.

"Screw you," the man said, his Southern twang like a steel guitar. "I'm the rude American. That's my cover. Works pretty well, too."

"In Syria?"

"In Syria, in the PI's, in fucking Tehran. Those little shits don't bother me. I've been shot so many times the bullets bounce off my bullets." He clapped his arm. The sound was like a grizzly slapping a tree trunk.

"Good to know."

"I was told you'd be wearing a regular Ayatollah beard."

"Plans change," Bolan said.

The bear of a man sighed. "Tell me about it."

"I didn't mean our plan," Bolan said. "Is there something wrong?"

"Wrong?" The man snorted. "Try driving a dune buggy over an hour's worth of desert with hemorrhoids."

"Personal problem. Thanks for sharing."

The man stood in front of Bolan and met him eye to eye, his girth almost twice that of the Executioner. He stared Bolan hard in the eye. The soldier stared back, liking the man despite himself.

The contact broke into a grin. "No time for games, then. You'll be wanting these?"

He held up a pair a key fobs. "Just push the start to hop the engine, this one releases the Semtex on the gas tank."

"Good to know," Bolan said.

As he took the fob, Bolan saw the tattoo on the inside of the man's enormous forearm. It was a modified version of the USMC Globe, Eagle and Anchor emblem. Instead of a globe the cutout's tattoo had a grinning skull.

"Keys are in it," Bolan said, jerking his head back toward the running FJ Cruiser.

"They gave you an ugly little piece of shit, didn't they?" The man grunted.

James spoke up from the edge of the vehicle. "*That's* what I said." He paused. "Get's a hell of a lot better mileage than a Suburban," he allowed.

"You armed? You need one of our pistols?" Bolan asked.

The man shook his head and stepped around Bolan to slide into the Toyota SUV. The vehicle rocked over on its frame as he got behind the wheel. The suspension actually groaned in protest.

"No, thanks," he said. "If one of these little idiots pulls me over, I'll whip out my dick and beat 'em to death with it."

James walked up and stood beside Bolan. "I like this guy," he said. "He's like a walking macho cliché, a real PC nightmare."

"PC's for people behind desks," the man answered. "Trigger pullers don't play that shit."

"Take it easy," Bolan told the man.

The man looked up at him and smiled for the first

time. "I set you boys up with some bang for your buck, so you give 'em hell for me."

"We'll work hard," Bolan said, carefully noncommittal.

The contact slammed the car door and carefully eased the SUV out onto the East Syrian Highway. The vehicle sped away and the lights clicked on about a quarter mile down the road.

Back behind the ruins of the adobe brick house Bolan slid his NVDs back on before turning to Calvin James.

"Let's go see what Satan Claus left us," he said.

IT WAS A LETHAL beauty.

Once they walked around the hill they found the Desert Patrol Vehicle sitting in the dark, its black frame hidden beneath camouflage netting just on the far side of the oil pipeline. Bolan hit the button on the fob and disengaged the charges placed on the fuel tank. Wasting no time the two commandos then pulled back the covering and began to assess what they had been given.

Formally known as the Fast Attack Vehicle, the new Chenowth Racing Products Desert Patrol Vehicle utilized a 4-stroke, V8 engine that could propel the weaponized dune buggy across rough terrain at incredible speeds.

"I wanna drive," James said.

"They made it for the SEALs first," Bolan laughed.

"Damn right," James said, his hand trailing on the strong, lightweight frame.

The two men quickly got down to business. From a metal box in the back they removed M-4 carbines, one of which was outfitted with an M-203 grenade launcher.

James loaded a fragmentation grenade into the M-203 and stood sentry while Bolan quickly stripped out of his suit and slid into the dark olive nomex flight suit provided in the vehicle equipment. The flight suit would serve to better guard against sand infiltration than a regular uniform. Over these Bolan laced up black canvas, jungle-issue combat boots.

When he was finished, he took up his M-4 and stood guard as James repeated the process. Once both men were outfitted they inspected the DPV's dedicated weapon systems, which included a brace of M-134 AT-4 anti-tank weapons, an M-60 machine-gun on the driver's side, a Mk 19 automatic grenade launcher on the passenger side and the new XM-312 .50-caliber heavy machine-gun, whose barrel was secured in the down position for the journey. Once the weapons check was completed the two men climbed into the three-passenger vehicle. James hit the ignition and the vehicle purred to life.

Bolan shot his failsafe azimuth, then plugged coordinates into his GPS system. He tapped James on the shoulder and pointed out a course paralleling the pipeline. The hard rubber tires bit deep into the sand and thrust the sleek vehicle forward.

Driving entirely through the use of their night-vision goggles the Americans slid off into the Syrian desert and headed toward their prey.

JAMES PUSHED the DVP hard, and it ate up the miles like a greyhound racer. The ride was rough, even with the improved suspension and they were dealing constantly with sand cutting into their exposed flesh, but the time they made was phenomenal.

As the first hint of light creased the horizon, they crested the final rise in the desert. Monzer al-Kassar's desert estate spread out in front of them in the uncertain light of their NVDs, set five miles off the main eastern highway behind a sharp defilade of shale stone and sand.

Bolan picked up the handset for his base unit, a PRC-117F. The communication kit interfaced easily with the Single Channel Ground and Airborne Radio System, or SINCGARS, outfitted with a VINSON device for security, and operating in the VHF-FM, 30-88 megahertz range. The VINSON devices utilized by Stony Man had been modified by Aaron Kurtzman to be symbiotic encryption units. Code generated by the sending unit was specific and random to only those VINSON, not generic.

"Element Dawn, this is Dark Horse. Over."

"Dark Horse, this is Element Dawn," Charlie Mott answered.

"We're at the gate," Bolan said. "We have overflight confirmation?"

"Affirmative," Mott answered. "Ground vehicles ID match. The money is in the account, Dark Horse."

"Roger, T-time two mikes. Over."

"Roger. Two mikes," Mott repeated. "You'll see me. Element Dawn, out."

"Dark Horse, out."

Bolan secured the handset into its cradle. He looked down the long slope of the desert hill toward the compound of Monzer al-Kassar. An hour ago an MQ-9 Reaper, a larger more capable improvement on the older RQ-1 Predator, Unmanned Ariel System, had come on scene.

After making a reconnaissance overflight, its camera had confirmed the make and license plates of vehicles used by Chao Bao, the Chinese operative, the three remaining Scimitar captains, Monzer al-Kassar and the Syrian intelligence officer. The money had been deposited in the account.

The Reaper UAS then powered up to a holding pattern at its fifteen kilometer ceiling.

Bolan looked at the sprawling, walled compound and began to prep his SOFLAM, Special Operations Forces Laser Marker. The handheld laser target designator Bolan operated would put the two, five-hundred-pound, laser-guided bombs carried by the Reaper directly on the al-Kassar palace.

The compound was lavish and the contrast it held to the stark and remote desolation of the Syrian desert only emphasized the ostentatious display of wealth. The main house was a four-story palace with all the hallmarks of traditional Arabic architecture. It held spires, arched windows, open courtyards with fountains and rooftop patios. Lights set just below the water's surface illuminated three separate swimming pools.

The landscaping around the main house gave the oasis a tropical feel, with palm trees and thick shrubs marking gardens of date trees. Both the driveway and paved footpaths connected the palace to guest houses, stables, tennis courts, private mosque and a helicopter landing pad. One side of the compound had been dedicated to a short runway capable of hosting small jets.

The palace complex, surrounded by a ten-foot-high, adobe-brick wall, was not just a residence. In addition to the runway and helipad there was a line of large warehouses set against the east wall beyond the landing strip, which intelligence had shown doubled as a shooting range. One of the guest houses was believed to serve as a fully functional clinic.

Servants quarters divided the palace from the industrial areas where semi-trailers were parked next to garages with service bays designed to accommodate aircraft and ground vehicles. It was rumored that air traffic controllers from the Syrian air force served three-month tours at the desert compound, and that it was a launching point for air force reconnaissance helicopters to monitor U.S. troop movements along the Iraqi border.

Nothing as obvious as gun towers lined the walls, but al-Kassar's bodyguards were vigilant and a small gate in the rear, on the northern side of the compound, was used for mounted patrols in customized black Hummers to conduct security sweeps of the desert outside the perimeter walls. Bolan could see two armored vehicles on opposite sides of the flatland below his position, now trundling slowly through the desert like giant, wheeled cockroaches.

Foreign jihadists from geographic locations as diverse as Chechnya and Punjab used the al-Kassar compound as a staging area for Iraq border infiltrations, just as Scimitar mules carried Afghanistan heroin *into* it. The al-Kassar compound was a fully functional, enemy Forward Operating Base in the war against narcoterror.

When the Scimitar connection had been presented to the director of National Intelligence and the Oval Office, it had served as a proverbial straw against the infamous compound. Bolan had been given the resources necessary to take out the militarized compound.

Syria had proved to be a fickle and unreliable partner in both the Iraq conflict and the larger war on terror.

On one hand Syria had been vigilant about American and European security inside the country. They had provided some intelligence on al Qaeda operations while protecting Hezbollah and Palestinian terror groups. The government had held suspects and interrogated prisoners on behalf of American interests, and they had been well rewarded for doing so.

At the same time the right hand helped, the left hand of the Syrian government stabbed with a poisoned dagger. Syria funneled foreign fighters, weapons, technologically advanced equipment, money and logistical supplies into Iraq in concert with Iran, doing much to help destabilize an already volatile situation.

With the heroin connection now starkly illuminated, Washington, D.C., had decided to emphasize to Syria that it could no longer play the "left hand nice, right hand bad" game of diplomacy, or more precisely, D.C. sought to emphasize that it, too, could play that particular game. Bolan had been given special authority through Hal Brognola to piggyback on JSOC capabilities.

He would be given what he needed to take out the al-Kassar compound while no official United States military or intelligence personnel would violate Syrian soil. Later there would be an apology for the strike, and it would be explained away as an "accidental" overshoot by B-52 bombers conducting operations along the Iraq border. It was a ridiculous cover story, designed to be blatantly so to send the message.

It allowed the Syrian and American governments to continue the pretense of normalized relations behind a wall of plausible deniability while a powerful message would be sent to the government in Damascus through back channels.

In addition, the death of a Chinese agent hosted by a Syrian narcoterrorist was a diplomatic free shot. The agent would be killed, Beijing would know why he'd been eliminated and would be unable to officially acknowledge the loss or risk having to explain what a Chinese official with a known special operations background was doing in Syria that close to the Iraq border in the company of drug smugglers.

Once again Mack Bolan had found himself at the tip of the spear.

CHAPTER TWENTY-EIGHT

Bolan intended to drop two, five-hundred-pound bombs on al-Kassar's palatial compound. He activated his SOFLAM and "painted" the main house with his laser pointer while beside him James spoke the activation code into the PRC-117F radio, alerting Mott in his Little Bird and the UAS operator in Camp KV, Iraq.

While Bolan held the SOFLAM steady, James climbed out of the front seat where he'd sat behind the Mk 48 light machine-gun, and into position behind the driver's seat where he unlimbered the XM-312 .50-caliber machine-gun. He racked the charging handle and seated a bullet in the chamber.

Adrenaline began to leak into his system as he waited for the bombs to fall. The carry racks on the sides of the DPV had been filled with light arms, grenades and rocket launchers. Each commando was outfitted with a lethal personal arsenal in addition to the weapons systems indigenous to the DPV. After the action started in the compound the weapons would be disposable with reloading being replaced in the initial strike by new weapons.

The place housed foreign jihadists, intelligence agents and elite bodyguard troops as well as some official Syrian military personnel. With the odds so heavily stacked against them, the ex-SEAL knew the Stony Man kill box could quickly become a deathtrap for the would-be ambushers.

Up in the desert stratosphere he saw a streak of fire then a second one. He forced himself to look away from the rain of descending death and to focus in on the two black, hard-shell Hummers patrolling the ground between their position and the back gate of the al-Kassar palace compound. They would be his first target once the hellfire began.

There was a screaming whistle out of the night and a sound like an airplane flying low. The twin GBU-12 bombs landed like the fists of angry gods. The explosions shattered the upper stories of the palace in twin balls of fiery retribution. The top floor disintegrated under the impact, and flames blew out the windows and doors on the bottom floors. The concussive force of the blast uprooted trees and bushes in the various yards and gardens. The third and fourth stories of the palace collapsed inward, and the structure raged into a screaming inferno.

"Jesus, *yes,*" James whispered, his satisfaction a bloody grim emotion in his gut.

The Reaper UAS began to circle down in altitude. Its camera rolled feeds that ran back through an AWACS bounce in the Atlantic to a room in the Pentagon, and Stony Man Farm where Hal Brognola and Barbara Price watched the unfolding action along with the Stony Man cybernetics team.

In the front of the DPV Bolan hurriedly secured the SOFLAM laser designator and slid across the seats and behind the steering wheel.

Out on the edge of the flames Charlie Mott's AH-J6 Little Bird swept into view. Bolan gunned the dune buggy and it sprang forward and raced down the hill, tearing into the dry, hard turf and spraying gravel wildly. He felt the rear end start to slide and he steered into it so that the fast attack vehicle straightened itself out and shot forward like a bullet from a gun.

Out ahead of them each of the exterior-mounted patrols in the hard-shell Hummers skidded to a stop at the sudden explosion. Top hatches sprang open, and gunners took up positions behind the swivel-mounted M-60D machine-guns. Neither Syrian had seen the approaching DPV and they kept their faces pointed toward the burning palace compound.

Blacked out and running hard, the DPV swept down on them like a cheetah cutting a weak animal out from the herd. One of the turret gunners suddenly shouted and pointed. From behind the wheel of the DPV Bolan saw the vehicle sentry gesture and followed the line of his pointing arm. The man had seen the helicopter.

"Take them!" Bolan shouted over the DPV's screaming engine. "They've spotted Charlie!"

James's .50 caliber XM-312 machine-gun had a maximum effective range almost twice that of the M-60D, and he ruthlessly exploited his superior firepower.

Above the compound the helicopter turned in the air, rotating like the gun turret of a tank. The 2.75-inch rockets from the twin, 7-tube launchers lit up like fireworks, and began striking the compound in streaks. Mott moved in a methodical sweep from left to right.

As he pivoted his fire, placing rocket after rocket on target, he took out grounded aircraft, parked vehicles and the guest houses running along the short runway. The effect was catastrophic.

Sitting helplessly on the pad a fourteen-passenger Sikorsky S-76 Spirit went up as Mott put a rocket in its fuel tank. The helicopter leaped into the air as fire mushroomed out and cast burning debris across the eastern half of the compound.

The nose of a Rockwell International Sabreliner 65 jet stuck out from the open doors of a Quonset hut-style hangar. Mott put a rocket through the sleek, jet-black windows and into the cockpit. The explosion was contained by the hangar, but the open doors served like a chimney and black smoke, clearly visible in the light of the raging fires, roiled out. Mott turned the Little Bird on a dime, smoothly swinging the tail around so that he faced the closest guest house. Lights had clicked on in the structure as al-Kassar's "guests" and employees scrambled to respond to the raid.

A rocket blasted through an upstairs window, knocking down interior walls and setting the house on fire.

Behind him, beyond the wall and out in the desert, patrolmen in a black Hummer twisted their M-60D machine-guns into play and drew down on the hovering death machine. Orange flames licked from the machine-gun muzzles, lead flying in earnest toward the little attack helicopter.

From behind Bolan, James opened up with the XM-312. The lightweight, heavy machine-gun had been pressed into service to replace the military's aging inventory of M-2s. With advanced muzzle brakes and chambering action, the recoil and weight of the XM-312 had greatly improved on the old M2, while maintaining a respectable rate of fire at just over 400 rounds per minute. The heavy sound of a .50-caliber weapon firing remained a powerful psychological weapon in its own right.

In his driver's seat Bolan felt the recoil through the frame of the dune buggy though it did nothing to slow the vehicle. He saw red tracers burn like laser bolts across his NVD goggles and arc out across the distance before falling on target.

The .50-caliber rounds tore into the first Hummer. The vehicle soaked up the rounds like a sponge. Out in the desert red tracer fire burrowed into the hard-shell Hummer, some rounds skipping off at wild angles, others disappearing into the vehicle's cab.

The top gunner fired his weapon hard, the muzzle-blast taking a star-shaped burst pattern in Bolan's goggles. He saw the man suddenly convulse and heave forward only to bounce off his weapon. A red-hot tracer round burned into the gunner's back and out his front where it bounced wildly off the roof. One moment the gunner had a right arm and in the next moment it was gone. The man slumped across the hood with wounds large enough to be seen even across the distance and in the uncertain light.

Bolan saw concentrated tracer fire slip through the side of the Hummer, and after a moment the racing vehicle suddenly veered off sharply to the right. It drifted for several dozen yards across the broken ground, then its front end hit a narrow wadi crevice and buried its nose in the far bank.

On the other Hummer the topside gunner's head snapped to the side to follow the sudden erratic path of its fellow patrol vehicle. He saw the wild red tracer fire and he swiveled, searching for the source of the incoming rounds.

Beyond the M-60 gunner Bolan could see Mott's chopper continuing its rampage. Vehicles exploded as semi-tractors, limousines and all-terrain vehicles were struck with equal enthusiasm.

By the time the rocket fusillade had finished, multiple bonfires of burning vehicles and structures raged across the compound, all of them minuscule in comparison to the blazing inferno of the main palace. Despite the heavy damage wrought on the majority of buildings, personnel scrambled around the compound, most wielding weapons of one sort or another.

Mott's last rocket went through the front door of the guest house farthest from the palace. It punched through the door like a breeze tossing paper and detonated inside, decimating the building.

Without hesitation Mott switched over to his M-134 7.62 mm miniguns. The electrically powered chain guns whirred to life and a cascade of machine-gun bullets began to douse the compound, tearing into buildings and knots of struggling narcoterrorists.

The machine-gun bursts struck the figures like chainsaw blades, hacking them to pieces and splashing guts and body parts around in sloppy, senseless patterns. As he fired, Mott worked the helicopter, drifting out toward the edge of his effective range to avoid any intensity of return fire likely to bring his lightly armored helicopter down.

Bolan cut the DPV hard, running up off the desert and onto a track used by the al-Kassar Hummers. The front wheel of the fast-attack buggy struck a head-size boulder in the dark and the steering wheel lurched hard in Bolan's grip.

The vehicle frame shuddered under the impact and the wheel shot into the air, tipping the racing DPV onto one side. Bolan turned the wheel hard and straightened out the buggy, throwing his weight hard to his right to keep the low-slung vehicle stable.

Tracer rounds cut across his front, and he realized they'd finally sped into the range of the Hummer's M-60D. Above him Calvin James cut loose with the XM-312 .50. Bolan worked his brakes and slid into position onto the track, now racing toward the back gate of the al-Kassar palace compound, several football fields away.

Once on the dirt track Bolan took his right hand off the steering wheel and grabbed the M-60 mounted in front of him. He freed it in its mounts and swiveled it around to engage the second Hummer.

The turret gunner leaned low over his weapon, and the Hummer turned in a tight half circle, spraying loose gravel like surf as the driver tried to meet the new threat of the DPV head-on.

A bullet sparked off the front of Bolan's vehicle and his finger found the trigger of the M-60. The weapon roared to life and rocked in his one-handed grip, straining against the vehicle-secured mounts.

Red tracer rounds from James's XM-312 tore into the engine hood and then windshield of the Hummer as the Phoenix Force commando walked his fire up toward the Syrian machine-gunner. Bolan followed his partner's lead, spraying a long, ragged burst in a tight Z-pattern to keep his rounds bouncing inside the Hummer's cab.

James found his target. The M-60D exploded into pieces as the .50-caliber slugs buzzed into it, shattering it beyond recognition in the blink of an eye. Half a second later the machine-gunner was vaporized above the sternum, reduced and shredded into bloody spray.

Bolan hit the brakes and cranked his steering wheel hard to slow his momentum. The DVP went into a power slide and stopped abruptly as the rudderless Hummer drifted off into the desert before petering out to a stop one hundred yards away. A wave of dust rolled over them as the DPV screeched to a full halt.

Working with efficient speed and ignoring the piping-hot barrel of the XM-312, James secured the weapon and dropped down into the passenger seat behind the automatic grenade launcher.

As soon as the Phoenix Force commando was in place, Bolan punched the throttle again. Both men were pushed hard back into their seats by the force of the acceleration. The engine revved to a full-throated scream as Bolan roared toward the back gate of the palatial compound.

Ahead of them flames climbed high into the air, and, sitting amid the blank dark of the vast Syrian desert, it seemed as if the chimneys of hell had been opened. Something exploded and a burning, unidentifiable mass shot into the air. Bolan saw tracer fire pouring toward a section of the compound he knew was the fuel reserve farm area. Mott's minigun burst seemed to go on forever, then there was a whump as the reserve fuel tanks for automobiles, aircraft and semi-tractors began to blow in succession like falling dominos. Jet fuel shot 150 feet into the sky.

The exploding fuel farm illuminated the area like a noonday sun and as the Stony Man hit team drew closer their NVDs were overworked by the brilliant light. Almost in tandem James and Bolan stripped off their AN/PVS-7s and tossed them into the seat behind them.

"Element Dawn to Dark Horse," Mott said, his voice alive with the energy of his adrenaline charge.

"Go ahead, Dawn," Bolan answered.

"Copy, alpha phase completed. I'm going to rise to observation platform as my miniguns are low. All first-strike targets engaged. All first-strike targets engaged. Element Dawn, out."

"Good job. Dark Horse, out," Bolan said.

The back gate to the compound loomed. It was a solid structure of heavy wood and wrought iron. James grasped the dual spade grips of the 40 mm grenade launcher and centered the weapon on the gate.

He fired an exploratory shell from the 32-round magazine, which arced out over the desert and exploded into the dirt at the front of the gate, raining dirt into the air like lava from a volcano.

James lifted the vented muzzle on the Mk 19 and began to fire in earnest, putting the rounds dead-center on his target and blowing the gate into flaming splinters. Each explosion showed as a flash of burning light spilling around clouds of dark smoke, then the gate was gone and Bolan could see clearly into the interior of the al-Kassar compound.

"Dark Horse, this is Element Dawn." Mott's voice broke over the earjacks in the two Stony Man operator's helmets.

"Go ahead, Dawn," Bolan answered.

"Inside the gate to your nine o'clock you have a response team orientated toward your position. I see long weapons and a RPG-7."

"Roger. Dark Horse, out," Bolan said.

He wrenched the wheel of the speeding DPV to the side, looped out wide to the right and then brought the nose grille back around toward the gate. Now instead of breaching the threshold straight-on through the smoking ruin of the gate, Bolan would guide the DPV through the breach at a diagonal line heading from outside right to inside left.

This would have the effect of orientating the weapons of the DPV straight onto the knot of defenders pointed out by the Mott's observation platform. Bolan fought the bouncing vehicle back under control, then took up the pistol grip of the M-60 machine-gun. Beside him James adjusted his grip on the dual spade handles of the grenade launcher.

The Desert Patrol Vehicle ate up the ground, clawing its way forward and spewing twin rooster tails of dirt out behind it. Bolan gunned the vehicle over a slight, rocky berm and muscled the dune buggy into position. The angles lined up and a trajectory window appeared, which Calvin James immediately exploited.

The launcher coughed a staccato pattern of high-explosive death. The weapon cycled with brute economy, throwing 40 mm shells downrange with devastating effect. The relatively slow-moving projectiles shot out in front of the speeding DPV and landed hard. The explosions provided deadly, unforgiving cover as the Executioner crossed into the al-Kassar compound.

Hell had come riding into Syria and Death rode beside him.

CHAPTER TWENTY-NINE

Bolan could just make out the knot of armed figures in the light of the burning fires. Smoke hung as thick as London fog between the walls of the palace compound and obscured the area from the sky. Both Charlie Mott and the camera eye of the Reaper UAS could only make out the unfolding action in random, patchy glimpses.

Shouting his alert to James, Bolan triggered the M-60 machine-gun set in front of him. The heavy, 7.62 mm slugs lanced out and sliced into the knot of confused gunners on flat, smooth rails of flight.

The first bullet struck the lead gunman low in the stomach, striking with the force of a baseball bat and penetrating the soft flesh and viscera without slowing. The man folded like a lawn chair, gasping at the sudden agony and a wave of bullets tore his screaming face from his body.

James turned the Mk 19 on its axis and lobbed two rounds at the group of fighters Bolan was engaging with his M-60.

Bolan's fire scythed into the formation, cutting them

off at the legs on one sweep of a Z-pattern burst then finishing them with the second pass. Two grenades slammed into their midst and exploded, tossing bodies into the air like parade confetti. Bolan gunned the patrol vehicle forward, skirting a low, ornate iron fence running around an Olympic-size swimming pool.

The soldier saw a line of burning two-story houses running between the palace and airstrip. He looked overhead but couldn't see where Mott was. He made to initiate radio contact but was suddenly taken under fire.

A stream of bullets cut toward him from a concrete pool house just behind him. The rounds struck the back of the Desert Patrol Vehicle and hacked apart equipment boxes. The bullets ricocheted wildly and cut the air immediately between the two men.

"Christ!" James shouted.

Instinctively Bolan started to cut to his right and face the attack but realized just as quickly that such a maneuver would leave James open to fire from that side and unable to use the grenade launcher as it was currently mounted.

Bolan slammed on the brakes, leaving the rear of the DPV orientated toward the pool house as more rounds burned around him. He bailed out of the vehicle, snatching up his M-4/M-203. James threw himself sideways across the seats to avoid the angle of fire, and green tracer rounds tore apart the steering wheel inches from his head.

Bolan rolled out of the DPV and hit the ground on his belly. He lifted up and looked for a target over the knobby rear wheel of the military dune buggy. Instantly bullets blew by him on all sides. He felt a slap and a sting on his right shoulder and something punched him in the head above his ear.

Hot blood poured down the side of his face and filled the sleeve of his uniform blouse. He ducked, his cheek resting on the dirty tread of the thick off-road tire at the back of the DPV, feeling the rough impact as more bullets slammed into the solid rubber. He brought his M-4/M-203 around the corner of the thick tire and angled its fire by estimation.

His finger found the metal trigger behind the shotgun breech of the attached grenade launcher and pulled it. The weapon recoiled in his hands with the solid, blue-collar kick of a 12-gauge shotgun. He heard the round land and explode, and he risked a peek around the tire. Earth fell in an avalanche along with pieces of a deck chair, about four feet in front of the gunman's position behind the concrete-block pool house.

Bolan threw his carbine's collapsible stock to his shoulder and began pouring fire around the building, keeping the rifleman pinned down. His bullets knocked chunks off the pool house and skipped across the deck encircling the pool. The carefully tended lawn began to burn.

"Get the 312 up!" Bolan shouted.

James scrambled over the bullet-ripped DPV seats and brought the XM-312 .50 online. The black bungee tie-down shot out of the DPV like a rubber band and landed on the ground yards away. James turned the machine-gun in a tight traverse and unloaded on the pool house.

Across fifty yards the .50-caliber gun blew the concrete block and rebar structure into dust. The rounds smacked hard into the building, punching through the walls without slowing and baseball-size chunks of mortar disintegrated, leaving gaping holes throughout the structure. Bolan saw a figure, shirtless and barefoot, wearing only pants, spin wildly out from the pool maintenance shed.

The man was tossed bleeding into the pool where he hung suspended in the water, floating facedown and turning the chlorinated blue darkly scarlet. Bolan rose swiftly and spoke into his throat mike.

"Dawn, this is Dark Horse," he said. "You have our twenty?"

"Roger. I have you by the pool but observation is spotty," Mott replied. "You want extraction? It's a hornet's nest."

"Negative, Horse Two and I will do target site assessment, prior to extraction."

"Roger, I'll try to cover your back when you go in, but the smoke is bad."

"Understood. Out," Bolan finished.

James dropped out of the DPV and began quickly arming himself from several of the light weapons secured around the frame of the dune buggy. In addition to his M-4 he grabbed a folding-stock Remington 870 pump-action shotgun, a Glock 18 pistol capable of 3-round bursts and a 10 mm Glock 17, as well as the grenades, knives and equipment already secured to his web belt.

"Let's go make sure no one missed the party," Bolan said.

James nodded as he pulled a timing pencil detonator from his uniform shirt's chest pocket, activated it and then squatted by the DPV gas tanks. He reached under and inserted the pencil into the plastique charge shaped along the seam, rearming it after the long drive across the Syrian desert.

"Let's go," he said.

THEY CUT ACROSS A STRIP of manicured lawn separating the rear pool complex from the patios and steps at the back of the now collapsed and burning palace. It was becoming immediately clear as they navigated the palace grounds that NSA intelligence had been dramatically incorrect about the number of enemy combatants contained in the compound.

After the overwhelming force and violence of the initial strike, resistance should have been sporadic and uncoordinated. Command and communications centers, staging areas and arsenals had all been struck and reduced to rubble. Despite that, there was such a large number of uninjured gunmen sweeping the palace complex that it was apparent that there had been a vastly greater number of paramilitary agents than reported.

Bolan and James found themselves in an anthill of running, screaming men, calling out to one another in an attempt to reorganize and repel the threat. Machine-gun teams were set up rapidly and engaged Charlie Mott in standoff duals, forcing the helicopter pilot to zip in and out of range as he took gun runs at multiple knots of fighters.

The Stony Man duo moved under fire toward the palace. They approached a long series of French doors issuing smoke through the blown-out glass. They moved in a bounding overwatch, modified to exploit speed, but basically consisting of one commando holding security while the next leapfrogged forward to the next point of offered cover.

As Bolan and James advanced, they could hear people screaming from around the compound, as well as a long ragged machine-gun burst answered immediately by Mott's M-134 minigun. The Executioner cleared the deck over a column of concrete pillars supporting a low, wide stone rail encircling the patio. The explosive force of the GBU-12 bombs had cracked and pitted its surface but failed to break the stone railing.

Bolan landed on mosaic tile, waves of heat from the burning building washing over him. A nearby stone bench offered cover, so he took up a position behind it, going down to one knee.

James passed Bolan's hasty fighting position in a rush and put his back to a narrow strip of wall set between two ruined patio doors. He kept his weapon at port arms and turned his head toward the opening beside him. From inside the dark structure flames danced in a wild riot.

The ex-SEAL nodded sharply and Bolan rose in one swift motion, bringing the buttstock of his M-4 to his shoulder as he breached the opening. He shuffled past James, sweeping his weapon in a tight pattern as he entered the building.

The Phoenix Force commando folded in behind him, deploying his weapon to cover the areas opposite Bolan's pattern. It felt as if they had rushed headlong into a burning oven. Heavy tapestries, Persian rugs and silk curtains burned bright and hot. Smoke clung to the ceiling and filled the room to a height of five feet, forcing the men to crouch below the noxious cover.

In a far corner the two men saw a sprawling T-shaped stair of highly polished wood now smoldering in the heat. A wide-open floor plan accentuated groupings of expensive furniture clustered together by theme. Before arriving in Damascus both commandos had studied the blueprints of the al-Kassar palace closely. The sprawling compound and ostentatious structure had been designed by a international architectural firm out of Istanbul, known for the lavish structures they had built for the sultans of Brunei and Oman.

Akira Tokaido, the Stony Man cybernetic team's young hacker, had breached the company's firewalls and snatched the blueprints of the palace without leaving a whisper of a trace to witness his infiltration. Both Bolan and James had committed the building interior to memory prior to their strike.

The bombs had rendered much of their memorization superfluous. Slowly the two men turned so that their backs were to each other, their weapon muzzles tracking through the smoke and uncertain light. Smoke choked their lungs and stung their eyes. The inert shapes of several bodies were around the room among pieces of shattered furniture.

Bolan moved slowly through the burning wreckage, approaching twisted bodies and searching the bruised and bloody faces for traces of recognition, looking for the cadre's leader. Around him the heat grew more intense and the smoke billowed thicker. James moved with the same quick, methodical efficiency, checking the bodies as they vectored in toward the stairs.

Bolan sensed more than saw the motion from the top of the smoldering staircase. He barked a warning even as he pivoted at the hip and fired from the waist. The 5.56 mm rounds chewed into the staircase and snapped railings into splinters as he sprayed the second landing. One of his rounds struck the gunman high in the abdomen. The Teflon-coated, high-velocity rounds speared up through the smooth muscles of diaphragm, sliced open the bottom of the lungs and cored out the left atrium of the gunman's pounding heart. Bright scarlet blood squirted like water from a faucet as the target staggered backward.

The figure, indistinct in the smoke, triggered a burst that hammered into the steps before pitching forward and striking the staircase. The faceless gunmen tumbled forward, limbs loose, and his head smacking into steps on the way down, leaving black smears of blood on the wood.

Bolan sprang forward, heading for the stairs. James spun in a tight 180-degree circle to cover their six as he edged out to follow Bolan. Silhouettes were visible outside through the blown-out frames of the patio doors, and he let loose with a wall of lead in a sloppy, figure-eight pattern.

One shadow fell sprawling across the concrete divider and the rest of the silhouettes scattered in response to James's fusillade. The Phoenix Force commando danced sideways, found the bottom of the stairs and started to back up. Above him he heard Bolan curse, and then the Executioner's weapon blazed.

To James's left a gunner reeled back from a window. Another came to take his place, the star-pattern burst illuminating a hate-twisted face. The Phoenix Force commando put a 3-round burst into his head from across the burning room, and the man fell away.

"Let's go!" Bolan shouted.

He let loose with a long burst of suppressing fire aimed at the line of French doors facing the rear patios as James spun on his heel and pounded up the steps past Bolan. Outside, behind the cover of the pillared railing, an enemy combatant popped back up from his crouch, the distinctive outline of a RPG-7 perched on his shoulder.

Down on one knee, Bolan fired a instinctive burst, but the shoulder-mounted tube spit flame in a plume from the rear of the weapon and the rocket into the devastated house. Bolan turned and dived up the stairs as the rocket crossed the big room below him and struck the staircase.

The warhead detonated on impact and Bolan shuddered under the force and heat, but the angle of the RPG had been off and the construction of the staircase channeled most of the blast force downward and away from where Bolan lay sprawled. Enough force surged upward to send the soldier reeling even as he huddled against the blast. He tucked into a protective ball and absorbed the waves of energy.

He lifted his head and saw James standing above him, his feet widespread for support and firing in short bursts of savage, accurate fire. Bolan lifted his M-4, and the assault carbine came apart in his hands. He flung the broken pieces away and felt his wrist burn. His hand became slick with spilling blood as the stitches from his garrote wound came apart under the abuse.

He ignored the hot, sticky feeling of the blood and cleared his Beretta 93-R from its underarm sling. He pushed himself up and turned over as James began to engage more targets. As he twisted he saw something move from the hallway just past the open landing behind his fellow warrior.

Bolan extended his arm with sharp reflexes and stroked the trigger on the Beretta. A 3-round burst struck the creeping enemy in a tight grouping high in the chest, just below the throat.

The narcoterrorist's breastbone cracked under the pressure, the back of the target's neck burst outward in a spray of crimson and pink as the 9 mm rounds burrowed their way clear.

"Go! Go!" James shouted.

The Phoenix Force commando swept his M-4 back and forth in covering fire as Bolan scrambled past him to claim the high ground. The Executioner pushed himself off the stairs and onto the second floor. Stepping over the bloody corpse of his target, he turned and began to aim and fire the Beretta in tight bursts.

Under his covering fire James wheeled on his heel and bounded up the stairs past Bolan. At the top of the landing he threw himself down and took aim through the staircase railing to engage targets below him in the open great room.

From their superior position the two Stony Man warriors rained death down on their enemies.

CHAPTER THIRTY

"Hold the stairs!" Bolan growled, rising to his feet. "I'll check the site, then we'll evac."

"Roger," James acknowledged as he coolly worked the trigger on his M-4.

Bolan moved quickly down the hallway. Smoke burned his throat and irritated his eyes, obscuring his vision as he hunted. He worked quickly, checking behind doors as he moved down the hall. Flames kept the corridor oven-hot and the hair and clothes on broken bodies smoldered as Bolan hunted to verify the dead.

In several places he found that the collapse of the two floors above had penetrated down onto the second story, cracking open the bedroom ceilings and dumping broken furniture and flaming debris like rockslides. Bolan scrambled over mounds of rubble and skirted charred holes dropping away beneath his feet.

Behind him Bolan heard James's smooth trigger work keeping the animals at bay. He refused to waste energy on being angry but deep inside of him he was furious at the NSA intelligence failure that had missed such a huge number of combatants in the compound. But he couldn't afford to let it cloud his attention now.

He came upon a body whose face looked as though it had been taken apart by a tire iron. It was puffy, bruised and covered in blood, but Bolan was still able to identify one of the Scimitar captains. He mentally crossed the man off his list and was thankful he hadn't been forced to use his forensic evidence kit yet.

He turned the corner in the L-shaped hallway and saw the corridor blocked. An avalanche of ceiling beams, flooring, ruined furniture and body parts had dropped through the third floor and completely obstructed the hall. Flames ran in fingers off the cave-in, spreading heat and destruction with rapid ferocity.

A bit of debris fell through the roof, and Bolan looked up. Dangling from the hole was a mahogany-colored Gucci executive briefcase made from dyed alligator hide. The case hung from a pair of blue-steel handcuffs attached to a blood-smeared arm.

"Well, look at that," he murmured.

Bolan raised his arm and touched the bottom of the alligator-hide case. He stood on his toes and grasped it with a firmer hold. Realizing he was going to have to yank the whole body down to get the case, Bolan pulled hard.

There was a brief moment of resistance, then the case came loose in his hand so suddenly he was overbalanced and went stumbling back. His heel caught on a length of wood and he almost fell. He backpedaled like a pass receiver, then cut to the side and came up against the wall.

He looked down at the case in his hand, which was

still attached to the wrist by the dark metal handcuffs. A man's arm hung from the dangling chain, ending in a ragged tear at the elbow. Bloody muscle and tendon hung in scraps from the open wound.

Sweating, Bolan looked up through the hole and saw only more flames. He felt a grudging acceptance that it was unlikely anyone in the floors above could have survived the twin bomb blasts. He dropped his gory artifact onto the hot ground and knelt on to one knee, pinning the disembodied forearm to the ground with his leg.

The soldier drew his boot knife, forced free the arm from the handcuff. He clutched the Gucci briefcase under one arm and rose. Quickly he opened the expensive satchel and scanned the pages he found there, saw their value and immediately zipped the case closed, satisfied.

He backed up to the edge of the corner and pulled a grenade from his web belt. The AN-M14 TH3 incendiary hand grenade weighed as much as two cans of beer and had a lethal radius of more than twenty yards. In the hallway its destruction would be concentrated, spreading fire and contributing greatly to the overall structural instability of the building.

Bolan yanked the pin on the hand grenade and let the arming spoon fly. He lobbed the compact canister underhand and let it bounce down the short stretch of hall before ducking around the corner to safety. The delay fuse was four seconds, which gave him plenty of time to reach safety.

Bolan moved in a fast crouch toward the once ornate landing where James fired down from his defensive vantage point to cover his teammate's search-and-destroy mission. Bolan spoke into his throat mike.

"Dark Horse to Element Dawn, I have a structural blockage, our operation is finished. Site destruction verified to acceptable factor of certainty. Over."

"Dawn to Horse, copy," Charlie Mott answered. Bolan could hear the beating of the Stony Man pilot's rotors and the muffled sound of his minigun bursts. "I am disengaging covering operations and proceeding to rendezvous point. Over."

"Dark Horse, out," Bolan answered.

Behind him the hand grenade exploded and jellied flames spewed out past the turn in the hall. Bolan felt the rushing waves of heat strike his back, increasing the intensity of the fires already burning by several factors.

"Coming toward you!" Bolan shouted as he moved.

He jogged back down the hallway toward where James lay in a prone marksman position. He moved through the hall at a quick pace, but the thickening smoke forced him to keep his head down and run almost bent over.

As he approached the Phoenix Force commando, Bolan yanked his second incendiary grenade from his web belt and pulled the pin. He kept the handle down as he called out to James, counting down the fuse.

"I found this briefcase. Let's boogey," he yelled, expanding on the message he had uttered over the com link to Charlie Mott.

James nodded without looking back, and Bolan let the spoon on his grenade fly free. Below him through the smoke he saw gunners leaving cover, then muzzle-bursts. The heavy hand grenade arched out over the stairs and dropped like a stone into the smoke and milling confusion.

It hit the stairs with a clearly audible thump and rolled across the now scarred and pitted tile of the great chamber. James rolled away from the edge as the grenade detonated with sudden, stunning sound and liquid fire splashed across the room.

Men screamed in pain and horror at the eruption as hungry jelly flames began to feed. The bottom of the stairs was instantly ignited by the intense heat and a sheet of flame sprang up, cutting the combatants off from Bolan and James.

The two men turned and raced down the hall and stopped at the first door, which they hurriedly entered. Bolan had already cleared the room on his initial sweep and they moved into the guest room quickly. French doors of the same design as those on the patio below opened onto a small terrace holding two comfortable lounge chairs and a black, wrought-iron table. The veranda overlooked the pools, and off to one side more men were running up from the airstrip to assault the house.

Bolan and James each removed a M-18 smoke grenade and primed the canisters. The Executioner threw his out the window and off to one side while James repeated the process to the other one. They held back from engaging targets to avoid calling attention to themselves until they were ready.

The grenade canisters bounced out and immediately began spewing thick green smoke, obscuring the area around the window from any enemy eyes. Patiently the two men waited for the billowing smoke to grow thicker. James primed an incendiary grenade as they waited.

"Let's go," Bolan snapped once he had judged their covering smoke to be thick enough.

"Go!" James agreed, and rolled the grenade across the floor back toward the bedroom door.

Bolan rose, holding his pistol and the briefcase in the same hand. He moved forward and grasped the wrought-iron railing in his free hand and leaped over the side. James's AN-M14 TH3 incendiary canister trundled across the distance between the window and the bedroom door.

He turned and rose as the grenade reached the doorway, stepping forward to grasp the railing. The flesh of his palm found the warm metal bar just as the bullets struck him.

The burst of machine-gun fire struck him hard in the back at a sharp angle, so that the 5.45 mm rounds penetrated his torso armor just to the left of the ceramic plate insertion and entered the big muscle near the spine before traveling along the curve of ribs to exit underneath the armpit. A fourth round hit the left cheek of his buttocks.

James felt the shock of impact, then heard his attacker screaming as the sound of the AKS-74 chattered hard across the room. The shock of impact sent the wounded American over the railing and he lost his weapon as he fell.

The ground rushed up to meet him and he hit it with the force of a car wreck. Pain lanced like lightning strikes through his body from the bullet wounds, and then the blunt trauma of his impact drove his breath from his lungs. James's eyes welled with a thousand points of brilliant light and then a black void rushed in and darkness claimed him.

BOLAN HIT THE GROUND and rolled, coming to his feet in the smoke. He popped up, bringing his weapon to bear, and heard weapon fire from the balcony above him. He heard James grunt with pain and then had an impression of something falling.

James sprawled across the ground at his feet. He went to one knee beside his brother-in-arms, and the smoke eddied just enough for him to see James lying still, his eyes closed.

The incendiary grenade detonated with a signature whoomp and blazing banners of flame shot out the open window above Bolan. With grim satisfaction he heard someone screaming in agony from above him, and he knew the man who had shot James was burning to death.

Bolan moved quickly. He did not stop to see if James was alive or dead. It did not matter. If the ex-SEAL was still alive, then Bolan had no time to treat or dress his wounds. If he were dead, then Bolan had no intention of leaving his body to the wolves to be displayed in mutilated splendor on terrorist Internet Web sites.

He looked at the briefcase lying on the ground beside the immobile commando. The blue bracelet of the handcuff was crusty with drying blood. Bolan knew there was only one way for him to carry both James and the briefcase while remaining capable of defending himself with his pistol in an efficient manner.

He set down his Berretta 93-R and snatched up the loose end of the handcuff before grabbing the limp arm of Calvin James just below his hand. He held the arm out and snapped the handcuff bracelet down, locking it into position around James's wrist.

Bolan grabbed James's arm and muscled the man

over his shoulder in a tight fireman's carry position. Using the burning room above his head as a compass point, Bolan turned and began to jog through the smoke out toward the back gate.

A figure rushed past Bolan in the smoke, nearly colliding with him. The soldier put a single 9 mm round through the confused man's head, then stutter-stepped over the body as it fell.

James was a big man and Bolan gasped for breath in the choking smoke as he labored to carry the fallen commando clear of the assault site. The Phoenix Force veteran's blood soaked into Bolan's fatigues and ran down his back.

Bolan got clear of the area obscured by his and James's smoke grenades. The air still stank of ash and blood and burning fires continued to pollute the desert air, but he was now better able to see. His eyes were red-rimmed and his throat raw from his coughing.

He hacked and spit as he turned, searching through the haze for the back gate. He heard the rotors of Mott's helicopter as it passed overhead. There was a burst of minigun fire and a hailstorm of spent shell casings rained down on Bolan from above.

He raced forward, the Beretta machine pistol up and tracking as he moved. Each step sent thumping shock waves through his body and into his tightly clenched teeth. The added weight of James's body slowed him, compromised his reactions, but not once did he think of leaving his companion behind.

The Executioner passed the burning remains of the Ford 350, and the flames had died down enough that he could easily see the charred, skeletal remains of the enemy gunmen trapped inside the vehicle cab when James's 40 mm HE rounds had found them.

He cut across the back stretch of irrigated lawn and saw a pile of multicolored balls next to a metal hoop stuck into the ground. He felt a jolt of incredulity as he passed the croquet set and found the asphalt road leading toward the rear gate.

Just beyond the ruins of the structure the smoke was being beaten back by the spinning rotors of Mott's helicopter. Bolan jogged toward the chopper, and he realized with a jolt of random thought that everyone back in the War Room at Stony Man would be able to see that James was down on the UAS Reaper's cameras.

The weapons package on the Little Bird had precluded the personnel carrying benches the helicopter had been outfitted with on the Baghdad raid so, once again, the aircraft had been prepped for a SPIE operation.

Bolan ducked underneath the hovering Little Bird where the tow rope dangled, outfitted with the loops necessary to secure his and the unconscious Calvin James's harness points. He felt the rotor wash beating down on him, throwing grit in his face, forcing him to squint against the windstorm.

His hands found the waist pack attached to the back of James's web gear, and he ripped it open, freeing OD-green packets of coagulation powder packed between 4x4 bandages and a cravat. He snatched three of them up, ripped them open with his teeth and began dumping them into James's wounds, trying to get the leaking blood to clot before they extracted from the assault.

"Hook it up, Striker!" Mott shouted over the radio, as the enemy advanced.

Bolan was already working frantically, double hooking James to the rope with carabiners before snapping his own on. He became aware of dirt kicking up around him and realized he was under fire. He picked the Beretta up again and turned.

"We're good! Go!" he shouted into his throat mike.

Immediately the engine changed pitch and the helicopter began to rise. Bolan shoved his pistol toward the back gate and fired one-handed. As the rope lifted off the ground, he hugged the lower half of James's limp body to prevent the unconscious payload from spinning.

The pistol in his fist burped 3-round bursts hard one after the other. He felt himself leave the ground and begin to float backward, his center of balance shifting from the hard earth beneath his feet to the connection points of his harness where carabiner attached to rope.

The air was cooler as he rose and he gasped, his lungs hungry for its freshness after the cordite and arson-smoke of the palace. He saw flashes of gunfire below him from the burning compound and knew they were still being engaged but had no perception of the rounds coming anywhere near close to him.

He felt James's blood clotting his already gummy clothes and when he lifted his head he saw the first bloody slivers of dawn on the jagged hills of the horizon. Behind him columns of black smoke rose into the sky.

Mott put the nose of the Little Bird down and ran for the border.

CHAPTER THIRTY-ONE

An elite team of U.S. Air Force flight nurses had taken possession of Calvin James at Camp KV airfield and whisked him to the main military hospital in Baghdad in a medevac helicopter. Bolan had waited at the base, isolated from the Marines and waiting for JSOC liaisons to clear him secure communications to Stony Man Farm.

Once the information was in Barbara Price's hands the translation activity had been undertaken at phenomenal speed. It was during this process that a team of Stony Man blacksuits was sent to Baghdad to oversee James's recovery and transportation to a secure wing of the U.S. naval hospital in Bethesda, Maryland. In the meantime Bolan learned that Rafael Encizo had been transported to Ramstein Air Force base in Germany where he had undergone further surgery. Encizo had regained consciousness that morning for the first time since the Baghdad grenade blast.

Bolan paced, waiting for word, wondering what in the briefcase could have been so explosive if the Scimitar's cell captains and foreign intelligence patrons had been taken out by the al-Kassar strike. The Chinese operation and the organization itself had been decapitated and reduced to shreds. Some isolated activities remained functioning, such as the Azerbaijani airport and some logistical centers in Al-Rutbah. But even those were rudderless and isolated now that communication links had been severed. Normal special operations or even regular conventional forces could finish up those as autonomous mop up operations.

When Price finally contacted Bolan, her message was simple. "The situation has changed. Come home."

Charlie Mott choppered Bolan to Amman where he found a ticket on the next international flight into Dulles International Airport waiting for him.

"You see the headlines?" Price asked.

The mission controller tossed a copy of the *Washington Post* onto the conference table of the War Room. It was a repeat of the stories Bolan had already read in the English versions of overseas newspapers. Hal Brognola chewed his cigar.

"About Hiba Bakr?"

"Yep, read for yourself."

The Toronto cleric had been released by Canadian authorities after appeals by the lawyers for the Ottawa Civil Liberties Chapter. They had found it easy to convince a judge at the federal arraignment that the original surveillance of the man had been a case of racial profiling in a crass attempt to curry favor with the government of the United States in its "so-called war on terror."

The decision was hailed as a triumph of Canadian independence in the press.

Bolan, long cynical to such things, pushed the paper away. Unlike many in his position he did not blame politics or any other such nefarious motivation on the part of the people who had labored so hard to gain the terror collaborator's freedom.

Mistakes had been made in the past with security and Canadian citizens. The U.S. had held its own part in those mistakes, including the kidnapping and harsh interrogation of a man later proved to be innocent. The water was muddy for many good people on the subject of security versus freedom.

"They'll be sorry," Bolan replied, looking up at Price. "He'll funnel money through bogus Islamic charities to terrorists, launder their money in the other direction or provide sanctuary to killers. I had hoped for a better outcome when I left him to the RCMP team, but I'm not surprised."

"He's Scimitar," Price said.

Bolan sat up, his face drawn into a tight mask. "What?"

"Hiba Bakr is Scimitar," Brognola confirmed.

"How? I thought the misinformation was that Scimitar, a coalition cell, was only a single man. I saw the intel, hell, *you* saw the intel. The names, the bios, the Chinese funding and organization orders, all of it."

"Bakr set up Scimitar the cell as a smoke screen for his activities. The cell set up the Scimitar cipher as smoke screen for themselves. The cell was not a cabal of equals like the New York City Five Families of the Mafia. It was a command-and-control administrative unit masquerading as autonomous confederacy."

"The captains answered to Bakr?"

"Yes, the documents in that briefcase proved it. The man you got them from was a courier. He was taking the joint Syrian-Chinese proposal to Bakr for his approval. The letters were a smoking gun, proving everything. The courier had a Damascus to Toronto flight booked in advance of the meeting. Even the Syrians and the Chinese had no idea the captains were simply a front for Bakr."

Bolan settled back into his chair. He rubbed his chin, getting used to the feel of his beard being gone. His face remained as inscrutable as a tombstone. He stopped rubbing his chin and carefully set his hands on the table.

He remembered Encizo lying on the ground in Baghdad. He remembered the feel of Calvin James's blood as it seeped through his shirt and congealed on his skin. He thought about watching the video of the man being tortured. Slowly his back teeth ground together and he forced his jaw muscles to relax. He let the air trapped in his lungs out in a slow, even bleed.

"Why was he living like that? Why the cover? If he was a millionaire, then why live in near poverty?"

"We think he is incognito for a specific purpose," Price answered. "The NSA was able to connect him to several UAE bank accounts once we knew to focus on him in that capacity. He's worth tens of millions. He has a palace in northeastern Sudan we can trace to him. He was in Canada for a reason. Whatever that reason is, it required him to play the role of impoverished cleric."

"Make no mistake, Striker," Brognola said. "He's the guy. You don't often get such an Easter egg of intelligence but the background checks out. We made the connections and double checked them. Bakr is Scimitar."

"I had him. All the globe-hopping, all the deaths…Rafe and Cal? It was a circle."

"We knew he was bad, but we didn't know he was that bad, Striker. You couldn't have executed him. What did you have? You left him for the Canadian intel guys, it's not your fault they blew it, Mack," Price argued.

The RCMP had him under surveillance. I went in there and compromised an investigation, tipped their hand and the guy walked. If I believed in what I was doing, I shouldn't have let the deal go down like it did. I had a room full of killers and facilitators of killers. I decided some of them weren't 'as bad' as others and I let them go."

"Mack—"Price tried again.

"No, Barb," Bolan said. "You don't think Bakr couldn't have walked us through every piece of that puzzle I put together? The hit on Ning-tan? Exactly what was going on in Baghdad? The true numbers of the al-Kassar compound? All of it."

"We couldn't have known." Brognola shook his head.

"We knew he was bad, right? We knew he was rotten. You either fight a war and you fight it with commitment, or you don't fight it. If you don't fight total war, then you always leave your enemy the option of going to the next level, of taking the conflict one step further than you were willing to go and then defeating you."

"We'll get him, Striker," Brognola said.

"From now on no more false lines. No more buying into the camouflage acts. A man is what a man does. If he does evil things and glories in them or does evil things and calls them good, then he is evil. No more hiding behind artificial designations like titles or occupations. If a man is bad then it doesn't matter if he wears a badge or wraps himself in holy robes.

"It no longer matters to me what a man *says* he is or how he hides his evil. If the time comes…then the time comes," Bolan finished.

Brognola caught Bolan's eye and held it. The Executioner did not turn away. Between them, Price turned her head from one expressionless face to the other.

"I signed on to this train a long time ago," Brognola said. "I intend to ride it through. All the way to the end."

"There is no way Scimitar gets to run a global narcoterror network funded by Syria and China and then walk away from court a free man. A free man preaching to a flock of isolated and disenchanted youths, issuing fatwas and calling himself a man of God."

"Not in the world of Stony Man," Brognola agreed.

"We'll get you back into Toronto," Price said.

"Good. Because I'm going to get Bakr."

Toronto, Ontario

BOLAN KNEW BAKR was afraid. He had come within a hairbreadth of dying when the Executioner had come calling last time. Since then his captains, couriers and contacts had been decimated, his people slaughtered, his facilities destroyed, his middlemen eliminated and himself imprisoned, though later released.

Carmen Delahunt had been able to utilize her old contacts in the FBI to communicate with the liaison in the Toronto office where information sharing was an intricate part of the international law-enforcement program. She had learned several useful facts.

First, she had discovered where the cleric now resided. Second, she had learned that upon his demands following the Executioner's last visit he was surrounded by Syrian bodyguards from the IMJ. Third, it was revealed that CSIS had been instructed to cease all activities in regard to the cleric that could lead to any international incident.

The Bakr was no longer the subject of any investigations, inquiries or actions by the Canadian government.

Bolan thought about his approach. The IMJ bodyguards would be security experts. Their VIP close-protection abilities would be augmented by electronic measures and countersurveillance expertise. Delahunt believed that Bakr himself had seen surveillance footage of Bolan and would be able to recognize him. Despite that, he believed such measures could be overcome by aggression and firepower, but Toronto was not Baghdad.

Bolan would need to get close.

He decided to exploit the weakness of the target. He decided to appeal to greed.

"THE IMAM IS NOT seeing anyone."

"My name is Michael McKay. I'm a freelance reporter for the Associated Press," Bolan said. "I would like to do an interview highlighting your employer's mistreatment at the hands of the Canadian government for *The Nation* magazine."

"No press." The man moved to slam the door shut.

Bolan put his foot in the jamb and halted the motion, the thick tread of his shoes absorbing the blunt force. The bodyguard looked up, his face growing red.

"Easy," Bolan said. "Give this to His Eminence. Tell him there are fifteen more just like it if he grants me the interview." Bolan held out his hand.

Suspicious, the bodyguard took the items Bolan handed him. One was a business card with the McKay cover name, press credential listing, and a contact number. The second item was a metal coin.

"It is not the policy of *The Nation* to pay for interviews. However, in the case of Imam Bakr, we are willing to make an exception as long as he grants us certain guarantees of exclusivity. We prefer to conduct such transactions in neutral currency."

The bodyguard looked at the heavy coin in his hand. "How many more?" he asked.

"Fifteen. The current value of each coin is six hundred dollars, U.S."

"We'll be in touch," the man said.

He stepped back and slammed the door hard in Bolan's face.

Fighting back a grin, Bolan turned and walked down the steps of the modest suburban house.

EARLY THE NEXT MORNING Bolan got the call on his disposable cell phone. He assumed Bakr had taken the time to use his foreign intelligence contacts to check out his cover story. That was understandable given the crumbling nature of the man's empire. But greed wasn't just a sin, it was a weakness.

He shut off the channel playing on his hotel suite's television and picked up the ringing cell phone.

"McKay, here," Bolan said.

"His Eminence will see you today, at 1:00 p.m. Fifteen is a good number, no cameras."

"I'll be on time," the Executioner said.

CHAPTER THIRTY-TWO

Bolan knocked on the door.

He held the heavy case loosely in his hand. The door swung open and the same bodyguard from the previous day stood in front of him. He held a metal-detector wand in his hands. He was not smiling.

"You're early," he said.

"I'm eager to get to work," Bolan answered.

"Step inside. Give the case to Ezzedine and hold your arms out."

The Syrian bodyguard stepped back and swung the door open wide. Bolan stepped across the threshold and entered the house. He saw a big man with a short haircut and a clipped mustache standing in the entrance-way. The man held out a strong hand and Bolan gave him the briefcase.

The bodyguard set it on a narrow, decorative wash-stand table by a coatrack in the entranceway. The home was split-level. They stood on a landing just inside the door, with a short staircase leading up and an identical one leading down. From upstairs he could hear an Arabic-language television program playing.

The metal wand moved quickly across Bolan, chirping only at his belt buckle. Bolan hooked his thumbs underneath the ornament and showed the bodyguard nothing was hidden behind it. The man grunted his satisfaction and waved the wand across the briefcase resting on the washstand.

The wand exploded with beeps.

"Open it," Ezzedine ordered.

"Sure," Bolan replied, and stepped forward.

As he moved he saw two more men in blazers appear above him, at the top of the stairs. He reached out and snapped open the locks on the briefcase. They popped like gunshots as the tight springs released the latches. Bolan lifted the lid and stepped back.

Both Ezzedine and the first bodyguard leaned forward. Fifteen gold coins lay nestled in cut-foam seats. The guard reached out with a finger toward one of the carefully positioned coins. Bolan slapped his hand like an exasperated mother with her misbehaving toddler.

"Imam Bakr touches," Bolan said. "You don't touch. I signed for that currency. If something happens to it, I'll have to sell my house. I'm not going to tell my wife we have to move."

"Are you afraid of your woman?" The first bodyguard sneered and the others chuckled behind him at the insult.

Bolan cocked his head to one side, pensive. "She can handle herself," he allowed. "Doesn't matter. I give the coins to the imam. If you don't like it, I leave and you tell him where his money went."

WHEN IT HAPPENED it happened fast.

The bodyguard team flanked Bolan as soon as he reached the top of the short flight of stairs. The two at the top turned and led him through a spacious living area with hardwood floors while Ezzedine and the team leader fell in behind him. He was effectively boxed in.

Bolan moved through the house toward a back hallway. He passed a kitchen where a woman in a modest dress and headscarf was cleaning. She did not look up as Bolan and the men walked past. The kitchen was spacious with a center island, an informal dining area and plenty of counter space framing the room along the walls. Close to Bolan, in the lee of the entrance arch, was an expensive stainless-steel refrigerator. In the far corner of the room a sliding-glass door opened up onto a cedar-wood deck.

From behind Bolan the lead bodyguard began to give instructions.

"You have twenty minutes, no more. You will put the briefcase on the desk and show the imam the money immediately. No pictures, no recording devices. You may take notes on the pen and tablet provided for you."

"Understood," Bolan answered as they neared the final door at the end of the hallway.

The two bodyguards ahead of him stopped at the dark wood-paneled door and Bolan waited, hands folded around the handle of the briefcase clasped in front of him. The bodyguards behind him were so close he could feel their breaths on the back of his neck.

One of the lead bodyguards opened the door and stuck his head around the corner and announced the

American in Arabic. A voice Bolan instantly recognized answered.

The bodyguard pulled his head out of the room and stepped out of Bolan's way.

"Go in," the man ordered.

Bolan stepped forward.

THE HECKLER & KOCH MP-5K had been introduced in 1976. Bolan carried the most modern variant of the weapon, the MP-5K A-4 with an ambidextrous, 4-position trigger selector unit. The "K" stood for Kurz, which was German for "short," and the machine pistol was a cut-down version of the immensely popular H&K MP-5 submachine-gun.

The weapon was squat, compact and capable of using the same 30-round magazine as the SMG, and Bolan had increased the lethality of his model by outfitting it with Russian armor piercing bullets. Stony Man's armorer, John "Cowboy" Kissinger had handcrafted the infamous "briefcase" configuration utilized by VIP protection specialists, with a hidden trigger in the handle.

The tray of metal coins had performed well in their subterfuge role to avoid closer visual inspection of the briefcase after tripping the metal sensor wand. Just as Bolan's well-crafted cover credentials had served to cloud the bodyguard's mind to exactly who Bolan actually was.

There would be no fooling Bakr however. Bolan was quite sure the man would never forget the Executioner's face. In fact, Bolan quite hoped his face would be the last thing the demagogue ever saw.

Bolan stepped through the door. He brought the briefcase up and held it in front of him like a food tray, the preferred position for optimal use of the hidden machine pistol. He walked into a large bedroom that had been converted into a home office space.

The cleric was seated behind an oak desk. He made to rise as Bolan entered, then his face went as white as a sheet as he recognized the man walking toward him.

"You!" he shouted.

Bolan turned, still holding the case like a food tray in both hands. His finger curled around the trigger hidden in the curve of the briefcase handle and depressed it. The bodyguard team was crammed together, nearly shoulder to shoulder in the hallway, big men packed into a tight kill box.

The machine pistol erupted in Bolan's hands. The briefcase shuddered with the vibrations of the automatic weapon's recoil. Bullets exploded from the shortened muzzle, the armor-piercing ammunition cutting into the knot of bodyguards from point-blank range.

The front two men shook and danced as the rounds sliced through their body armor, shredded their flesh from their bones and carved tunnels into their internal organs. Bolan dropped the rear of the briefcase slightly, elevating the muzzle, and the tight pattern burrowed shots underneath the exposed chins of the first two men, cracking their skulls.

The men stumbled back into Ezzedine and the team leader. Both men, professionals, stepped back to avoid being tangled up in the corpses of their murdered team members. Both men went for shoulder holsters underneath their blazers. Professionalism wasn't enough to save them.

The pair absorbed the impact of Bolan's long, ragged burst with jerky, uncontrolled movements. They tumbled together in a dog pile of bodies and the Executioner followed them down, tracking their motion until he was sure it was safe to turn his back on the Syrian agent.

He spun, saw the imam coming at him with a curved, bejeweled ceremonial dagger. The bearded man's face was twisted with rage and desperation, and though in his midfifties the narcoterror leader was a solidly built man.

Bolan blocked the dagger trust with the briefcase. The blade plunged through the outer wall of the case and buried deep inside. The soldier twisted the briefcase hard and ripped the dagger from Bakr's hand.

The cleric lunged forward as he released the handle on his dagger and wrapped his arms around Bolan's body in a clumsy two-leg take-down.

The briefcase tumbled off to the side and both men collapsed to the floor. The hard jar rattled through Bolan's body, and he snapped his teeth together as he landed on the floor. He sprawled out on his back and Bakr thrust himself forward, his hands clawing for his adversary's face like the talons of a desert hawk.

Bolan did a short, abdominal crunch and rose, the point of his left elbow shooting out and striking the lunging narcoterrorist in the face. Bakr grunted under the impact and the skin of his cheek split open. He threw a wild right haymaker that Bolan blocked with his left forearm.

The Executioner extended his thumb and lashed out, catching the man in his eye socket. Bakr screamed and instinctively his hands flew to his face. The soldier drew back his right arm and hammered a fist into the side of his opponent's unprotected face.

The man's head rocked to the side just as Bolan's left fist lashed into his face. The impact forced a low moan from the man and he sagged, stunned. As the befuddled terror leader's hands fell away Bolan struck him twice more, cracking his nose.

Blood spilled in a waterfall over Bakr's bruised and swelling lip, and his eyes, scrunched tight against the damaged orb, suddenly relaxed as the man sagged unconscious. Bolan shoved the limp body away and started to rise.

The sudden scream from behind him was high and shrill and utterly terrified.

Bolan looked up and saw the woman standing in the hall, her hands clasped to her face. Her gaze kept jumping back and forth between the pile of dead Syrians and the battered cleric.

She screamed again, and Bolan cursed as he scrambled to his feet.

The woman watched Bolan rise, and her eyes spread wide in terror. She screamed a third time and turned to run. Bolan leaped forward, clearing the pile of corpses blocking the hallway. His foot came down in blood and his shoe twisted on the slippery surface but he did not go down.

He raced down the hall after the screaming woman and, like a tiger bounding after its prey, caught her in the living room. He reached out and threw her into a couch.

Hauling the terrified woman to her feet, he headed back toward the hallway, forced to drag her limp body as she remained immobile in terror.

"If you speak English," Bolan said, "just shut up and listen. I won't kill you. You are to tell the imam's followers that I am from al-Kassar. He is being punished for al-Kassar. Do you understand?"

Confused, the woman looked up at him and nodded. "Al-Kassar," she said. Bolan didn't waste time trying to ascertain if she spoke English or was merely repeating the only word of his speech that she understood.

Reaching the first door he found a bathroom, scrubbed to a gleaming cleanliness, no doubt by the very woman he now held. He pushed her onto a rug next to the tub and secured her hands and feet with plastic ties. He moved quickly, uncertain of how long Bakr would remain incapacitated.

After hurriedly shoving part of the woman's head covering into her mouth to stifle her screams, he rose, moved quickly out of the room and closed the door behind him. He looked down the hall and saw Bakr pluck a black pistol from underneath the arm of one of his dead bodyguards.

The two men locked eyes across the stretch of hallway.

The cleric noted Bolan's empty hands with their bloody, torn knuckles. He smiled. The Executioner turned and dived as the narcoterrorist lifted his pistol.

The weapon exploded. Bolan heard the air snap as the bullets passed over his body as he hit the hardwood floor, and rolling through the archway into the big, modern kitchen.

Moving quickly he twisted and jumped up onto the granite countertop beside the refrigerator positioned next to the kitchen entrance. He heard footsteps pounding on the hardwood floor and pressed himself back around the corner of the massive appliance.

Bakr turned the corner and entered the kitchen. He held his pistol in both hands as he raced forward. Bolan reached out and snapped the door of the refrigerator open.

The heavy stainless-steel door slammed into the startled cleric and the man stumbled back, the 9 mm handgun skidding across the floor like a flat stone skipping across a lake. Bolan leaped around the corner of the door.

He raised his right foot and his heel caught the falling man under the chin. Bakr's head snapped back from the blow, and he was laid out on the floor.

As Bakr started to rise, Bolan charged forward and dropped onto Bakr's chest. Bleary-eyed, the cleric looked up at the big American, but all he saw was a fist the size of a boulder as it sped down to impact his face. Bolan struck the man twice more, battering him into unconsciousness with ruthless power.

The Executioner leaned close and whispered to the unconscious man.

"You'll talk," he promised. "When you get to where I'm sending you, you'll talk and fewer people will die. You'll get better food than we give our own soldiers and you'll be able to pray five times a day, if that's even something you really do. But you'll talk," he assured him.

Bolan slowly sat up.

"You will talk."

LOOK FOR

CRITICAL EFFECT
by Don Pendleton

In St. Louis, a rogue scientist unleashes an experimental pathogen on innocent victims. Stony Man targets the disturbing intel and launches an offensive that stretches from Munich to America's heartland. It's a worst-case scenario linking a radical Middle Eastern group with Europe's most sophisticated smugglers—along with a killer virus manufactured for mass destruction.

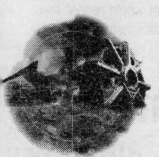

STONY MAN®

*Available June 2008
wherever you buy books.*

ROOM 59

A nuclear bomb has gone missing. At the same time Room 59 intercepts a communiqué from U.S. Border Patrol agent Nathaniel Spencer. But as Room 59 operatives delve deeper into Mexico's criminal underworld, it soon becomes clear that someone is planning a massive attack against America...one that would render the entire nation completely defenceless!

Look for

aim AND fire

by

cliff RYDER

Available July 2008
wherever you buy books.

GOLD EAGLE

GRM593